P9-DVQ-148

Back by Popular Demand

A collector's edition of favorite titles
from one of the world's best-loved
romance authors. Harlequin is proud to
bring back these sought after titles and
present them as one cherished collection.

BETTY NEELS:
COLLECTOR'S EDITION

A GEM OF A GIRL
WISH WITH THE CANDLES
COBWEB MORNING
HENRIETTA'S OWN CASTLE
CASSANDRA BY CHANCE
VICTORY FOR VICTORIA
SISTER PETERS IN AMSTERDAM
THE MAGIC OF LIVING
SATURDAY'S CHILD
FATE IS REMARKABLE
A STAR LOOKS DOWN
HEAVEN IS GENTLE

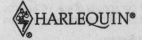

HARLEQUIN®

Betty Neels spent her childhood and youth in Devonshire before training as a nurse and midwife. She was an army nursing sister during the war, married a Dutchman, and subsequently lived in Holland for fourteen years. She now lives with her husband in Dorset, and has a daughter and grandson. Her hobbies are reading, animals, old buildings and, of course, writing. Betty started to write on retirement from nursing, incited by a lady in a library bemoaning the lack of romantic novels.

Mrs. Neels is always delighted to receive fan letters, but would truly appreciate it if they could be directed to Harlequin Mills & Boon Ltd., 18-24 Paradise Road, Richmond, Surrey, TW9 1SR, England.

Books by Betty Neels

HARLEQUIN ROMANCE
3355—DEAREST LOVE
3363—A SECRET INFATUATION
3371—WEDDING BELLS FOR BEATRICE
3389—A CHRISTMAS WISH
3400—WAITING FOR DEBORAH
3415—THE BACHELOR'S WEDDING
3435—DEAREST MARY JANE
3454—FATE TAKES A HAND
3467—THE RIGHT KIND OF GIRL
3483—THE MISTLETOE KISS
3492—MARRYING MARY
3512—A KISS FOR JULIE

Don't miss any of our special offers. Write to us at the following address for information on our newest releases.

Harlequin Reader Service
U.S.: 3010 Walden Ave., P.O. Box 1325, Buffalo, NY 14269
Canadian: P.O. Box 609, Fort Erie, Ont. L2A 5X3

BETTY NEELS

FATE IS REMARKABLE

COLLECTOR'S EDITION

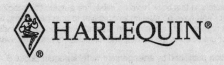

HARLEQUIN®

TORONTO • NEW YORK • LONDON
AMSTERDAM • PARIS • SYDNEY • HAMBURG
STOCKHOLM • ATHENS • TOKYO • MILAN • MADRID
PRAGUE • WARSAW • BUDAPEST • AUCKLAND

If you purchased this book without a cover you should be aware
that this book is stolen property. It was reported as "unsold and
destroyed" to the publisher, and neither the author nor the
publisher has received any payment for this "stripped book."

ISBN 0-373-83395-4

FATE IS REMARKABLE

First North American Publication 1971.

Copyright © 1970 by Betty Neels.

All rights reserved. Except for use in any review, the reproduction or
utilization of this work in whole or in part in any form by any electronic,
mechanical or other means, now known or hereafter invented, including
xerography, photocopying and recording, or in any information storage
or retrieval system, is forbidden without the written permission of the
publisher, Harlequin Enterprises Limited, 225 Duncan Mill Road,
Don Mills, Ontario, Canada M3B 3K9.

All characters in this book have no existence outside the imagination of
the author and have no relation whatsoever to anyone bearing the same
name or names. They are not even distantly inspired by any individual
known or unknown to the author, and all incidents are pure invention.

This edition published by arrangement with Harlequin Books S.A.

® and TM are trademarks of the publisher. Trademarks indicated with
® are registered in the United States Patent and Trademark Office, the
Canadian Trade Marks Office and in other countries.

Printed In U.S.A.

CHAPTER ONE

IT was quiet in the consulting room, if the difficult, rasping breaths of the patient were discounted. From somewhere behind the closed door came the steady, subdued roar of a great many people, interrupted at intervals by a nurse's voice calling the next in line. Sister Sarah Ann Dunn stood quietly, holding layers of woolly garments clear of the patient's shoulders, so that Dr van Elven could get at them in comfort. He was a large man, and very tall, and the patient was fat. He bent, his handsome grizzled head an inch or so from the starched bib of Sarah's apron, his grey eyes looking at nothing while he listened and tapped, then listened again. Presently he came upright with the deliberation which characterised all his movements, said, 'Thank you, Sister,' and turned his back, as he always did, while she dealt with hooks and eyes and zips. She fastened the last button, gave its owner a reassuring little pat and a friendly smile, and said, 'Mrs Brown is ready for you, sir.' It was one of the nice things about her, that she never forgot people's names, however hard pressed she was. Patients were still people to her, and entitled to be treated as such. Dr van Elven strolled back from the X-rays he had been studying, glanced at her briefly from eyes half shut, and nodded. It was her cue to leave him with his patient for a few minutes—an arrangement which suited her very well, for it gave her time to have a quick look round OPD and make sure that everything was going smoothly.

The hall was still quite full, for it was the orthopaedic consultant's afternoon as well as the gynaecologist's clinic and the medical OP she was taking. Both staff nurses were busy, but she could only see one student nurse. She made her way along the benches and turned into the narrow passage leading to the testing room. There were two nurses in it, carrying on such an animated conversation that they failed to see her for several seconds. When they did, they stopped in mid-sentence, their eyes upon her, presenting very much the same appearance, she imagined, as she had done when she had been caught in a similar situation as a student nurse. She said now, half smiling:

'If you two don't do your work, we shall all be late off duty, and there's no point in that, is there? If you're not doing anything here, go back to Staff Nurse Moore, please.'

She didn't wait to hear their apologies, but gave them a little nod and went back the way she had come, hurrying a little in case Dr van Elven was waiting. All the same, she stopped for a brief word with several of the patients sitting on the benches, for after three years as OPD Sister, she was on friendly terms with a number of them.

Mrs Brown was on the point of going as she went into the consulting room, and the doctor said at once:

'Ah, Sister, I have been suggesting to Mrs Brown that she should come in for a short time, so that I can keep an eye on this chest of hers—I daresay you can fix a bed? In three or four days, I think; that will give her time to make arrangements at home.'

He was looking at her steadily as he spoke and she said immediately:

'Yes, of course, sir. I'll get someone to write and tell Mrs Brown which day to come.' She smiled at the elderly, rather grubby little woman sitting in front of the doctor's desk, but Mrs Brown didn't smile back.

'It's me cat,' she began. ''Oo's going ter look after 'im while I'm in?' She sat silent for a moment, then went on, 'I don't see as 'ow I can manage. . .'

'Perhaps the RSPCA?' suggested Sarah gently.

Mrs Brown shook her head in its shapeless hat. ''E'd pine. I'm sorry, doctor, for you've been ever so kind. . .'

He sat back in his chair, with the air of a man who had all day before him, and nothing to do. 'Supposing you allow me to—er—have your cat while you are in hospital, Mrs Brown? Do you feel you could trust him to my care?'

Mrs Brown's several chins wobbled while she strove for words. It was, to say the least, unusual for an important gentleman like a hospital specialist to bother about what became of her Timmy. She was still seeking words when he continued, 'You would be doing me a great favour—my housekeeper has just lost her cat after fifteen years, and is quite inconsolable. Perhaps looking after your Timmy for a week or so might help her to become more resigned.'

The old lady brightened. 'Oh, well now, that's different, doctor. If 'e's going ter make 'er 'appy, and it ain't no trouble. . .'

She got up, and he got to his feet too. 'No trouble—I'll see that your cat is collected just before you come in, Mrs Brown. Will that do?'

Sarah ushered her out, competently, but without haste, laid the next case history on the doctor's desk, put up the X-rays, and waited. He finished what he was writing, closed the folder and said in his rather pedantic English:

'A pity Mrs Brown wasn't referred to me earlier. There's very little to be done, I'm afraid. Chronic bronchitis, emphysema, and congestive heart failure, not to mention all the wrong diet for I don't know how many years.' He picked up the next folder, frowning. 'If her home conditions were not too bad, I could patch her up enough to get her back there for a little while. . .'

Sister Dunn said nothing, for she knew that nothing was expected of her. She had been working for Dr van Elven for a number of years now; he was rather a taciturn man, kind to his patients, considerate towards the nursing staff, and revealing on occasion an unexpected sense of humour. She was aware that he was not, in fact, addressing her, merely speaking his thoughts out loud. So she stood quietly, patiently waiting for him to rid his mind of Mrs Brown. The little pause in the day's work did not irk her in the least; indeed, it gave her the opportunity to decide which dress she would wear that evening for dinner with Steven—the newish black would have been nice, but she particularly wanted to look young and gay. It would have to be the turquoise crêpe again. He had seen it a good many times already, but it suited her and she thought he liked it. Besides, it made her look a lot younger than her twenty-eight years. . .she looked a little wistful for a moment, although there was not the slightest need, for she looked a lot younger anyway, and was possessed of a serene beauty which she would keep all her life.

Her face was oval, with wide grey eyes, extravagantly lashed by nature; she had a delicious nose, small and straight, and a soft curving mouth. Her hair curled a little and she wore it neatly pinned when she was in uniform, and loose in an unswept swirl around her neck when she was off duty. She had a pretty figure too, and a quiet, pleasant voice—everyone who knew her or had met her wondered how it was that she had reached the age of twenty-eight without getting married. She sometimes wondered herself; perhaps it was because she had been waiting for someone like Steven to come along—they had known each other for three years now, and for the last two she had taken it for granted that one day he would ask her to marry him. Only he hadn't—she knew that he wanted a senior post, and just lately he had been talking about a partnership. Last time they had been out together he had observed that there was no point in marrying until he was firmly established.

She frowned a little, remembering that last time had been more than a week ago. He had telephoned twice since then to cancel the meetings they had arranged. He was Surgical Registrar at St Edwin's, and she had always accepted the fact that his work came first and because of that she had made no demur and no effort to waylay him in the hospital; but tonight should really be all right—she hoped that they would go to that restaurant in Monmouth Street where the food was good and the company gay. She suddenly wanted to be gay.

She came out of her brown study with a start to find Dr van Elven staring at her with thoughtful eyes. She smiled.

'I'm sorry, sir,' she said. 'Do you want the next patient? It's old Mr Gregor.'

The doctor went on staring. 'Yes. I have studied his X-rays, and read his notes through twice, Sister.' His voice was dry.

She went faintly pink. She liked Dr van Elven very much; they got on well together, although she sometimes felt that she didn't know him at all. She knew from the hospital grapevine that he was unmarried, that he had had an unhappy love affair when he had been a young man, and that now, at forty, he was a prize any woman would be glad to win. Rumour had it that he had plenty of money, a flourishing practice in Harley Street, and a beautiful house in Richmond. Sarah considered privately that the reason that they got on so well was because they had no romantic interest in each other. But now she had annoyed him.

'I really am sorry, sir,' she said with a genuine humility, because his time was precious and she had been wasting it. 'I—I was thinking.'

'So I could see. If you would perhaps postpone your thoughts we could get finished and you will be free to enjoy your evening.'

The pink in her cheeks deepened. 'However did you know I was going out?' she demanded.

'I didn't,' he answered blandly. 'I was thought-reading. And now, Mr Gregor, please, Sister.'

The rest of the afternoon passed smoothly. The last patient came and went; Sarah started to pile X-rays and Path. Lab. forms and notes in tidy heaps. Dr van Elven rammed his papers untidily into his briefcase and stood up. He was almost at the door when Sarah asked:

'Are you really going to look after Mrs Brown's cat, sir?'

'You doubt my word, Sister?'

She looked shocked. 'My goodness, no. Only you don't look as though you like cats. . .' She stopped, fidgeting with the papers in her hands.

He said in surprise, 'Have you looked at me long enough to form even that opinion of me?' He laughed in genuine amusement, so she was able to laugh too.

'You look like a dog man,' she observed pleasantly.

'You're quite right, Sister. I have two dogs—it is my housekeeper who is the cat-lover. But my dogs are well-mannered enough to tolerate Mrs Brown's cat.' He turned on his heel. 'Goodnight. I hope you have a pleasant evening.'

His remarks diverted her thoughts into happy channels. She hurried up with her work, sent the nurses off duty and closed the department for the day. Tomorrow they would be busy again, but now she was free. She walked briskly across the courtyard in the direction of the Nurses' Home, and halted halfway over to allow Dr van Elven's car to pass her. It whispered past, as elegant as its driver, who lifted a gloved hand in salute. She watched it slide through the big double gates, and wondered for the hundredth time why the doctor should need a car as powerful as an Iso Grigo to take him to and from his work. Maybe he took long trips at weekends. She felt suddenly rather sorry for him, because she was so happy herself, with an evening in Steven's company before her, while Dr van Elven had only a house-keeper to greet him when he got home.

When she went down to the Home entrance half an hour later, she could see Steven's car outside the gates. She had put on the blue crêpe and covered it with an off-white wool coat against the chilly March wind. She walked to the Mini Cooper, wondering why he hadn't come to the Home as usual; but when he opened the door for her to get in beside him, she forgot everything but the pleasure of seeing him again. She said, 'Hullo, Steven,' and he returned her smile briefly and greeted her even more briefly. She looked at his dark good-looking face and decided that he was probably tired; which was a pity, because she was looking forward to their evening out. He started the car and said with a cheerfulness which seemed a little forced:

'I thought we'd go to that place you like in Monmouth Street,' and before she could reply launched into an account of his day's work. When he had finished she made a soothing reply and then, thinking to amuse him, told him about Dr van Elven's offer to look after Mrs Brown's cat. He was amused, but not in the way she had intended, for he burst out laughing and said to shock her:

'Good lord, the man's a fool—bothering about some old biddy!'

Sarah breathed a little fast. 'No, he's not a fool—he's just a kind man, and Mrs Brown's going to die in a month or so. The cat's all she has!'

Steven glanced at her with impatience. 'Really, Sarah darling, you're just as much a fool as your precious old van Elven. You're not going to get very far if you're going to get sentimental over an old woman.'

He applied himself to his driving, and she sat silent, biting back the sharp retort she would have liked to make. They had often argued before, but now it was almost as if he were trying to make her angry. He parked the car, and they walked the short distance to the restaurant, talking meanwhile, rather carefully, of completely impersonal things. It was warm in the small room but relaxing and carefree. They had a drink and ordered *entrecôte mon Plaisir*, which was delicious, and then cherry tart, and all the while they continued to talk about everything and everyone but themselves. They were drinking their coffee when Sarah said:

'I've got a week's holiday soon. I'm going home—I wondered if you'd like to drive me down and stay a couple of days,' and the moment she had said it, wished it unsaid, for she had seen the look on his face—irritation, annoyance and even a faint panic. He said far too quickly:

'I can't get away,' not quite meeting her eye, and she felt a cold hand clutch at her heart. There was an awkward silence until she said in a level voice, 'Steven, you're beating about the bush. Just tell me whatever it is—because that's why you brought me here, isn't it, to tell me something?'

He nodded. 'I feel a bit of a swine. . .' he began, and looked taken aback when she said briskly, 'I daresay you do, but you can hardly expect me to be sympathetic about it until I know what the reason for that is.'

She looked calm and a little pale; her hands were clenched tightly in her lap, out of sight. She knew, with awful clarity, that Steven was about to throw her over; a situation she had never envisaged—no, that wasn't quite correct, she told herself honestly.

She had wondered a great deal lately why he never mentioned marriage any more.

He said sulkily, 'I'm going to be married. Old Binns' daughter.' Mr Binns was his chief. The sensible side of Sarah's brain applauded his wisdom—money, a partnership, all the right people for patients. . .

'Congratulations.' Her voice was cool, very composed. 'Have you known her long?'

He looked astonished, and she returned the look with calm dignity, the nails of one hand digging painfully into the palm of the other. If he was expecting her to make a fuss, then he was mistaken.

'About eighteen months.'

Her beautiful mouth opened on a gasp. 'Why didn't you tell me? Or was I being held as a second string?' she wanted to know in a kind of interested astonishment which made him say quickly:

'You don't understand, Sarah. We've had a lot of fun together, haven't we? But you always thought in terms of marriage, didn't you? You must see—you're not a child. If I want to get on—and I do—I must get some money and meet the right people.'

'Do you love her?' asked Sarah.

He blustered a little. 'I'm very fond of her.'

She looked down her exquisite nose and said with feeling, 'Oh, the poor girl! And now I should like to go back, please—I've a heavy morning tomorrow.'

On the way to the car, he asked in a surprised voice, 'Don't you mind?'

'That's a question you have no right to ask as it's of no consequence to you. In any case, I certainly don't intend answering you.'

'You're damned calm,' he answered on a sudden burst of anger. 'That's the trouble with you—calm and strait-laced; we could have had a grand time of it, if it hadn't been for your ridiculous moral upbringing!'

Sarah settled herself in the car. 'It's a good thing in the circumstances, isn't it?' she observed with icy sweetness.

But she wasn't icy when she got to her room. She went along for a bath, and exchanged the time of day with the other Sisters she met in the corridor, refusing a cup of tea on the plea of being tired, and finally shut her door so that at last she was alone and could cry her eyes out. She cried for loneliness and misery and the thought of the empty future and the wasted years, and, because she was a nice girl, she cried for Miss Binns.

The next day was nightmarish, made more so by the fact that it was Mr Binns' out-patients and Steven would be with him that afternoon. She went to her dinner, white-faced and heavy-eyed, and encouraged all those who asked in the belief that she was enduring a heavy cold. She allowed Mr Binns to think the same when he remarked upon her jaded looks, carefully avoiding Steven's eye as she did so. She went about her work with her usual briskness, however, talking to Steven, when she had to, in her usual friendly manner and uttering calming platitudes to the patients as they came and went.

Mr Binns was a brilliant surgeon, but he was a thought too hearty in pronouncing judgment—no one likes being told that some vital organ is in need of repair—and Mr Binns, she suspected, tended to lose sight of the person in the patient. She wondered sometimes if he was quite so cheerfully abrupt with his private patients, and thought it unlikely. She studied him, sitting behind the desk, a shade pompous, faultlessly dressed and very sure of himself, and the unbidden thought streaked through her mind that in twenty years' time Steven would be just like him. This thought was closely followed by another one—most unexpectedly of Dr van Elven, who, although just as sure of himself and dressed, if anything, even more immaculately, had never yet shown himself to be pompous, and whose patients, however trying, he always treated as people.

The day ended at last. She went over to the Home, had a bath and changed out of uniform and went along to the Sisters' sitting room. As she went in, there was a sudden short silence, followed by a burst of chat. She smiled wryly. The grapevine was already at work; it was something she would have to face sooner or later. Luckily she knew everyone in the room very well indeed; she might as well get it over and done with. She caught Kate Spencer's eye—she had trained with Kate; they had been friends for a number of years now—and said cheerfully, 'I expect the grapevine has got all the details wrong—it always does, but the fact remains that Steven is going to marry Mr Binns' daughter. It isn't anyone's fault, just one of those things. Only it's a bit awkward.'

She sat down on one of the easy chairs scattered about the pleasant room and waited quietly for someone to say something. It was Kate who spoke.

'Of course it's Steven's fault. I bet,' she continued with her unerring habit of fastening on the truth, 'he's not in love with her. She's Dad's only daughter, isn't she? There'll be some money later on, and a partnership now.'

She glanced at Sarah's face, which was expressionless, and said with devastating candour, 'I'm right, aren't I? Sarah? Only you'll not admit it.'

She made a small snorting noise, indicative of indignation and echoed by everyone else in the room, because Sarah was liked and Steven had played her a rotten trick. A small dark girl who had been curled up by the fire and had so far said nothing got to her feet.

'There's a new film on at the Leicester Square. Let's all go—if we're quick we can just manage it, and we can eat at Holy Joe's on the way back. It's only spaghetti for supper anyway.'

Her fortitudinous suggestion was received with a relief everyone did their best to conceal. They were all sorry for Sarah, but they knew her enough to know that the last thing she wanted from them was pity. They went in a body to the cinema, sweeping her along with them, and afterwards had a rather noisy supper at Joe's. It was after ten as they walked back through the mean little back streets of the East End to the hospital. It was a long walk, but they had agreed among themselves that it would be a good idea to tire Sarah out, so that she would sleep and not look quite so awful in the morning as she had done all day.

But she didn't sleep that night either—she still looked beautiful when she went on duty the next morning, but she had no colour at all, and her eyes were haggard. She would have to see Steven; work with him, talk to him until dinner time. It was Mr Peppard's surgical OP, and Steven would naturally be there too. She could of course tell one of the staff nurses to take the clinic and make herself scarce at the other end of the department, but pride forbade her. She did the usual round, making sure that patients were being weighed, tests done, X-rays fetched, and Path. Lab. forms collected. It was almost time for the clinic to open when she had done. She went into her office—she would have time to sketch out the off-duty rota before nine o'clock. She had barely sat down at her desk when Steven came in. Sarah looked up briefly, said 'Good morning' with quiet affability and went on with her writing. He stood awkwardly by the door, and when she didn't say anything else, said sulkily:

'I'm sorry, Sarah. I didn't know you were so serious about it all—I mean, we were only good pals, after all. I never said I'd marry you. . .'

Sarah put down her pen at that, gave him a haughty look, and said with deliberation, 'Aren't you being just a little conceited, Steven? No, you never asked me to marry you, so aren't you anticipating my answer? The one I might have made, that is. There's no point in raking over a dead fire, is there?' She had gone rather red in the face, and was regrettably aware that her lip was trembling. She went on sharply, 'Now do go away; I want to get this done before Mr Peppard comes.'

He went then, and she was left to sit alone, staring in front of her, the off-duty rota forgotten.

She went to first dinner, leaving Staff to finish Mr Peppard's clinic. Dr van Elven had his OP at one-thirty—he liked his patients ready and waiting when he arrived, and as he didn't keep other people waiting himself, Sarah did her best to achieve this state of affairs, although it often meant a wild race against time between the clinics. It was one of her lucky days, however. She was ready to start, with the first patient waiting in the little dressing room and the nurse outside already hovering over the second, and there were still five minutes to go. She had had no time to tidy herself. She began feverishly to do so now—showering powder over her pretty nose in a vain effort to cover its redness, and putting on far too much lipstick. She was tucking her hair into a neat pleat, her mouth full of pins, when Dr van Elven stalked in. He was never early—she was so surprised that she opened her mouth and all the pins scattered on the floor. He put down his case on the desk and went and picked them up for her and handed them back gravely. He gave her a quick, searching glance as he wished her good afternoon; a look which she was convinced saw right through the powder. She was annoyed to feel herself blushing—not that it mattered, for he was standing, half turned away from her, reading up the first patient's notes.

For some reason which she couldn't understand, she didn't want him to know about Steven. Of course, in time, he was bound to find out—news leaked through even to the most exhalted of the senior staff. He had been one of the first to know when she had started going out with Steven; she remembered with awful clarity how he had asked her lightly if she would like being a surgeon's wife. She thought that she had no more tears left, but now, at this most awkward of moments, they rose in a solid lump into her throat. She swallowed them back resolutely and heard his calm voice asking her to fetch in the first patient. He looked up as he spoke and gave her a long steady look, and she was all at once aware that he knew all about it. She lifted her chin and went past him to the door to bring in his patient.

The clinic was a long one that afternoon. The medical registrar was on holiday; it meant that one of the house physicians was dealing with blood samples and blood sugars and any of the various tests Dr van Elven wanted done at once. He was nervous and therefore a little slow; when they stopped for five minutes to snatch a cup of tea cooling on its tray, there was still a formidable number of patients to see. Of these, two had to be admitted immediately, and several were sent to X-Ray, which meant that Dr van Elven had to sit patiently while the wet films were fetched by a nurse. It was six o'clock by the time the last patient had gone. Sarah had never known him so late before, and even now he evinced no desire to go home. He sat writing endless notes, and even a couple of letters, because the secretary had gone at five-thirty. Sarah cleared up the afternoon's litter around the department locking doors and inspecting sluices and making sure that there were no patients lurking in the cubicles. When she got back, he had apparently finished, for the desk was cleared of papers, and his case was closed. He got up as she went into the consulting room.

'Mrs Brown is to come in the day after tomorrow, I believe, Sister?'

Sarah said yes, she was, and had he fetched the cat.

'Not yet,' he answered seriously. 'I wonder if you would do me the favour of coming with me to Mrs Brown's—er—home? It seems to me to be a good idea if we were to take her to Richmond with the cat; she could meet my housekeeper and then go on to hospital. If you were there too... I believe that you are free on Saturday mornings?'

She was always free on Saturday mornings—she wondered why he asked, because after all these years he must surely know. But she had nothing to do; it would fill the hours before she came on duty after dinner. She replied:

'Yes, certainly, sir. Shall I meet you there?' She thought a moment. 'Mrs Brown lives in Phipps Street, doesn't she?'

The doctor nodded. 'Yes. But I will fetch you from the Home. Would eleven o'clock suit you?'

He waited only long enough for her to murmur a rather surprised Yes before he went, calling a brief goodnight over his shoulder.

She went to the front door of the Home exactly on the hour on Saturday morning to find him waiting. The Iso Grigo looked sleek and powerful, and it was very comfortable. Dr van Elven got out and walked round and opened the door for her—something Steven had seldom done. Her spirits lifted a little, to drop to her shoes as the car slid to the gate and purred to a halt to allow Steven's Mini to pass them, going the other way. She had a glimpse of his face, gazing at her with a stunned surprise, then he had passed them and they themselves were out in the street. She remembered then that it was Steven's

habit to play squash each Saturday and that he
invariably returned at eleven. She wondered if the
man beside her knew that, and decided that he didn't,
but her flattened ego lifted a little—the small incident
would give Steven something to think about.

She felt all of a sudden more cheerful and was able
to utter a few pointless remarks about the weather, to
which Dr van Elven made courteous replies in a
casual voice. He was so relaxed himself that she
began to relax too and even to feel pleased that she
had dressed with such care. She had read once, a
long time ago, when such advice seemed laughingly
improbable, that it was of the utmost importance for
a girl who had been jilted to take the greatest pains
with her appearance. Well, she had. She had put on
her new tweed suit—a rather dashing outfit in
tobacco brown—and complemented it with brown
calf shoes and handbag. She felt pleased that she had
taken such sound advice, and pondered the advis-
ability of getting a new hat until, obedient to the
doctor's request, she peered out of the window to
look for number 169. Phipps Street was endless,
edged with smoke-grimed Victorian houses, the
variety of whose curtains bore testimony to the
number of people they sheltered; the pavements were
crowded with children playing, housewives hurrying
along with loaded baskets, and old men leaning
against walls, doing nothing at all. Sarah said on a
sigh, 'How drab it all is—how can they live here?'

The doctor eased the car past a coal cart. 'And yet
you choose to work here.'

'Yes. But I go home three or four times a year—
I can escape.' She broke off to point out the house
they were making for, and he brought the car to halt
between a milk float and an ice-cream van with a
smooth action which earned her admiration. They
had barely set foot upon the pavement before a small
crowd had collected. The doctor smiled lightly at the

curious faces around them and applied himself to the elderly knocker upon the front door. Several faces from various windows peered out, and after a good look, the windows were opened. The nearest framed a large man with a belligerent eye. ''Oo d'yer want?' he enquired without enthusiasm.

Dr van Elven said simply, 'Mrs Brown.'

'Ah,' said the man, and disappeared, to reappear a moment later at the door. 'You'll be the doctor,' he remarked importantly. 'Second floor back. Mind the stairs, there's a bit of rail missing.' He stared at them both and then stood back to let them pass him into the small dark hall. 'I'll keep an eye on that there car,' he offered.

'Thank you.' The doctor had produced some cigarettes from a pocket of his well-cut tweed suit and offered them silently. The man took one, said, 'Ta' and waved a muscled arm behind him. 'Up there.'

They mounted the stairs with a certain amount of caution, the doctor restraining her with a hand on her shoulder. She remembering the missing rail. They were on the first landing when Sarah said:

'You don't smoke cigarettes—only a pipe.'

He paused, a step ahead of her, and smiled over his shoulder.

'How—er—observant of you. They're useful to carry around in these parts; they smooth the way, I find.'

They went on climbing and she wondered why he talked as if he was in the habit of frequenting similar houses in similar streets. Most unlikely, she decided, when he lived in Richmond and had rooms in Harley Street and a large private practice to boot.

The second landing was smaller, darker, and smelled. The doctor's splendid nose flared fastidiously, but he said nothing. Sarah had wrinkled her own small nose too; it gave her the air of a rather

choosy angel. The doctor glanced at her briefly, and
then, as though unable to help himself, he looked
again before he knocked on the door before them.

They entered in answer to Mrs Brown's voice,
and found themselves in a small room, depressingly
painted in tones of spinach green and margarine, and
furnished with a bed, table and chairs which were
much too big for it. Mrs Brown was sitting in one
of the chairs and when she attempted to get up, said
breathily, 'Well, well, this is nice and no mistake. I
ain't 'ad visitors for I dunno 'ow long.' She beamed
at them both. ''Ow about a nice cuppa?'

Rather to Sarah's surprise, the doctor said that yes,
he could just do with one, and drew forward an
uncomfortable chair and invited her to sit in it. The
twinkle in his eye was kindly but so pronounced that
she said hastily, 'May I get the tea while you and
Mrs Brown talk?' and left him to lower himself cau-
tiously on to the chair, which creaked in protest under
his not inconsiderable weight.

Making the tea was quite a complicated business,
for it involved going out on to the landing and filling
the kettle from the tap there, which presumably
everyone adjacent to it shared, and setting it on the
solitary gas ring in a corner of the room. She found
teapot, cups and sugar, and was hunting for the milk
when Mrs Brown broke off her conversation to say:

'In a tin, Sister dear, under the shelf. I can't get
down to the milkman all that easy, and tinned milk
makes a good cuppa tea, I always says.'

The tea was rich and brown and syrupy. Sarah sat
in the chair which the doctor had vacated and
inquired for Timmy.

Mrs Brown put down her cup. 'Bless 'im, 'e knows
I'm going.' Her elderly voice shook and Sarah made
haste to say kindly, 'Only for a week or so, Mrs
Brown, and you'll soon feel so much better.'

'That's as may be,' Mrs Brown replied darkly. 'I

wouldn't go to no 'ospital for no one but Doc 'ere.'
She drew a wheezy breath. 'Timmy, come on out ter
yer mum!'

Timmy came from under the bed—an elderly, lean
cat with battle-scarred ears and magnificent whis-
kers. He climbed into the old lady's lap, butted her
gently with his bullet head, and purred.

'Nice, ain't 'e?' his owner asked. 'Pals, we are—
don't know as 'ow I wants ter go. . .'

Dr van Elven turned from his contemplation of
the neighbouring chimney pots. His voice was gentle.

'Mrs Brown, if you will consent to go to hospital
now, and stay for two weeks, there will be no chance
of you waking up one morning and not feeling well
enough to get out of bed. You remember I explained
that to you. What would happen to Timmy then?
Surely it is better to know that he is safe and cared
for now than run the risk of not being able to look
after him?' He picked up her coat from the bed.
'Shall we go? You will be able to see where he will
be and who will be looking after him.'

He sounded persuasive and kind and quite sure of
what he was talking about. The old lady got up, and
allowed herself to be helped into her coat, put on the
shapeless hat with a fine disregard as to her appearance, and pronounced herself ready. When they
reached the pavement, the small crowd was still
there, kept firmly under control by the man who had
opened the door to them. He accepted the remainder
of the cigarettes from the doctor, shut the car doors
firmly upon them and saluted smartly.

''E's me landlord,' Mrs Brown informed them
from the back of the car. 'Real gent 'e is. Let me
orf me rent.' She settled back, Timmy perched on
her lap, apparently unimpressed by his surroundings.
Sarah didn't look at the doctor, but she had the feeling that they were thinking the same thing. She was
proved right when he murmured:

'*Bis dat qui cito dat.*'

She said. 'Oh, Latin. Something about giving, isn't it?'

The man beside her chuckled. 'He who gives quickly, gives twice.'

'That's what I thought too, only in English. He didn't look as though he'd give a crumb to a bird, and I don't suppose he could really afford to lose the rent, even for a couple of weeks.'

Dr van Elven said briefly, 'No,' then glanced at his watch. 'You're on at half past one, are you not? It's just gone half past eleven. Time enough; we'll go by the back ways.'

He knew his London, that was evident; he didn't hesitate once, but wove his way in and out of streets which all looked alike, until she wasn't at all sure where they were. It was a surprise when they crossed the river, and she recognised Putney Bridge. They turned into Upper Richmond Road very shortly after, then into Richmond itself and so to the river. The doctor's house was one of a row of Georgian bow-fronted houses set well back from the road, with their own private thoroughfare and an oblique view of the water, which was only a couple of hundred yards away. It was surprisingly peaceful. Sarah got out of the car and looked around her while the doctor helped Mrs Brown to get out. It would be nice to live in such a spot, she thought, only a few miles from the hospital, but as far removed from it as if they were upon another planet.

The doctor unlocked the front door with its gleaming knocker and beautiful fanlight and stood aside for them to go in. The hall was a great deal larger than she had thought from the outside, and was square with a polished floor and some lovely rugs. There was a satin-striped wallpaper upon which were a great many pictures, and the furniture was, she thought, early Regency—probably Sheraton. The baize door at the back of the hall opened and a woman came towards them. She was tall and bony and middle-aged, with dark brown eyes and pepper-and-salt hair; she had the nicest smile Sarah had seen for a long time. The doctor shut the door and said easily:

'Ah, there you are, Alice.' He glanced at Sarah and said, 'This is my good friend and housekeeper, Alice Miller. Alice, this is Sister Dunn from the hospital, and this is Mrs Brown, of whom I told you, and Timmy.' He threw his gloves on to a marble-topped wall table. 'Supposing you take Mrs Brown with you and show her where Timmy will live, and discuss his diet?'

Sarah watched the two women disappear through the door to the kitchen and looked rather shyly at Dr van Elven.

'Come and see the splendid view from the sitting room,' he invited, and led the way to one of the doors opening into the hall. The room was at the back of the house, and from its window there was indeed an excellent view of the river with a stretch of green beyond. It was almost country, and the illusion was heightened by the small garden, which was a mass of primulas and daffodils and grape hyacinths backed by trees and shrubs. There was a white-painted table and several chairs in one corner, sheltered by a box hedge; it would be pleasant to sit there on a summer morning. She said so, and he replied, 'It is indeed. I breakfast there when it's fine, for it is difficult for me to get out of doors at all on a busy day.'

She didn't reply. She was picturing him sitting there, reading the morning paper and his post—she wondered if he had any family to write to him. She hoped so; he was so nice. He had gone to the ground-length window and opened it to let in two dogs, a basset hound and a Jack Russell, whom he introduced as Edward and Albert. They pranced to meet her, greeted her politely and then went back to stand by their master.

He said, 'Do sit down, won't you? We'll give them ten minutes to get to know each other. There are cigarettes beside you if you care to smoke.'

She shook her head. 'No thanks. I only smoke at parties when I want something to do with my hands.'

He smiled. 'You won't mind if I light my pipe?'

'Please do. What will you do about Mrs Brown, sir?'

'What I said. Pull her together as far as we can in hospital and then let her go home.'

Sarah looked horrified. 'Not back to Phipps Street?'

He raised his brows. 'Phipps Street is her home,' he said coolly. 'She has lived there for so long, it would be cruel to take her away, especially as she has only a little of life left. I shall arrange for someone to go in daily and do everything necessary, and I think the landlord could be persuaded to clean up the room and perhaps paint it while she is away.'

Sarah nodded, highly approving. 'That would be nice. Yes, you're right, of course. She'd be lost anywhere else.'

He had lighted his pipe; now he stood up. He said, quite without sarcasm, 'I'm glad you approve. I'm going to fetch Mrs Brown—will you wait here? I shan't be long.'

When he had gone, she got up and began an inspection of the room. It was comfortable and lived-in, with leather armchairs and an enormous couch drawn up before the beautiful marble fireplace. The floor was polished and covered with the same beautiful rugs as there were in the hall. There was a sofa table behind the couch and a scattering of small drum tables around the room, and a marquetry William and Mary china cabinet against one of the walls. A davenport under one of the windows would make letter writing very pleasant. . .it had a small button-backed chair to partner it; Sarah went and sat down, feeling soothed and calmer than she had felt for the last two days or so. She realised that she hadn't thought of Steven for several hours; she had been so occupied with Mrs Brown and the ridiculous Timmy—it had been pure coincidence, of course, that Dr van Elven should have asked for her help; all the same she felt grateful to him. He couldn't have done more to distract her thoughts even if she had told him about the whole sorry business.

Her gratitude coloured her goodbyes when they parted in the hospital entrance hall, he to go off to some business of his own, she to take Mrs Brown to Women's Medical. But if he was surprised by the fervour of her thanks, he gave no sign. It was only later, when she was sitting in the lonely isolation of OPD that the first faint doubts as to whether it had been coincidence crept into her mind. She brushed them aside as absurd at first, but they persisted, and the annoying thing was that she wasn't sure if she minded or not. There was no way of finding out either, short of asking Dr van Elven to his face, something she didn't care to do; for if she was mistaken, she could imagine only too vividly, the look of bland amusement on his face. The amusement would be kindly, and that would make it worse, because it would mean that he pitied her, a fact, which for some reason or other, she could not bear to contemplate.

She drew the laundry book towards her, resolutely emptying her mind of anything but the number of towels and pillow cases she could expect back on Monday.

CHAPTER TWO

SARAH went to see Mrs Brown on Sunday. She went deliberately during the visiting hour in the afternoon, because she thought it unlikely that the old lady would have any visitors. She was right; Mrs Brown was sitting up in bed in a hospital nightie several sizes too large for her, looking very clean, her hair surprisingly white after its washing—a nurse had pinned it up and tied a pink bow in it as well.

'How nice you look, Mrs Brown—I like that ribbon.' Sarah drew up a chair and sat down, aware of the glances Mrs Brown was casting left and right to her neighbours as if to say 'I told you so'. She made a resolve then and there to pop in and see her whenever she could spare a minute, and enquired after the old lady's health.

Mrs Brown brushed this aside. ''E sent a message,' she stated. 'Timmy's 'ad a good sleep, 'e said, and eaten for two.' She fidgeted around in the bed and all the pillows fell down, so that Sarah had to get up and rearrange them. 'One of them young doctors told me this morning.' She frowned reflectively. 'They knows what they're doing, I suppose? Them young ones?'

'Yes, Mrs Brown.' Sarah sounded very positive. 'They're all qualified doctors and they're here to carry out the consultant's wishes.'

'So all them things 'e did to me 'e was told ter do by the doc?'

Sarah nodded. 'That's right. Now is there anything I can do for you while you're here? Was anyone going to get your room ready for you to go back?'

The old lady looked astonished. 'Lor', no, ducks.

'Oo'd 'ave the time? Though I daresay someone'll pop in and do me bed and get me in some stuff.'

Sarah made a noncommittal reply to this remark, and made a mental note to go round to Phipps Street one evening and make sure that there really was someone.

She didn't see Steven again until Tuesday morning, when Mr Binns had an extra OP clinic. They had barely exchanged cool good mornings, when he was called away to the wards, and didn't return until all but two of the patients had gone. It was already past twelve, and they were behind time. Dr van Elven had a vast clinic at one-thirty. For once she was glad of Mr Binns' briskness; he took no time at all over the last patient—a post-operative check-up—thanked Sarah with faint pomposity, and hurried away with Steven beside him. She sent the nurses to dinner, had a few words with Staff, who had come on duty to take the gynae clinic, and then got on with the business of substituting Dr Binns' paraphernalia for that of Dr van Elven. She had almost finished when Steven returned.

He said abruptly as he came in, 'Where the hell were you going on Saturday with old van Elven?'

Sarah's heart gave an excited jump. So he minded! She stacked the case notes neatly and consulted her long list of names before she replied, in a calm voice she hardly recognised as her own:

'Is it any business of yours? And if you refer to Dr van Elven, he's not at all old, you know.'

He gave an ugly laugh. 'You're a sly one—pretending to be such a little puritan and playing the hurt madam with me! How long have you been leading him by the nose? He's quite a catch.'

He was standing quite near her. She put down her list and slapped his face hard, and in the act saw Dr van Elven standing at the doorway. As he came into the room he said quietly, 'Get out.' His voice had the menace of a knife, although his face was impassive.

Sarah watched Steven standing irresolute, one hand to a reddened cheek, the look of surprise still on his face, and then turn on his heel and go. She had never expected him to brazen it out anyway. Dr van Elven was the senior consultant at St Edwin's, and could, if he so wished, use his authority. She didn't look at him now, but mumbled, 'I'm late for dinner. . .'

'Sit down,' he said placidly, and she obeyed him weakly. She had gone very white; now her face flamed with humiliation and temper—mostly temper. She shook with it, and gripped her hands together in her lap to keep them steady. Dr van Elven went over to the desk in a leisurely fashion and put down his case. He said, not looking at her, in a most reasonable voice:

'You can't possibly go to the dining room in such a towering rage.'

He was right, of course. Sarah stared at her hands and essayed to speak.

'You know about me and Steven.'

'Yes. But I see no need to enlarge upon what must be a painful subject.'

Sarah choked on a watery chuckle, 'I'm behaving like a heroine in a Victorian novel, aren't I?' She gave him a sudden waspish look. 'I'm furious!' she snapped, as though he hadn't commented upon her feelings already. He said 'Yes,' again and gave her a half smile, then bent over his desk, leaving her to pull herself together. Presently he remarked:

'That's better. We have a large clinic, I believe. How fortunate—there's nothing like hard work for calming the nerves. Might I suggest that you go to your dinner now? I should like to start punctually.'

She got up at once, unconsciously obedient to his quietly compelling voice. 'Yes, of course, sir. I've been wasting time.'

She fled through the door, feeling that somehow or other he had contrived to make the whole episode not worth bothering about. She even ate her dinner, aware that he would ask her if she had done so when she got back and would expect a truthful answer.

There was not time to ask her anything, however. When she returned the benches were overflowing. The air rang with a variety of coughs, and as it was raining outside, the same air was heavy with the damp from wet coats and the redolence of sopping garments which those who had arrived first had had the forethought to dry out upon the radiators. Sarah went swiftly into the consultants' room, saw that Dr van Elven was already sitting at his desk, adjusted her cuffs and said in her usual serene tones:

'Shall I fetch in the first one, sir? Mr Jenkins— check-up after three weeks as in-patient.'

He gave her a brief, impersonal glance, nodded and returned to his writing. 'I've seen his X-rays— I'll want some blood though. Will you get Dr Coles on to it?'

She fetched in Mr Jenkins, waited just long enough to make sure that she wouldn't be wanted for a moment, and flew to find the Medical Registrar. Dr Coles was tucked away in the little room near the sluice, going through Path. Lab. forms and various reports, so that later, when Dr van Elven wanted to know some detail about one of his patients, he would know the answer. He looked up as she went in and said pleasantly:

'Hullo, Sarah. Is the chief already here? I'm still choking down facts and figures.' He grinned and she smiled at him warmly. He was a nice man, not young any more, and apparently not ambitious, for he seemed content to stay where he was, working in hospital. He got on well with the consultant staff and was utterly reliable and invariably good-natured. He was reputed to be very happily married and was apt to talk at length about his children, of whom he was very proud. He got up now and followed her back past the rows of patients. Mr Jenkins was still describing the nasty pain that caught him right in the stomach, and Dr van Elven was listening to him with the whole of his attention. When the old man paused for breath, though, the doctor said, 'Hullo, Dick', and smiled at his Registrar. 'What did you make of Mr Jenkins when he was in?'

The two men became immersed in their patient, leaving her free to make sure that the one to follow was ready and waiting in the dressing room, and that everything that Dr van Elven might want was to hand.

The afternoon wore on, the small room gradually acquiring the same damp atmosphere as the waiting hall. Sarah switched on the electric fan, which stirred up the air without noticeable improvement. She switched it off again and Dr van Elven said:

'Don't worry, Sister,' and then, surprisingly, 'I am a little ashamed that I can drive myself home, warm, and dry for I imagine, from their appearance, that quite a number of my patients haven't even the price of a bus fare, and even if they have, won't be able to get on a bus.' He caught her eye and smiled. 'How about tea?'

Over their brief cup, the men discussed the next case and Dr Coles told them about his eldest son, who was doing rather well at school. It was while Sarah was piling their cups and saucers on to a tray that Dr van Elven remarked quietly, 'Mrs Brown tells me that you visit her regularly, Sister. That is good of you.'

Sarah whipped the next patient's notes before him and said in a matter-of-fact voice, 'Well, I don't think she has any relations or friends to come and see her, sir. And you know how awful it is for a patient to be the only one in the ward without visitors.'

He eyed her thoughtfully. 'I imagine it must be a miserable experience. She is responding very well, you know. I must see about getting her home.'

Sarah was on the way to the door. She paused and looked back at him.

'How's Timmy?' she asked.

'The perfect guest—his manners, contrary to his appearance, are charming.'

They finished at last—she sent the student nurses off duty, left Staff to clear up the gynae clinic on the other side of the department, and began her own clearing up. Dr Coles had gone to answer a call from one of the wards, and she was alone with Dr van Elven, who was sitting back in his chair, presumably deep in thought. She bustled about the little room putting it to rights and piling the case notes ready to take back to the office. She was trying not to remember that it was just a week since she had gone out to dinner with Steven, but her thoughts, now that she was free to think again after the afternoon's rush, kept returning to the same unhappy theme. She had quite forgotten the man sitting so quietly at the desk. When he spoke she jumped visibly and said hurriedly:

'I'm sorry, sir, I didn't hear what you were saying.'

He withdrew an abstracted gaze from the ceiling, stared at her from under half-closed lids, and got up. At the door he said quietly:

'It gets easier as the days go by—especially if there is plenty of work to do. Good night, Sister Dunn.'

Sarah stood staring, her mouth open. He was well out of earshot when she at length said 'Good night' in reply.

There was a message for her when she got over to the Home, from Steven, saying that he had to see her, and would she be outside at seven o'clock. To apologise, she surmised; but he could have done that

in his note, and she had no intention of running to
his least word. She changed rapidly; she had a good
excuse to go out, and was glad of it. She would go
and see about Mrs Brown's room. There was actually
plenty of time, but as Dr van Elven had said, being
busy helped.

Phipps Street looked depressing; the rain had
stopped, but the wind was fresh and the evening sky
unfriendly. Sarah banged on the front door and the
same man opened it to her. He looked at her sus-
piciously at first, perhaps because she was in a
raincoat and a headscarf and looked different, but
when he saw who she was he opened the door wide.

'It's you again, miss. Thought you'd be along.
Come to 'ave a look, I suppose, and do a bit o'
choosing. 'Ow's the old girl?'

Sarah edged past him. 'She's fine—and settled
in very nicely, though of course she's longing to
come home.'

He lumbered ahead of her up the miserable
staircase.

'Well, o'course. 'Oo wants ter stay in 'ospital
when they got a good 'ome?'

They had reached the little landing and he flung
open Mrs Brown's door with something of a flourish.
It was empty of furniture—of everything, she noted
with mounting astonishment. Two men were painting
the woodwork; one of them turned round as she went
in, greeted her civilly and asked if she had come to
choose the wallpaper. Her grey eyes opened wide
and she turned to the landlord. 'But surely you want
to decide that?' she wanted to know.

'Lor' luv yer, miss, no. What should I know about
fancy wallpaper?' He let out a great bellow of laughter and went out, shutting the door behind him. Sarah
looked around her. The room was being redecorated
quite lavishly. The hideous piping which probably
had something to do with the water tap on the landing

had been cased in: one of the men was fitting a new sash-cord to the elderly window frame he was painting. The paintwork was grey, the walls, stripped of several layers of paper, looked terrible. There were several books of wallpaper patterns in the centre of the room, on the bare floor. After an undecided moment, Sarah knelt down and opened the first of them. The man at the window said:

'That's right, ducks, you choose something you like; we'll be ready to 'ang it soon as the paint's dry.'

She gave him a puzzled look. 'Well, if there's no one else.'

She was contemplating a design of pink cabbage roses when she heard someone running upstairs and the door was opened by Dr van Elven. He nodded to the two men, and if he was surprised to see Sarah, she had to admit that he didn't show it. He said, 'Hullo. What a relief to see you—now you can choose the wallpaper.'

She had to laugh. 'It's like a conspiracy—when I got here the landlord seemed to think that was why I had come, and so did this painter. I really only came to see if there was any cleaning to do before Mrs Brown came home.'

'Not for ten days at least.' His tone was dry.

She was annoyed to feel her cheeks warming. 'Well, I wanted to get away from the hospital.' She turned back to the pattern book, determined not to say more, and was relieved when he said casually:

'That's splendid. Have you seen anything you like?'

'Mrs Brown likes pink,' she said slowly, and frowned. 'Surely if the landlord is having this done, he should choose?' She looked up enquiringly, saw his face and said instantly: 'You're doing it.' She added, 'Sir.'

'My name is Hugo,' he said pleasantly. 'You are, of course, aware of that. I think that after three years we might dispense with sir and Sister, unless we are actually—er—at work. I hope you agree?'

She was a little startled and uncertain what to say, but it seemed it was of no consequence, for he continued without waiting for her reply:

'Good, that's settled. Now, shall we get this vexed question of wallpaper dealt with?'

He got down beside her as he spoke, and opened a second book of patterns, and they spent a pleasant half hour admiring and criticising in a lighthearted fashion until finally Sarah said:

'I think Mrs Brown would like the roses. They're very large and pink, aren't they, and they'll make the room look even smaller than it is, but they're pretty—I mean for someone who's lived for years with green paint and margarine walls, they're pretty.'

The man beside her uncoiled himself and came to his feet with the agility of a much younger man. 'Right. Roses it shall be. Now, furniture—nothing too modern, I think, but small—I had the idea of looking around one or two of those second-hand places to try and find similar stuff. Perhaps you would come with me, Sarah. Curtains too—I've no idea. . .'

He contrived to look so helpless that she agreed at once.

'Would eleven o'clock on Saturday suit you?' he asked. She gave him a swift suspicious glance, which he returned with a look of such innocent blandness that she was instantly ashamed of her thoughts. She got to her feet and said that yes, that would do very well, and waited while he talked to the two men. When he had finished she said a little awkwardly:

'Well, I think I'll go now. Goodnight, everyone.'

The two workmen chorused a cheerful, ''Night, ducks,' but the doctor followed her out. On the stairs he remarked mildly:

'What a shy young woman you are!' and then,

'Let me go first, this staircase is a death-trap.'

With his broad back to her, she found the courage to say, 'I know I'm shy—it's stupid in a woman of my age, isn't it? I try very hard not to be; it's all right while I'm working. I—I thought I'd got over it, but now I seem worse than ever.'

Her voice tailed away, as she remembered Steven. They had reached the landing and he paused and turned round to look at her. 'My dear girl, being shy doesn't matter in the least; didn't you know that? It can be positively restful in this day and age.'

They went on down to the little hall and Sarah felt warmed by the comfort of his words; it was extraordinary how he put her at her ease, almost as though they were friends of a lifetime. She stood by the door, while he, in a most affable manner, pointed out to Mr Ives, the landlord, the iniquity of having a staircase in the house that would most certainly be the death of someone, including himself, unless he did something about it very soon. Mr Ives saw them to the door, and stood on the pavement while the doctor opened the car door for Sarah to get in. It was only when they were on their way back to St Edwin's that she realised that there had been nothing said about taking her back. The doctor had ushered her into his car, and she had got in without protest.

She hoped he didn't think she'd been angling for a lift. 'I could have walked.' She spoke her thoughts out loud. 'You're going out of your way. . .'

She looked at him, watching the corners of his eyes crinkle as he smiled.

'So you could. I'm afraid that I gave you no opportunity—you don't mind?'

She said no, she didn't mind, and plunged, rather self-consciously, into aimless chatter, in which he took but a minimal part. At the hospital, she thanked him for the lift.

'I could have easily walked. . .' she began, and

stopped when she saw Steven standing outside the Home entrance. The doctor saw him too; he got out of the car in a leisurely way, and strolled to the door with her; giving Steven a pleasant good evening as they passed him. He opened the door, said 'Good night, Sarah' in an imperturbable voice, urged her gently inside and shut the door upon her.

Steven wasn't at the surgical clinic the following day. Mr Binns had the assistance of Jimmy Dean, one of the house surgeons; he and Kate were in love, but he had no prospects and neither of them had any money. It would be providential if Steven left when he married Mr Binns' daughter, so that Jimmy could at least apply for the post. He was good at his job, though a little slow, but Sarah liked him. But Steven was with Mr Peppard when he arrived to take his clinic on Thursday morning—and as soon as opportunity offered, he asked shortly:

'Why didn't you answer my note—or wasn't I supposed to know that you had a date with van Elven?'

Sarah picked out the X-ray she was looking for. She said in a voice it was a little hard to keep steady because he was so near, 'I had arranged to go out; not, as you suppose, with Dr van Elven—and anyway, what would be the purpose of meeting you?'

She walked briskly to the desk, and remained, quite unnecessarily, throughout the patient's interview. She was careful not to give Steven the opportunity to waylay her again, a resolve made easier by the unexpected absence of a part-time staff nurse who usually took the ear, nose and throat clinic. She put a student nurse in her place because there was no one else, which gave her a good excuse for spending the greater part of the morning making sure that the nurse could manage. Mr Peppard went at last, with Steven trailing behind him. He gave her a look of frustrated rage as he went, which, while gratifying her ego, did nothing to lessen her unhappiness.

It was a relief to see Dr van Elven's placid face when she came back from dinner. His 'Good afternoon, Sister' was uttered with his usual gravity, but she detected a twinkle in his grey eyes as he said it. Perhaps he was remembering that the last time they had seen each other, they had been kneeling side by side on a dusty floor, deciding that pink cabbage roses would be just the thing. . .but if he was thinking of it too, his manner betrayed no sign of it.

The clinic went smoothly, without one single reference to Mrs Brown or her rooms; it was as if none of it had happened. And he didn't mention Saturday at all. Sarah decided several times during Friday, not to go at all, and indeed, thought about it so much that Mr Bunn, the gynaecologist, had to ask her twice for the instruments he required on more than one occasion—such a rare happening that he wanted to know if she was sickening for something.

She was still feeling uncertain when she left the Nurses' Home the next morning—supposing Dr van Elven had forgotten—worse, not meant what he had said? But he hadn't; he was waiting just outside the door. He ushered her into the Iso Grigo, and she settled back into its expensive comfort, glad that she was wearing the brown suit again.

He said, 'Hullo, Sarah. I'm glad you decided to come.'

'But I said I would.'

He smiled. 'You have had time enough to change your mind. . .even to wonder if I would come.'

It was disconcerting to have her thoughts read so accurately. She went pink.

'Well, as a matter of fact, I did wonder if you might forget, or—or change your mind.' She added hastily, 'That sounds rude; I didn't mean it to be, only I feel a little uncertain about—well, everything.'

He sat relaxed behind the wheel. 'That's natural, but it won't last.' His mouth curved in a smile. 'You look nice.'

Her spirits rose; she smiled widely and never noticed Steven's Mini as it passed them. She had forgotten all about him, for the moment, at least.

The morning was fun. They chose the furniture for Mrs Brown with care, going from one dealer to the other, until it only remained for them to buy curtains and carpets. They stood outside the rather seedy little shop where Sarah had happily bargained for the sort of easy chair she knew Mrs Brown would like.

'We'll go to Harrods,' said the doctor.

She looked at him with pitying horror. 'Harrods? Don't you know that it's a most expensive shop? Anyway, it'll be shut today. There's a shop in the Commercial Road. . .'

Mindful of the doctor's pocket, she bought pink material for the curtains, and because it was quite cheap, some extra material for a tablecloth. She bought a grey carpet too, although she thought it far too expensive and said so, but apparently Dr van Elven had set his heart on it. When they were back in the car she pointed out to him that he had spent a great deal of money.

'How much?' he queried lazily.

She did some mental sums. 'A hundred and eighty-two pounds, forty-eight pence. If it hadn't been for the carpet. . .'

He said gravely, 'I think I can manage that—who will make the curtains?'

'I'll do those—I can borrow Kate's machine and run them up in an hour or so. They cost a great deal to have made, you know.' She paused. 'Dr van Elven. . .'

'Hugo.'

'Well, Hugo—it's quite a lot of money. I'd like—
that is, do you suppose. . .'

He had drawn up at traffic lights. 'No, I don't
suppose anything of the sort, Sarah.'

She subsided, feeling awkward, and looked out of
the window, to say in some surprise, 'This is New-
gate Street, isn't it? We can't get back to St Edwin's
this way, can we?'

His reply was calm. 'We aren't going back at the
moment. I have only just realised that you'll miss
first dinner and not have time for second. I thought
we might have something quick to eat, and I'll take
you back afterwards. That is, if you would like that?'

She felt that same flash of surprise again, but
answered composedly.

'Thank you, that would be nice. I'm on at two
today—I had some time owing.'

They went down Holborn and New Oxford Street
and then cut across to Regent Street, and stopped at
the Café Royal. Sarah had often passed it and wondered, a little enviously, what it was like inside; it
seemed she was to have the opportunity to find out.
They went to the Grill Room, and she wasn't disappointed; it was pretty and the mirrors were
charming if a trifle disconcerting. The doctor had
said 'something quick'; she had envisaged something
on toast, but on looking round her she deduced
that the only thing she would get on toast would be
caviare. She studied the menu card and wondered
what on earth to order.

'Something cold, I think,' her glance flew to her
watch, 'and quick.'

Quick wasn't quite the word to use in such surroundings, where luncheon was something to be
taken in a leisurely fashion. She caught her companion's eye and saw the gleam in its depths, but all
he said was:

'How about a crab mousse and a Bombe Pralinée

after?' He gave the order and asked, 'Shall we have a Pernod, or is there anything else you prefer?'

'Pernod would be lovely.' She smiled suddenly, wrinkling her beautiful nose in the endearing and unconscious manner of a child.

'What a pity that we haven't hours and hours to spend over lunch.' She stopped, vexed at the pinkening of her cheeks under his amused look. 'What I mean is,' she said austerely, 'it's the kind of place where you dawdle, with no other prospect than a little light shopping or a walk in the park before taking a taxi home.'

'You tempt me to telephone Matron and ask her to let you have the afternoon off.'

He spoke lightly and Sarah felt a surprising regret that he couldn't possibly mean it. 'That sort of thing happens in novels, never in real life. I can imagine Matron's feelings!'

They raised their glasses to Mrs Brown's recovery, and over their drinks fell to discussing her refurbished room, which topic somehow led to a variety of subjects, which lasted right through the delicious food and coffee as well, until Sarah glanced at her watch again and said:

'Oh, my goodness! I simply must go—the time's gone so quickly.'

The doctor paid the bill and said comfortably:

'Don't worry—you won't be late.' And just for a moment she remembered Steven, who was inclined to fuss about getting back long before it was necessary. Dr van Elven didn't appear to fuss at all—as little, in fact, as he did in hospital. She felt completely at ease with him, but then, her practical mind interposed, so she should; they had worked together for several years now.

They didn't talk much going back to the hospital, but the silence was a friendly one; he wasn't the kind of man one needed to chat to incessantly. There

wasn't much time to thank him when they arrived
at the Nurses' Home, but though of necessity brief,
her thanks were none the less sincere; she really had
enjoyed herself. He listened to her with a half smile
and said, 'I'm glad. I enjoyed it too. I hope I'm not
trespassing too much on your good nature if I ask
you to accompany Mrs Brown when I take her home.'
He saw her look and said smoothly, 'Yes, I know
she could quite well go by ambulance, but I have to
return Timmy, so I can just as well call for her on
my way. Would ten o'clock suit you? And by the
way, I've found a very good woman who will go
every day.'

Sarah said how nice and yes, ten o'clock would
do very well, and felt a pang of disappointment that
once Mrs Brown was home again there would be no
need for her to give Dr van Elven the benefit of her
advice any more. She stifled the thought at once; it
smacked of disloyalty to Steven, even though he
didn't love her any more. She said goodbye in a sober
voice, and later on, sitting in the hollow stillness of
OPD, tried to pretend to herself that any minute now
Steven would appear and tell her that it was all a
mistake and he wasn't going to marry Anne Binns
after all. But he didn't come—no one came at all.

The week flew by. She saw Steven several times,
but never alone; she took care of that—although she
thought it likely that he didn't want to speak to her
anyway. Perhaps, she thought hopefully, he was
ashamed of himself, although there was no evidence
of it in his face. She went out a great deal in her
off-duty too—her friends saw to that; someone
always seemed to be at hand to suggest the cinema
or supper at Holy Joe's. She made the curtains and
the tablecloth too, and took them round on Friday
evening. Hugo van Elven had said nothing to
her about Mrs Brown or her room—indeed, upon

reflection, she could not remember him saying anything at all that wasn't to do with work.

Mr Ives let her in with a friendly, ''Ullo, ducks.' Sarah responded suitably and was led up the stairs, pausing on the way to admire the repair work he had done. When they reached the top landing he opened Mrs Brown's door with something of a flourish and stood back, beaming.

'Nice little 'ome, eh?' he remarked with satisfaction. Sarah agreed; despite the pink roses, which seemed to crowd in on her the moment she set foot inside the room, and the superfluity of furniture, it was just what she was sure Mrs Brown would like. She undid her parcel and spread the cloth on the table, and gallantly helped by Mr Ives, hung the curtains. She had been to visit Mrs Brown several times during the week and had contrived to bring the conversation round to the subject of colours. Mrs Brown had been quite lyrical about pink. Sarah stood back and surveyed her handiwork and thought that it was a good thing that she was, because there was pink enough and to spare. Mr Ives obviously had no such qualms.

'Nice taste that doc's got—couldn't 'ave chosen better meself.'

She agreed faintly, thinking of the gracious house at Richmond with its subdued colours and beautiful furniture. She told Mr Ives the time they expected to arrive and he nodded, already knowing it.

'Doc told me last night when 'e was 'ere. Brought a bottle of the best with 'im too.' He saw Sarah's look of enquiry. 'Brandy,' he explained, 'I'm ter keep it safe and give Mrs Brown a taste now and then like; just a teaspoon in 'er tea. Brought me a bottle for meself too. I'll keep an eye on the old gal like I promised; I got Doc's phone number, case 'e's wanted.'

He led the way down the stairs again and bade

her goodbye after offering to escort her back to St Edwin's. 'Don't know as 'ow the doc would like yer out at night,' he observed seriously.

Sarah, a little overcome by such solicitude, observed in her turn that it was highly unlikely that the doctor would care a row of pins what she did with her free time, and in any case, it was barely nine o'clock in the evening. She spoke briskly, but Mr Ives was not to be deterred.

'I dunno about that,' he said in a rather grumbling voice, 'but I knows I'd rather not be on the wrong side of the doc. Still, if yer won't yer won't. I'll stand 'ere till yer get ter the end of the street—yer can wave under the lamppost there so's I can see yer.'

Sarah did as she was told. She had a sneaking feeling that she would prefer to keep on the right side of the 'doc' too.

Mrs Brown was sitting in a wheelchair in the ward, waiting for her when she went along to collect her on Saturday. She looked better, but thinner too— probably worry about Timmy and her little home and all the other small things that were important to old people living alone. Sarah sighed with relief to think that the old lady would have a nice surprise when she got home. Dr van Elven greeted them briefly at the entrance, stowed Mrs Brown in the back of the car, motioned Sarah to get in the front and released Timmy from his basket. Neither he nor Sarah looked round as he drove to Phipps Street. Mrs Brown's happiness was a private thing into which they had no intention of prying.

There were several neighbours hanging around when they arrived, and it took a few minutes to get into the house. The doctor, without speaking, scooped up the old lady, trembling with delight and excitement, and trod carefully upstairs, leaving Sarah and Timmy and Mr Ives to follow in his wake. On the landing he nodded to Sarah to open the door.

Mrs Brown didn't quite grasp what had happened at first, and when she did she burst into tears. It seemed the right moment to make a cup of tea. Sarah bustled around while Mrs Brown composed herself and began incoherent thanks which only ended when she sat in her new armchair with a cup and saucer in her hand. She had calmed down considerably by the time the door opened and a pleasant-faced, middle-aged woman with a cheerful cockney voice came in. Sarah had no difficulty in recognising her as the 'very good woman' the doctor had found, and it was obvious before very long that his choice had been a happy one; the two ladies were going to get on splendidly. They got up to go presently, and Dr van Elven drove Sarah back to the hospital, saw her to the door of the Home, thanked her politely and drove away again. It was barely twelve o'clock. Sarah went up to her room; a faint stirring of disappointment deep inside her which she refused to acknowledge as regret because he hadn't asked her out to lunch.

She saw Steven on Monday—he came in at the end of Dr MacFee's diabetic clinic. Dr MacFee had just gone, and the place was more or less empty when Steven walked in, taking her quite by surprise. She stood looking at him, waiting for him to speak first, and was inwardly surprised to find that the sight of him, though painful, was bearable.

'I suppose you expect me to apologise,' he began. 'Well, I don't intend to. All I can say is, I'm glad we split up before I found out what a. . .'

He caught her belligerent eye. 'A what?' she enquired with icy calm. 'I should be careful what you say, Steven—I'll not hesitate to slap you again!'

He flung away. 'I wish you joy, that's all I can say!' he shouted, as he strode through the empty waiting hall. She watched him go. He was very good-looking, and when he wasn't angry, charming too.

She sighed and went to her dinner, wondering why he should wish her joy.

Dr van Elven's clinic was, as usual, splitting at the seams. Sarah, nipping from one patient to the other, weighing them, taking them to the Path. Lab., to X-ray, helping them in and out of endless garments, wished that he wasn't quite such a glutton for work. She'd had to send two of her nurses up to the wards for the afternoon because a number of the staff were off with 'flu. Now and again, when she made a sortie into the waiting hall for another patient, she glimpsed Staff at the other end with the one junior nurse they had been left with; they were busy in Gynae too. She went back into the consulting room to find Dr van Elven dealing, with commendable calm, with the attack of hysterics which his patient had sprung on him.

Dick Coles went as soon as they had finished and Sarah began to tidy up, although she longed for tea. It would be too late to go to the Sisters' sitting room; she would have to make her own when she got to her room.

The doctor was sitting at the desk, absorbed in something or other. Sarah supposed that he was in no hurry to go home—it wasn't as if there was a wife waiting for him. . . She finished at length, picked up the pile of notes she intended dropping into the office on her way, and went to the door. When she reached it she said, 'Good night, sir,' then stopped short when he said 'Come back here, Sarah, and sit down. I want to talk to you.'

She did as she was asked, because when he spoke in that quiet voice she found it prudent to obey him. She sat in the chair facing him, the notes piled on her lap; she was tired and thirsty and a little untidy, but her face was serene. She looked at him across the desk, smiling a little, because in the last few days she had come to regard him as a friend.

He sat back, meeting and holding her glance with his own, but without the smile. He said, 'Sarah, will you marry me?'

CHAPTER THREE

His words shocked the breath out of her; she gaped at him until he said with a touch of impatience, 'Why are you so surprised? We're well suited, you know. You have lost your heart to Steven; I—I lost mine many years ago. We both need companionship and roots. Many marriages succeed very well on mutual respect and liking—and I ask no more than that of you, Sarah—at least until such time as you might feel you have more to offer.'

She said bluntly, her grey eyes candid, but still round with astonishment:

'You don't want my love? Even if I didn't love someone else?'

He settled back in his chair, his eyes half closed so that she had no idea of what he was thinking.

'I want your friendship,' he answered blandly, 'I enjoy your company; you're restful and beautiful to look at and intelligent. I think that on the important aspects of life we agree. If you could accept me on those terms, I think I can promise you that we shall be happy together. I'm forty, Sarah, established in my work. I can offer you a comfortable life, and I should like to share it with you. . .and you—you are twenty-eight; not a young girl to fall in and out of love every few months.'

He got up and came round the desk to stand beside her and she frowned a little, because it was annoying to be told that she was twenty-eight. The frown deepened. He had implied that she was too old to fall in love! As though she had spoken her thoughts aloud he said gently:

'Forgive me if sounded practical, but I imagine

you are in no mood for sentiment, but I hope very much that you will say yes. I shall be away next week—perhaps it will be easier for you to decide if we don't see each other.'

She got up slowly to face him, forgetful of the case notes, which slid in a kind of slow motion to the ground, shedding doctors' letters, Path. Lab. reports, X-ray forms and his own multitudinous notes in an untidy litter around their feet.

'You're going away?' Even to her own ears her voice sounded foolishly lorn. She tried again and said with determined imperturbability:

'I'll think about it. I'm rather surprised—you must know that, but I promise you I'll think about it.'

The words sounded, to say the least, inadequate. She looked at him helplessly and he took a step towards her through the papery confusion at their feet and looked down. He said on a laugh, 'My God! It looks as though we're going to spend this evening together anyway!'

It was surprising how much she missed him, which on the face of things was absurd, for she had rarely seen him more than twice or three times a week in the clinics. She had always been aware of her liking for him, but hadn't realised until now how strong that liking was. Perhaps it was because she had always felt she could be completely natural with him. She had lain awake a long time that first night, remembering how he had got down on his knees beside her and spent more than an hour helping her to sort out the chaos on the floor, without once referring to their conversation. She was forced to smile at the memory and went to sleep eventually on the pleasant thought that he considered her beautiful.

She had little time to ponder her problems during the days which followed. The clinics were full and she didn't allow her thoughts to wander. Steven came and went with Mr Binns and Mr Peppard and Sarah steeled herself to be casually friendly with him. Mr Coles, who took Dr van Elven's clinic in his absence, was of course quite a different matter; there was no need to be on her guard with him. He worked for two, taking it for granted that she would keep up with him, and still contrived to talk about his family. There was another baby on the way, and he was so obviously pleased about it that Sarah felt pleased too.

'How many's that?' she enquired. 'There are Paul and Mary and Sue and Richard. . .'

He interrupted her with a chuckle. 'Don't forget the current baby—Mike. Hugo's already staked his claim as godfather—that makes the round half dozen. He never forgets their birthdays and Christmas. We have to warn the children, otherwise he goes out and buys them anything they ask for. Pity he's not married himself. . .it's at least fifteen years since that girl threw him over.' He shrugged his shoulders. 'He deserves the best, and I hope he gets it one day.'

She visited Mrs Brown too, and found her happy and content, sitting by the new electric fire with Timmy on her lap. Sarah made tea for both and listened while Mrs Brown sang the praises of her daily helper.

'A gem,' she declared, 'and it don't cost me a farthing to 'ave 'er.' Sarah agreed that it was a splendid arrangement and wondered if the doctor had had a hand in that as well. It was surprising and rather disconcerting to find that she knew so little about him. . .less, apparently, than her hostess, who disclosed during the course of conversation that he had been in to see her, and that now he had gone to Scotland. 'It's ever so far away,' she confided to an attentive Sarah. 'Up in the 'ills, and 'e can see the sea. 'E's got a little 'ouse and 'e does the garden and goes fishin' and walks miles.' She chuckled richly. 'Good luck to 'im, I says; nicer man never walked.'

She stroked Timmy. 'Do with a few more like 'im.'

Sarah agreed with a fervour which surprised her even more than it surprised Mrs Brown, although upon reflection she was forced to admit to herself that 'nice' was a completely inadequate word with which to describe Hugo van Elven. She found herself beginning to count the days until his return, which wouldn't be until the Friday afternoon clinic. Once or twice, she thought of writing to her mother and asking her advice, but how could she seek advice from someone who had never met Hugo; someone, moreover, who still thought that she would one day marry Steven? It was something she would have to decide for herself, but it wasn't until Thursday night that she admitted to herself that she had made the decision already. Hugo van Elven represented a quiet haven after the turbulence of the last few weeks; she believed they had a very good chance of being happy together; she felt completely at ease with him, and now that she thought about it, she always had done, and she was aware, without conceit that he liked her. He needed a wife to run his home and entertain for him, and bear him company—she thought that she could do those things quite satisfactorily. It worried her that there was no love between them, but Hugo had said that companionship should suffice, and it seemed to be all that he wished for. Perhaps, later on, their deep liking for each other might turn to affection.

She went to sleep on that thought, and when she woke in the morning, she knew that her mind was made up. Any small doubts still lurking, she resolutely ignored, firmly telling herself that they were unimportant.

She knew she had been right when he walked in. He said 'Good afternoon, Sister' in a perfectly ordinary voice and gave her the briefest smile, then turned to the pile of notes on his desk and said resignedly, 'Oh, lord, I wonder where they all come from!'

Sarah was putting out wooden spatulas. ''Flu,' she said, and gave his downbent head a grateful look. She had been nervous, almost shy at the idea of seeing him again, trying to imagine what they would say, and he was making it all very easy. She went on, 'They go on working, or take someone's cough cure because they don't like to bother the doctor, and then he sees them and sends them to you with bronchitis. Did you have a pleasant holiday?'

He nodded absently, not looking at her. 'Delightful, thank you. First one in when you're ready, Sister.'

She was actually on the point of leaving after the clinic was finished, when he came back. He and Dick Coles had gone away together, leaving her to clear up—and without him saying a word! She felt deflated; she hadn't expected him to overwhelm her with questions when they met, because he wasn't that kind of man, but she had expected him to ask her if she had made up her mind. She turned to switch off the desk light, and found him at the door.

He asked abruptly, 'Are you tired?' And when she said 'No,' he went on briskly, 'Good. May I take you out to dinner?' His mouth curved in a faint smile. 'I've been wanting to ask you that all the afternoon, but each time I was on the point of doing so, you either confronted me with another patient or waved a bunch of notes under my nose.' He was still smiling, but his eyes searched her keenly. 'Shall we be celebrating, Sarah?'

At that she smiled too and the cold lump of unhappiness she had been carrying around somewhere deep inside her warmed a little. They might not be able to give each other love, but there were other things—understanding and friendship and shared pleasure in shared interests; they each had a great deal to offer. She turned out the light and went past him into the waiting hall where the cleaners were swabbing the floor under the harsh lights, because the daylight, however bright, rarely penetrated its vastness. She looked up at him, her smile widening, and said:

'Yes, Hugo, we'll be celebrating. What time shall I be ready?'

The expression on his face was hard to read. 'Seven-thirty? Wear something pretty, we'll go to Parkes'.'

Sarah went over to her room, tea forgotten, her mind a jumble of thoughts, the chief of which was what she should wear. She was rummaging through her wardrobe when Kate appeared in the doorway of her room. She leant against the wall, swinging her cap.

'What are you doing?' she wanted to know. 'Surely you're not going to spend the evening tidying clothes? A pity I'm not off duty, there's that marvellous film I wanted to see and Jimmy's on duty until Sunday.' She strolled over to the bed and eyed the jumble of dresses upon it. 'That pink thing looks nice,' she commented. 'Isn't that the one you bought. . .' her voice tailed off, because she had remembered that Sarah had bought it to go out with Steven.

Sarah was tearing off her apron. 'Yes—I'm going to wear it tonight.'

Her friend eyed her with interest. 'Sarah! You're never. . .?'

Sarah was wriggling out of her dark blue cotton dress. 'I'm going out to dinner with Hugo van Elven, and don't you dare tell a soul, Kate.'

Kate whistled piercingly, 'Cross my heart,' she promised, 'though you're making history, ducky. He's never so much as lifted an eyebrow at a female creature within these walls.' She went reluctantly to the door. 'I'm late. Come and see me when you get in. I'll stay awake.' She started to run along the corridor towards the stairs. 'Have fun!' she called as she went.

Sarah had almost reached the bottom of the stairs when the doubt suddenly beset her that perhaps she was making a mistake. She was actually on the point of turning round and going back to her room when she saw Hugo standing in the hall, looking elegant in his black tie and very much at ease. He was talking to Home Sister, of all people, one of the most dedicated gossips the hospital had ever known. Sarah greeted him briefly under that lady's interested eye and they went out to the car together, leaving her to gaze after them, already rehearsing her bit of news ready for the supper table.

Sarah arranged herself carefully, with an eye to the pink dress.

'Of course we would have to meet Sister Wilkes! She—she talks rather a lot, you know. She'll put two and two together and make ten.'

Hugo idled the car out of the hospital forecourt. 'Do you mind? Everyone will know soon enough, I imagine. They'll see the announcement in the paper. In any case, I should have cause to be grateful to her.'

'Whatever for?'

'Because if I hadn't waited inside instead of out in the car, and if she hadn't been there, I think you would most probably have changed your mind and disappeared on the staircase like Cinderella.'

Sarah stole a look at his profile to see if he was smiling. He wasn't.

'You're rather disconcerting,' she said at last. 'How could you possibly know that—that. . . Oh, dear! Did you feel like that too?'

This time he did smile. 'No. I have no doubts, and I hope that you will have none either.'

He didn't give her a chance to answer, but began a rambling sort of conversation which lasted until they reached the restaurant, where it was supplanted by a leisurely discussion as to what they should eat. They decided on *quenelles* in lobster sauce with *feuilleté de poulet à la reine* and then *Monte Bianco* because Sarah confessed to a passion for chestnuts. The waiter was barely out of earshot when Hugo spoke.

'Will you marry me, Sarah?' His voice was friendly and almost casual, and she was conscious of a vague disappointment until he smiled—a warm smile, compelling her to smile in return. She said, a little shyly:

'Yes, Hugo, I'll marry you.' Her voice was steady, as was her gaze as their eyes met across the elegantly appointed table. The pleasant feeling of warmth she had felt before returned and strengthened at the admiration in his. He lifted his glass in a toast, and for the first time in several weeks, she felt almost happy. Perhaps it was because of this that she realised, some two hours later, that not only had she helped Hugo to compose an announcement of their engagement, she had also accepted his offer to drive her down to her home when she went on holiday, and what was more, had invited him to stay the weekend. And, last but not least, she had agreed most readily to marry him in exactly one month's time.

They had parted on the steps of the Nurses' Home and she had enjoyed it when he kissed her lightly on one cheek before opening the door for her. She crept to her room, so that Kate should not hear, and undressed with haste. In bed, thinking about it, she decided she had probably had a little too much champagne, so that Steven's image had become dulled enough to allow her to find pleasure in Hugo's kiss, even though she was aware that he could have done a lot better.

When he came to fetch her on Sunday morning, however, he contented himself with a cheerful 'Hullo there,' stowed her cases in the boot, herself into the seat beside him, and then, with a wave to the various faces watching them from a variety of windows, drove the Iso unhurriedly through the gates. It was still early—barely nine o'clock. London was comparatively free of traffic and it was a mild spring day. Sarah had put on a knitted dress the colour of the April sky above them. She settled into her seat, confident that she had made the most of herself, looking forward to her holiday.

She had telephoned her mother the previous evening, so that by the time they arrived she hoped that her parents' natural surprise would have been tempered to a mildness that wouldn't be too obvious. Her father, a retired colonel, was inclined to be peppery and speak his mind. Her mother was sweet and a little vague, but occasionally disconcerted those around her by being devastatingly candid. She said rather uncertainly:

'I hope you'll like my mother and father, Hugo.'

He allowed the Iso to ooze past a dawdling taxi. 'I see no reason why I shouldn't. . .it's much more likely that they won't like me, you know. I am, after all, a usurper—' he glanced at her and went on deliberately, 'They must have supposed that you and Steven would marry.'

Sarah stared ahead of her. She said carefully, 'Yes, I think they did, though we never discussed it. They. . .they teased me sometimes about it. They only met him twice, when he took me down, and then he didn't stay. They were surprised when I told them yesterday—about us, I mean, but I'm not a young girl to be rash.'

He agreed with her gravely and without looking at her so that she failed to see the gleam in his eyes.

'No, I should hardly call you rash. But you are a beautiful young woman, Sarah. I shall be proud of my wife.'

She blushed. 'I hope you always will be.' She added without guile, 'You're very good-looking too, although I don't suppose you like to be told that.'

He chuckled. 'No. But I'll let it pass this once. After all, we must be frank with each other, must we not?'

They were on the A30 now. Hugo passed three crawling cars and raced ahead of them down the empty road. He sat relaxed at the wheel, checked the car's controlled rush momentarily at a crossroads, gave her head once more and glanced at Sarah. 'Do you drive, Sarah?' he asked.

'Yes, at home—a little. I think I should be scared in London.'

'I've a Rover TC 2000. You shall try it out, and if you like it you shall have it for your own use— you'll need a car, you know. I'm almost never home during the day and you'll want to get out and about.'

He spoke carelessly and Sarah was conscious of a faint chill, but before she had time to think about it, he went on, 'Another thing. I've a small cottage in the north-western Highlands; I wondered if you would like to go there for a week or two after we're married—it's very quiet and remote and the scenery is magnificent.'

She was grateful he hadn't said honeymoon. 'Mrs Brown told me you had a house in Scotland. Yes, I'd like that very much—it sounds delightful. What do you do there? Fish?'

'Yes—and walk, and there's a garden I work in, although a man in the village below looks after it— his wife sees to the house.'

'Where is it?' she wanted to know.

'Wester Ross, overlooking Loch Duich. It's about forty miles from Inverness. The cottage is perched on the hillside. There's a tiny village—I suppose you would call it a hamlet—a mile below and a small place called Dornie four or five miles away.'

'I shall like it,' Sarah declared positively. 'Now I know why you've got an Iso Grigo. It must be five hundred miles.'

'Five hundred and seventy-two. Sometimes in the summer I do the through trip.'

She made a small protesting sound and he laughed.

'Oh, it's not as bad as it sounds, because I stop to rest and eat. But we'll take two days over it when we go and stop the night somewhere this side of the border.'

They were beginning to leave the spreading fingers of London behind them now. It wouldn't be long before they were in Basingstoke.

'There's a good road through Laverstock to Andover,' she offered, 'and you can turn off at the crossroads before you reach the town and take the Salisbury road.'

He nodded. 'We'll do that—we can stop at Overton and have coffee at the White Hart.'

'Oh, you've been this way before.'

'Yes, years ago.' He spoke shortly, and she knew with the same certainty as though he had told her that he had been with the girl he had wanted to marry. Impulsively she said:

'Hugo, I don't mean to pry, but if you want to— to talk about her—the girl you loved—love, I won't mind; it helps to talk about such things, and I think I know how you feel.'

There was a small tremor in his voice when he answered; she thought it was emotion. 'Thank you, Sarah. I think perhaps I shall tell you about her, but not, I think, until we have been married for a while and have a complete understanding of each other.'

It wasn't quite a snub, but she coloured a little none the less because there were other questions, and perhaps he was a man who didn't brook questioning. She asked in a dogged voice:

'May I know something about your family?

Mother is bound to ask. . .' she hesitated. 'Of course, I know what the grapevine says about you, but that isn't always very accurate.'

He said on a laugh, 'I should imagine not, although I think you must know that I'm not English. That at least is true.' He glanced sideways at her and she nodded. 'My parents live in Holland, north of Arnhem. My father is a retired doctor. I have three sisters, they're ten years or more younger than I— they're all married with children. Two of them live in Holland, my youngest sister lives in France. There are cousins and aunts and uncles, of course, though I see very little of them, save for three aunts who live together in Alkmaar.'

'You don't want to live in Holland?'

'Not at present—maybe, when I retire, I would go back, but that would depend on your wishes too. My father came to England in the twenties; he had a Leiden degree—he took a degree at Cambridge too. He met my mother here—she was visiting her grandparents, as her mother was an Englishwoman. They married and returned to Holland where I was born. I followed my father's pattern—Leiden and then Cambridge. It was there that I met Janet and I decided to stay in England. I had inherited the house at Richmond and it was already a second home to me. Even when there was no reason for me to remain there any longer, I had my work and friends in England, and Holland is near enough for me to go over whenever I wish.' He paused and went on in a lighter tone, 'I think we must go there in the late summer so that you may be welcomed into the family.' He was silent for a moment, then enquired blandly, 'Is there anything else you would like to know?'

She heard the blandness so that her voice was stiff. 'No. Thank you for telling me what you have. Please understand that I have no intention of being inquisitive, but if I'm to marry you I must know the——the bare bones of your life. I can assure you,' she went on, getting haughtier with each breath, 'I'll not trouble you with any unnecessary questions.'

He didn't answer, but to her surprise pulled the car on to the side of the road and stopped. He looked serious enough, but she had the suspicion that he was secretly laughing at her.

'I'm not sure what I have said, that you should be so high and mighty. My dear girl, you may ask as many questions as you wish and I'll engage to answer them as truthfully as I am able——and if I don't wish to give you an answer, I shall say so, and I hope you will do the same. And there is no question of your inquisitiveness or any other such nonsense, so let us have no bees in our bonnets on that score.'

Sarah saw him smile. His large hand covered hers for a moment. She stared at it; it was a nice hand, cool and firm and reassuring. She said a little awkwardly, 'I expect I shall say a great many silly things until I. . .' she paused. 'If you'll bear with me——you see I can't help thinking that I. . .' she stopped.

'Will be jilted again?' He asked the question cheerfully. 'That is something I can promise you won't happen——I can give you proof of that.' He searched through his pockets and eventually found a small box. There was a ring inside——a magnificent diamond in an old-fashioned setting. He picked up her left hand and fitted it on. 'There,' he said, 'now you have the token of my firm intention to marry you.'

She was a little breathless. 'It's beautiful,' she managed at length. 'How extraordinary that it fits—— is it old?'

'It's been in the family for two hundred years or so——and it's not at all surprising that it should fit. There is a legend that it fits only upon the finger of the woman destined to be a van Elven bride.'

Sarah was holding her hand up the better to admire the ring. 'I feel like Cinderella. Thank you very much, Hugo—I'll wear it with pride.' She said, giving him a quick glance through her lashes, 'I'm sorry I was silly just now.'

He bent his head and kissed her on the cheek—a casual friendly salute that made no demands of her, and started the car again. 'Never silly,' he stated positively. 'And now what about that cup of coffee?'

Sarah found the rest of the trip delightful; she had always thought Hugo to be taciturn, but now, away from his work, she realised how mistaken she had been. He was amusing and considerate and restful. She had never met a man who was so completely untroubled. By the time that they had reached Salisbury they were on the best possible terms with each other. He skirted the town and took the Blandford road, and after about ten miles, she said, 'You turn right at Sixpenny Handley, then right again after a mile.'

The very small village was tucked away between the folds of the hills. There was a large church, a small pub, a manor house, a scattering of cottages and a handful of pleasant houses standing on their own. They had to go through the village before they reached Sarah's home; it stood back from the lane, its grey stonework brightened by the spring flowers which filled its garden. Hugo turned in at the propped-open gate and drew up at the front door which was immediately opened by Sarah's mother, a woman in her fifties and still wearing the traces of a beauty as splendid as her daughter's. She was beautifully groomed and well dressed. She was clasping a knife and a cauliflower closely to her. Sarah embraced her warmly, took the knife and the cauliflower from her with an air of having done it before, and introduced Hugo. Mrs Dunn shook hands, studying him in a manner which might have shaken a lesser man and then said sweetly:

'So much better than Steven, darling.' She smiled at them both. 'Come inside, my dears. Your father is in the sitting room.'

They followed her, and as they went Sarah felt the pressure of Hugo's hand on hers. It was surprising, but she was sure that he was more at ease than she herself was. Her father was sitting behind the *Sunday Times* which he put down as they entered. He kissed her heartily and stared at Hugo as she introduced him. Apparently he liked what he saw, for after a series of polite but guarded questions, answered equally politely, he felt free to pour the sherry.

As the day wore on, it was obvious to Sarah that her parents found Hugo an acceptable son-in-law. It was a pity that she had no opportunity to have five minutes alone with him, in order to find out what he thought of them. When she and her mother at length went up to bed, leaving the two men to talk, he went to the door with them and after ushering her mother through it, put out a detaining hand.

'Do you take the dogs out before breakfast?' he asked quietly, 'because if you do, I should like to come with you.'

'Half past seven—in the kitchen,' Sarah said promptly, so glad that he wanted to be alone with her that she smiled widely, so that the dimple in her cheek made her look like a little girl again. 'Good night, Hugo.'

She went to sleep almost at once, thinking with pleasure of the morning.

She was down first and had made the tea when he arrived. They sat in the deep window seat drinking it, while the dogs whimpered with impatience at their feet. It was a lovely morning, with a clear blue sky and almost no wind, nor any sound other than the birds singing and someone a long way off, calling the cows. Sarah had put on an oatmeal-coloured skirt and a matching silk shirt-blouse, and had slung a vivid pink cardigan across her shoulders. She tried not to notice Hugo studying her over his mug of tea and was pleased out of all proportion when he remarked:

'You look nice, Sarah. I like the way you dress—you even wear your uniform with *éclat*.' He added speculatively, 'I wonder who I shall get in your place?'

Sarah felt a sudden vague surprise that she hadn't thought of that at all, and now that she did, the idea of another girl taking her place at Hugo's clinic didn't please her at all. She looked thoughtful without being aware of it and was secretly delighted when he observed:

'Someone like Sister Evans would do nicely.'

Sister Evans was fiftyish, homely in appearance and cosy in manner—and she was happily married. Sarah looked at him to see if he was joking, but although his grey eyes were alight with laughter he went on soberly enough: 'Not even the grapevine could do much about her, could it?' He put down his cup. 'I must see what I can do.'

They went out of the back door, the Colonel's two labradors and Sarah's mother's corgi circling around in a very frenzy of excitement. They went through the kitchen garden and opened the little arched door in its wall and so into a lane that presently became a path which wound up the bare hill before them. At the top they paused to admire the view.

'Magnificent, isn't it?' Sarah remarked. 'When I feel miserable sometimes, I think of this view.'

'And have you felt miserable, Sarah?'

'You know I have. Oh, not only just these last few weeks—I think I knew in my heart that Steven wouldn't marry me, only I pretended to myself that

he would. I know now that I've been pretending for
almost three years. I suppose I shall get over it—
perhaps I don't love him as you've loved your Janet,
because I believe I shall recover, and you never have,
have you?'

He had bent to pat one of the dogs so that she
couldn't see his face.

'I gather the grapevine has you very well
informed,' was all he said.

On the way back, he caught her hand and held it
lightly as they walked and told her a little of his
work. He was a busy man; it seemed that she would
see very little of him during the week. She remarked
upon this in a rather wistful voice, to have it pointed
out to her bracingly that they would spend most of
their evenings together and that weekends were usually free. She agreed and on a happy thought,
enquired if he took his dogs for a walk each morning.

'Yes, always. Would you come with me? It would
be pleasant and give us time to talk, just as we have
been talking this morning.' He stopped and turned
her round to face him. 'No regrets?' he asked.

'No, none. It's funny, but you don't seem
strange—I mean, it's as though I've known you for
a long time.'

He smiled down at her. 'But, my dear girl, you
have—three years, is it not? One gets to know someone very well indeed when one works with them.'

They started to walk again. 'What will you do
with Mrs Brown?' asked Sarah.

'Leave her where she is for as long as possible.
In fact, I think she would prefer to die there rather
than go back into hospital—I should imagine that
she has a couple of months—maybe less.'

'You won't mind if I go and see her sometimes?
And do you suppose we could find a home
for Timmy?'

He said at once. 'Of course you can go and see

her when you like. I shall have to visit her when we get back; her own doctor is away ill and I suggested I took her over until he is back again. As for Timmy, he can come to us—Alice will be delighted.'

It wasn't until they were in the kitchen garden again that she asked:

'Do you like Mother and Father, Hugo?'

'Very much,' he replied promptly. 'And I'm sure they will get on excellently with my parents. Your mother wasn't disappointed that we want to be married quietly?'

Sarah smiled. 'Yes, she was really. I suppose mothers always want their daughters to wear white satin and a veil.'

'Do you want to wear white satin, Sarah? We could easily arrange. . .'

She sounded quite apprehensive. 'Oh, no. I'd like it to be just us and our mothers and fathers.'

His voice was smooth. 'Would you have worn white satin if you had married Steven?'

She was a truthful girl. 'Yes. I used to think about it sometimes—girls do, you know. But that isn't the reason why I want a quiet wedding with you. That sounds silly because I'm not sure what the reason is; but when I am, I'll tell you.'

He loosed her hand, and put a great arm around her shoulders.

'You're a nice girl, Sarah,' he said placidly. He somehow made it sound like a delightful compliment.

She was sorry to see him go that evening, at the end of a day which had seemed too short. They had been to see the vicar about the wedding, and on the way home had sat on a fallen tree trunk in the warm sunshine and talked like old friends. They parted like old friends too, although he hadn't kissed her, but taken her hand and said in a casual manner:

'I'll be back at the weekend, Sarah. Enjoy your holiday.'

And he had gone, leaving her with the feeling that she would have liked to have gone back with him.

But the week went quickly. Her mother, showing an unexpectedly practical turn, whisked her off to Salisbury to buy clothes, an undertaking much enhanced by the size of the cheque which her father had given her. Moreover, the village sheltered among its inhabitants a dressmaker of incredible skill; a retiring, middle-aged little woman, who on casual acquaintance looked incapable of hemming a duster, but who in the privacy of her Edwardian front parlour became a kind of *haute couture* fairy godmother. Sarah spent a sizeable part of each day closeted with this paragon, listening to her soft country voice discussing patterns and materials, and later to stand, more or less patiently, to be pinned and fitted. . .but whenever she could escape the mild hubbub of a quiet country wedding, she took the dogs and wandered for miles, thinking about Hugo, and regrettably, of Steven.

If her parents thought of Steven, though, they gave no sign of it, nor, she was glad to discover, did they talk incessantly of Hugo—it seemed that they had accepted him and were content. Just as she would be content, she told herself with a rather painstaking frequency, once she could forget Steven.

There were flowers for her mother during the week, with a correct note from Hugo and a letter for herself—a brief letter written in his small, almost unreadable handwriting. It was the kind of friendly note she occasionally had from her brother. She read it several times, but by no flight of imagination could it be altered into anything else. She sighed without knowing it, and put the letter in the frivolous beribboned sachet which held her handkerchiefs, telling herself that that was what she wanted anyway—what he had promised to be—a friend and companion, who would maybe, over the years, develop an affection for her as she would for him—once she had Steven out of her system.

He had said that he would arrive in time for lunch on Saturday. It was a glorious warm morning; even after she had done a few chores around the house and arranged the flowers, and done her hair and then done it again, there were a couple of hours to spare. She whistled up the dogs and strolled away, up the hill behind the house. She was lying on her back in the short springy grass, with a fine disregard for her twice-done hair, when Hugo sat down beside her. Sarah sat up at once.

'Hugo! I was going to be home, waiting for you.' She put a questing hand up to her flyaway hair. 'I'm all untidy.'

He studied her with deliberation. 'I like it like that—have you had a pleasant week?'

She told him. 'And you?'

'Busy—busier than I need have been without your capable help.'

Sarah paused in her half-hearted efforts to tidy her hair. 'Oh, Hugo, how nice of you to say so.'

'Not only I but Peppard and Binns—they wanted to know if you would continue to work after we were married.'

Her grey eyes were enquiring. 'What did you say?'

'An emphatic no. My dear girl, there's no need for you to work, and think how my practice would suffer if it got about that my wife went to work!'

He was smiling and she knew that he was joking, but not altogether.

'Yes, of course. But I'd work willingly if you ever needed help. . . I mean with money.' She glanced at him, but his face was inscrutable. He chose a blade of grass with care and began to chew it.

'Thank you, Sarah. Spoken like a true friend. As a matter of fact I wanted to talk to you about money. I've plenty—a good income from the practice and enough of my own to be independent. Later, when we're married, I'll take you to old Simms, my lawyer, and we'll have everything in writing. In the meantime there will be a quarterly allowance for you—paid in on our wedding day.' He mentioned a sum which made her sit up very straight indeed.

'All that? For me? Just for three months? It's enough for a year!' She had an enlightening thought. 'Of course, that's the housekeeping as well.'

He laughed. 'No, it's not. You run the house as you think fit and give me the bills each month—if you're too extravagant I'll tell you. And if you ever need money, Sarah, you are to ask me for it.'

She said obediently. 'Yes, Hugo,' although she couldn't see how she could possibly spend all that money. Her voice must have betrayed her doubts, for he said with firmness:

'Leave me to worry about it, Sarah.' He chose another blade of grass. 'I've letters from my mother and father for you—would you like to read them now?'

He lay stretched out beside her while she read them. They were kindly letters, a little formal perhaps, but then they had never seen her, while Hugo was their son and they must have known about Janet. She wondered what they were really like—she would know, of course, on her wedding day.

Hugo's placid voice interrupted her thoughts. 'Should we be going back?' he asked. 'Your mother mentioned one o'clock.'

They were within sight of the little door in the wall of the kitchen garden when he stopped. 'Sarah, I have an engagement present for you.'

He put a small box into her hand and she opened it, conscious of delight that he should have thought of it, and caught her breath at the diamond and pearl earrings in it. She said, a little breathless:

'Hugo, they're superb! I love them. They're

marvellous, only I—you. . .' She stopped and started again, her voice very level. 'Don't you see, Hugo? they're so lovely, such a magnificent gift. . . I don't deserve them. I don't expect you can understand. . .'

He interrupted coolly, 'You mean because we're not in love? Don't be a goose, Sarah.' He gave her a half-mocking, wholly friendly smile. 'I came down in the Rover; she's yours too—you shall drive her back tomorrow.'

She said in a shaky voice, 'Hugo, you're too good to me,' and stretched up and kissed him on one cheek, just above his jaw, because she couldn't reach any higher.

'Thank you very much. I've never had anything quite as beautiful, and they match perfectly with my ring.' She touched the earrings gently with a fore-finger, her beautiful head full of half realised thoughts which she shrugged aside to say, 'I'll try and be a perfect driver, too.'

He laughed gently. 'I'll answer that when we get to London tomorrow.'

The journey back went well, despite the fact that Sarah made the initial mistake of going into reverse, and had on several separate occasions clashed the gears in a manner which caused her to flush most becomingly. Hugo, however, ignored these small mishaps and kept up a soothing flow of small talk which restored her confidence, so that she drew up before the house in Richmond with something of a flourish, to be rewarded with his quiet:

'You'll do, my girl. Just a little more practice.'

Sarah went pink with pleasure; she would have minded very much if he had levelled criticism at her, although she was aware that she had merited it. Somehow, his good opinion of her mattered a great deal. It was therefore in a mood of relaxed content that she accompanied him into the house, to eat the delicious supper Alice had prepared for them, and afterwards to inspect her future home. They wandered around the rooms, quietly content with each other's company.

It was a lovely house; the furniture, although antique, had a pleasantly used air about it; the chairs were comfortable, the colours subdued. She approved of everything and roundly declared that she had no wish to alter any of it. Presently they went upstairs and she looked with something like awe at the beautiful room which was to be hers. It was at the back of the house and had a little iron balcony overlooking the garden. The furniture was Sheraton and the floor-length curtains chintz in muted pinks and blues, colours which were echoed in the carpet and bed coverlet. There was a bathroom leading off on one side, and a dressing room on the other side of the room, and Hugo said easily:

'My room is in the front of the house, so you can spread yourself as much as you like.'

His own room was smaller, and although the furniture was just as beautiful, it looked cold. Sarah decided that she would make sure that there were always flowers there. There were more bedrooms, all equally charming; even the small attic rooms had been furnished with care. On their way downstairs again, she paused by a big door at the back of the landing; she had seen it as they had gone up, but Hugo had walked straight past it.

'Where does this door lead to?' she wanted to know, and was chilled when he said, 'Nowhere in particular.' Which was nonsense, of course—he didn't want her to know. She promised herself that she would find out as soon as she was able. Meanwhile: 'The house is charmingly furnished,' she remarked lightly. 'Who did it?'

Hugo said rather shortly, 'I did, a long time ago. Nothing's been changed, merely replaced from time to time.'

He led the way downstairs, and Sarah followed him, digesting the unpleasant thought that probably he had done it all for Janet. A little subdued, she suggested that perhaps she should be getting back to St Edwin's.

It seemed strange to be back in uniform again and to see Hugo when he came to take his clinics. He addressed her with his usual polite formality, and at the end of the first one went away with Dick Coles, to reappear after ten minutes.

'It's fortunate that this state of affairs will only last for another week or so,' he observed from the door, 'for I find it both ridiculous and difficult to address you as Sister.'

Sarah giggled. 'I thought you'd gone,' she said, and was conscious of a surge of relief. 'I know it's silly, but you're—different here, you know. It seems as though none of it is true.' She picked up a pile of papers and prepared to go.

'In that case, I had better make it true, had I not, Sarah?' He had come to stand near her. 'How long will it take you to change?'

'Ten minutes—no fifteen.' She stood looking at him, the pile of notes clasped to her apron bib, her lovely face aglow. She hoped suddenly that he would kiss her. He did—a light, unhurried kiss on her mouth, the effect of which was entirely spoilt by his saying prosaically:

'I'll wait outside the Home. Don't dress up—we'll go and see Mrs Brown and then find somewhere quiet to eat.'

It was to be the forerunner of many such evenings—sometimes spent at Richmond, dining alone in the quiet dining room and sitting afterwards, talking—there was so much to say; Sarah found the time too short. Twice they went to the theatre and once to the Mirabelle because Hugo thought that she should have the opportunity to wear the earrings. Then again to Mrs Brown's rose-decked room, to drink strong tea and receive a wedding gift—a knitted teacosy of a breathtaking red, which its donor declared would go very well with a nice brown teapot. Sarah thought of the delicate silver Queen Anne tea-pot which was in Hugo's house and agreed with her, vowing silently that she would use it on her early morning tea-tray whether it matched the china or not.

She had had a wedding present from her friends in the hospital too, and spent her last evening there going from ward to ward, wishing them goodbye. It was on her way over to the surgical block to see the night Sisters that she met Steven. She would have passed him, but he stopped her with an outflung hand.

'I suppose you expect me to wish you happiness, Sarah. Well, I don't. You're a fool; van Elven's not the man for you—he's still wrapped up in his first love, and you're still mourning me. . .'

Sarah dragged her arm free and said furiously, 'That's a lie!' then stopped to fight the tears of rage which choked her. Hugo's voice behind her, quiet as always, but full of chilling menace, said:

'My friend, it seems I must tell you to get out yet again—and I should go if I were you, otherwise I might be tempted to use persuasion.'

She began to cry as Steven turned on his heel, and as he went she found herself swept into Hugo's arms to be comforted. After a minute or two of snivelling she was able to raise a tear-stained face and say in a furious voice:

'I'm so ashamed of myself, Hugo. And I'm not crying because I'm unhappy; I'm so—so angry.'

She dragged the back of her hand across her eyes like a child and accepted his proffered handkerchief. Presently she smiled at him in a watery fashion. 'Whatever do you think of me?' she asked.

Hugo put the damp handkerchief into a pocket,

still holding her with one arm. 'Remind me to tell you some time— Where were you going? I know we had agreed not to go out tonight, but when I got home I changed my mind and came back to see if you would come out after all. You see how I have got used to your company... We can have supper somewhere.'

'I'd like that very much—I missed you too. I must just say goodbye to Sister Hallett and Sister Moore— I can do the rest of my packing in the morning. We're not going until ten, are we?' She hesitated. 'You wouldn't like to come with me? They'll be in the duty room on Surgical.'

He didn't answer, only took her arm and walked with her down the long, deserted corridor, waited while she said her goodbyes, and then walked back to the Home with her. It was a lovely May evening. They lingered a moment outside the door and he said:

'Wear that blue thing with the pleats. We'll go to a place I know of in Jermyn Street.' She nodded and before she went inside said on an impulsive rush, 'Hugo, you're so nice—I wish. . .'

His voice sounded curt. 'What do you wish?' he asked.

She heard the curtness. 'Oh, nothing.' She paused, feverishly trying to think of the right thing to say. 'I expect we shall be a great comfort to each other,' she achieved finally. Up in her room, changing rapidly, she paused to laugh ruefully. Her well-meant remark had been a stupid one, but it had been impossible to put her thoughts into words, especially as she wasn't sure what those thoughts were.

She was thinking about it when she sat beside him in the Iso Grigo, driving away from her parents' home after the wedding. He was nice, and he was a comfort; it was as though he had known of the last-minute uncertainty which assailed her. She had got up early and taken the dogs for a walk, and halfway up the hill Hugo had been waiting for her. He was wearing an open-necked shirt and elderly flannels, and she had put on an old cotton frock and hadn't bothered with her hair. All he had said was:

'No one would ever think to see us now that we'll be getting married in an hour or so,' and then had gone on to talk about everything else under the sun. By the time they had got back to the house, getting married to him had seemed a perfectly sensible and ordinary thing to do.

She had liked his parents too—they had been kind, and charming to her mother and father as well. If they had felt any doubts about their son's marriage, they had given no sign. Her dress had been a success too, and although Hugo had had no time to tell her so, she was aware that he had liked it. The white ribbed silk, made up into the elegantly simple pattern she had chosen, had been just right for the lovely weather, and the little hat she hadn't been quite certain about had been the right choice after all. She glanced down at the plain gold ring on her finger, and then looked sideways at Hugo's hand on the wheel. She had been diffident about asking him if she might give him a ring too, and had been surprised when he had agreed without demur. He had put the heavy signet ring he always wore on the other hand. He interrupted her thoughts:

'You made a delightful bride, Sarah—I don't think I realised how beautiful you are.' He smiled fleetingly. 'I enjoyed my wedding.'

She smiled back at him, and settled back beside him as he sent the car speeding on the first stage of their journey to the cottage in Wester Ross.

CHAPTER FOUR

It was barely half past one, for they had married at the early hour of half past ten. The day was bright and warm and the country looked fresh and green. Hugo had told her that they were to spend the night at Windermere, a journey of almost two hundred and fifty miles—a distance, Sarah realised, of no consequence to the Iso Grigo, nor for its driver, who drove with the casual air of a man taking his wife to do the shopping. But she had travelled enough with him by now to know that the casual air was deceptive. He said now:

'And did you enjoy your wedding too, Sarah?'

It surprised her that upon reflection, she had. Wedded friends had told her that they had scarcely realised that they were being married, what with worrying about their veils and the bridesmaids and whether the best man had the ring. But she had had no veil and no bridesmaids, and the best man, a cousin of Hugo's who had flown over from Holland just for the ceremony, evinced no nervous fumbling at the last minute; he had been as calm as the bridegroom, who had been very calm indeed. She had been free to think her own thoughts, knowing that anything that needed taking care of would be dealt with by Hugo without fuss. She answered reflectively:

'Yes, I did—very much.'

He glanced at her briefly and smiled and she thought that he was on the point of speaking, but when he didn't she went on:

'I like your mother and father, Hugo.'

'And they liked you. I've promised we will go

76

over before the summer is over, so that you can get to know each other. I can show you something of Holland at the same time.'

'Tell me about them—and about Holland too?' she invited.

She listened happily to his quiet deep voice, marvelling at the stupid idea she had always entertained that he was taciturn. When he chose to talk he had a dry wit which was never unkind, and an amusing way of describing things and people. She pondered the strange fact that although her heart was broken, she could so enjoy Hugo's company. They reached Tewkesbury and the M5 without her having solved the problem.

'Dull, but quick,' was Hugo's comment as he allowed the car to run up to seventy and then kept her there. But it wasn't dull at all. Sarah forgot her problems; she felt happy and content, and delighted with her companion—it was like being with a life-long friend to whom she could voice her thoughts; she amended that to almost all her thoughts. They had talked frankly about their future together and Hugo had made it plain in the nicest possible way that he was content to wait indefinitely until such time as she felt that Steven no longer mattered quite as much—he had said it in such a way that she had gathered the impression that he didn't care overmuch, and had felt unreasonably hurt, only to chide herself for being foolish, for if Hugo had told her that he loved her, she would have refused him out of hand. To marry someone who loved you when you yourself were in love with someone else seemed to her to be a towering wickedness. As it was, she and Hugo had a deep regard for each other and nothing more, and upon that they would build their marriage.

Just before they reached Manchester he turned off the motorway into Knutsford where they had a rather late tea. Sarah, who was hungry, ate her way through

an assortment of sandwiches, an odd scone or two
and a variety of cakes with an unselfconscious
pleasure, for, as she remarked to Hugo, she had been
much too nervous to eat her breakfast and too excited
to do more than nibble at the delicious titbits which
her mother had provided for the wedding breakfast.
She beamed at him across the table.

'You weren't nervous at all, were you, Hugo—or
excited?' She drew in a breath. 'Of course, it isn't
quite—quite. . .well, I suppose you feel different if
you love someone very much.'

She had gone a little pink, but made no attempt
to evade his gaze.

He said, with the merest hint of a smile, 'So I am
led to believe—but I am neither nervous nor excit-
able by nature. Shall we go? It's roughly seventy-five
miles to Windermere; we should arrive in good time
for a late dinner. The food's rather good, I believe.'

She got up. 'Oh, I'm so glad.' She looked at him
doubtfully. 'I don't mean to sound greedy—only I'm
mostly hungry, especially now I shall have time to
eat. In hospital one eats fast, either because one has
to be on duty in a few minutes, or because one is
off duty and doesn't want to miss a minute of it. It's
ruinous to a proper appreciation of food.'

They were walking back to the car and Hugo took
her arm and said:

'The first time I took you out, you begged for
something quick.'

'And such a gorgeous place too!' she sighed, and
he answered quickly:

'We'll go there again soon, and you shall take as
long as you like.'

He was fastening her seat belt. She said to his
downbent head, 'You don't mind—I mean, that I
like food?'

He laughed, looking all at once much younger. 'I
find it delightful to be with someone who enjoys

herself—quite a lot of women pretend not to be interested in what they eat; which is nonsense, of course.' He started the car and said, smiling, 'There's some quite good scenery presently; that should give you an appetite.'

The hotel was old and rambling and lay, delightfully, by the lake. Their rooms overlooked the water and the fells beyond; the slow falling sun touched everything in sight with gold; the water of the lake looked like smooth shot silk. Sarah flung her hat on the bed and ran on to the balcony in order to have a better look, and found Hugo on the balcony alongside. 'It's lovely,' she cried enthusiastically. 'I've never seen anything like it.'

'Wait until you see the cottage,' was all Hugo would say, and 'I'm coming for you in five minutes.'

She was ready, with her bright hair brushed and a face nicely powdered and lipsticked. They went down, arm in arm, to the almost empty dining room and ate *filet de sole Grand Duc* and *chicken Marengo* and drank champagne, then Sarah found room for a water ice while Hugo watched her lazily over his coffee. Afterwards they strolled along the road beside the lake, it was almost dark, although the sky was still a deep turquoise in the west. Everything around them smelled delicately sweet and they hardly spoke until Sarah asked, 'What time do we go tomorrow?'

'We've about three hundred and thirty miles to go—if we leave at nine, allowing stops for lunch and tea and the condition of the roads, which will slow us down a little, we should get there about six. Are you tired?'

'No, not really.' She said with quick intuition, 'Shall we go for a walk before breakfast—would there be time?'

'Yes, if you don't mind getting up early... I'll ask them to call you at seven.'

The morning was even more beautiful than the

evening had been. They walked in the opposite direction this time and discussed the pleasures of getting up early, something they were both used to, as their jobs demanded it. The sun struck warm upon them, early though it was, and Hugo looked up at it and murmured, ' "Busie old foole, unruly Sunne," although perhaps that's a little out of context.'

'John Donne,' said Sarah, pleased that she knew what he was talking about, 'and most inappropriate, if I remember the rest of the poem.'

He burst out laughing and caught her by the hand. 'You know, Sarah,' he said, 'I think that we are going to enjoy life together.'

They stopped for lunch at Crianlarich, with Ben More and Ben Lui looming majestically on either side of them, and arrived in Inverness after a journey through scenery which had left Sarah speechless and round-eyed. Its grandeur, however, had by no means detracted from her enjoyment of her tea, although she found so much to talk about that Hugo had to press her to try a second slice of fruit cake. She took it absently.

'How many years have you had the cottage?'

He thought. 'Five—no, six; I come up twice a year, and when I can manage it, a third time as well.'

'Shall we—that is, shall I come with you?'

He raised surprised eyebrows. 'My dear girl, of course, unless there is anything else you would prefer to do.'

Sarah shook her head. 'I can hardly wait to get there.' The road ran along the edge of Loch Ness, but at Invermoriston Hugo turned away from it on to a narrow road and slowed the car's pace.

'We're almost there,' he said, and she could hear the happiness in his voice.

'It's beautiful and lonely and makes everything else seem unreal.' She craned her neck in order to see as much as possible of the grandeur around them and then stole a glance at him. 'Aren't you tired?'

'Not really. I enjoy it too much. I know the road quite well now, you see, which helps considerably.'

Sarah said, 'Only the direst of circumstances would make me drive all this way; I should be terrified by myself. Supposing I got a puncture, or ran out of petrol?'

Hugo laughed and said in a comfortable reassuring voice:

'The country looks empty, doesn't it? But you're far less likely to be overlooked here than in London. Would you really not drive up here?'

'No—at least, only if I were desperate.'

Loch Duich looked at its loveliest in the early evening light. The mountains of Kintail hung in the near distance, looking like some splendid, gigantic backdrop to a natural stage scenery of incredible beauty. A couple of miles along the loch's edge, and Hugo turned the car again, up a winding little road which appeared to go nowhere but presently unravelled itself into a tiny huddle of cottages, pressed against the side of the hill. He stopped the car at the last cottage and got out and knocked on its stout door. He had told Sarah that Mrs MacFee was one of the most remarkable women he had ever met, and when she had asked why, he had said:

'She's forty, sandy-haired and plain-faced and beautiful. She has a brood of children like angels and a husband who is the best shepherd in the district. She's completely content with her lot—so is he. Each time I meet them I'm cut down to size.'

Sarah knew exactly what he had meant when the door opened and Mrs MacFee appeared. She had no beauty at all, and yet she appeared beautiful. She went straight to the car and spoke to Sarah in her soft Highland voice, then gave Hugo a large old-fashioned key, and stood waving as they drove on up the hill.

'I usually leave the key under the water-butt,' Hugo explained, 'and so does Mrs MacFee, but I guessed she would have it with her today.' He gave her a wicked look. 'Everyone loves a bride, even in these lonely parts.'

Sarah giggled. 'You've got it wrong—that only applies to arriving at the church, all dressed up.'

'Which reminds me—your dress was quite perfect, Sarah, so was that ridiculous hat. You looked quite beautiful.'

She said, 'Thank you, Hugo,' in a demure voice and went on, 'Mrs MacFee is exactly as you described her, and I see what you mean. How do you manage about food?'

'Over the years we've worked out a very good system. When I leave, Mrs MacFee goes up to the cottage and re-stocks the cupboard, gets in coal for the Aga, makes up the beds, scrubs and polishes and so forth and leaves everything in apple-pie order— in fact, she leaves it so that if I were to arrive unexpectedly, I could walk straight in and live in comfort for at least a month. MacFee grows vegetables in the garden—and there's a potato clamp, and apples and onions in the shed. What more could I want?'

The last few yards were steep, and he slowed the car to walking pace and turned it sharply between the gateposts set in the old stone wall bordering the lane. The cottage stood a little way back; it was whitewashed, with a grey slate roof and small windows either side of its door. It was alone in the little lane, but Sarah had no feeling of loneliness as she inspected it. It was cosy and solid and looked as though it had grown out of the mountains all around it. The front door opened directly into a minute lobby and thence to the living room, which held a pleasant clutter of furniture—comfortable chairs, several small tables, well-filled bookshelves flanking a stone

fireplace, and a variety of oddments conducive to
comfort, all so well arranged that the small room
looked larger than it was. The floor was wooden,
covered to a large extent by thick handmade rugs.
The crimson serge curtains and the brass oil lamp
on the table beside the easy chair drawn up to the
fireplace added a colourful little glow to the room,
so that she sensed how pleasant it would be to draw
the curtains against a cold evening and light the lamp.
The kitchen was beyond—small, expertly planned,
and equipped down to the last saltspoon. There was
a scrubbed table against one wall, partnered by two
rush-bottomed chairs and crowned by a bowl of fruit,
witness of Mrs MacFee's thoughtfulness. The Aga
took up most of the opposite wall, with the stairs,
neatly hidden behind a narrow arched door, beside it.

'Go on up,' suggested Hugo, 'while I fetch the
cases in.'

There were two small bedrooms upstairs, divided
by a bathroom. The whole floor was carpeted by
a pale amber which showed up the white-painted
furniture very well. The curtains at the small
windows were blue and white chintz with splashes
of yellow. There were fitted cupboards cleverly built
into the unequal angles of the walls and some beautiful candlesticks; pewter and old, each with its snuffer.
The front room was the larger of the two, with a
small Pembroke table under the window, bearing a
shieldback mirror, a fine linen runner, exquisitely
embroidered, and a little vase of garden flowers—
Mrs MacFee again. She thought that the room would
be hers, and Hugo confirmed this when she went
downstairs to the kitchen. He had lighted the Aga,
and the fresh aromatic tang of pine as the kindling
blazed, filled the small room. He had taken off his
jacket and was leaning against the wall, waiting to
replenish the stove. He looked content, as though he
had come home. . .for a second, Sarah had the feeling

that she didn't know him at all. He looked so very different from the rather silent, immaculate doctor she had worked for. Then he glanced up and she knew that he wasn't changed in the least; it was she who was seeing him as he really was. They smiled at each other.

'Come up to the end of the garden and see the view,' he invited. The garden was long and narrow, with a path running up its centre to the boundary hedge—the village, a tiny cluster of rooftops, lay a mile or so below them, and lower still and further away was the road running alongside Loch Duich.

'We'll unpack, shall we? and then go down to Dornie for a meal. There's a splendid little hotel there.'

Sarah was disappointed; she was as good a cook as she was nurse; she was anxious to display her talents, but she said nothing. After all, they would be at the cottage for two weeks at least; plenty of time to demonstrate her ability to cook.

The days passed—long slow days of lovely weather, made longer because they got up early. It was the new Hugo Sarah was still learning to know who got up just after six and made tea and brought her up a cup. He was dressed and out in the garden by the time she got down to get breakfast; chopping wood or weeding or cutting back a hedge—he had a boundless energy which she had never suspected of him. At breakfast, that first morning, she had said, 'You're so different. I'd never thought of you as someone who could be so—so practical—chopping wood, and washing up and gardening and making tea in the morning.'

She caught his mocking eye and blushed brightly.

'My poor Sarah, have you been disillusioned? Perhaps I have the best of the bargain, for you are a famous cook.'

She had laughed then, and they had left the little

house in Mrs MacFee's capable hands and packed a picnic basket and roamed the lower slopes of the mountains until the early evening, when they went back to the cottage and Sarah surpassed herself in the roasting of a superb joint of Angus beef.

They went somewhere different each day; sometimes to spend hours fishing, a sport at which Hugo excelled, but which Sarah didn't much care for because of taking out the hook, but she was content to sit as still as a mouse while he went after his trout. He took her to Inverness one day, and she bought a quantity of wool to knit him an Aran sweater. This, together with an assortment of books from the sitting room, kept her contentedly occupied while Hugo fished. They might not speak for an hour, for she knew better than to start up a conversation, but that didn't matter, for her sense of companionship had deepened with the days. There was no need to talk, but it was pleasant to look up from time to time and see him, pipe in mouth, standing motionless and enormous in his waders, and to be ready with a wifely word of praise at the right moment.

But it wasn't all fishing—they went to Skye, taking the car with them, and spent the night at Portree, so that Sarah might have a chance to see as much of the island as possible. And he took her along the coast road too, north to Lochinver, and then inland to Lairg, where they lunched and then on to Dingwall and Loch Garve, where they left the car to allow Sarah to stare spellbound at the Falls of Rogie. She gazed in silence, and presently put out a hand and slipped it into Hugo's. After a minute, he loosed it gently and put an arm around her shoulders and drew her close, and for all that his touch was casual, Sarah felt a small thrill at it, instantly dispelled by his placid voice bringing her down to earth again with some rather prosaic facts and figures.

They went on to Achnasheen after that, where they

had tea at a hotel overlooking Strath Bran, and then on to the Strome Ferry, and so home. After their meal they sat in the small living room, still light with the late sun of an early summer evening, and later, when she was in bed, Sarah couldn't remember what they had talked about, only wonder at the endless things they had to say to each other. She thought, fleetingly, of Steven and wondered if Hugo thought of Janet, and hoped, hazily and half asleep, that he didn't. She yawned, listening to Hugo walking about downstairs, shutting doors and seeing to the Aga, and, lulled by these homely sounds, she went to sleep.

They stayed just over two weeks at the cottage, and when they finally locked its door and put the key under the water-butt in the garden, Sarah felt as though she had turned the last page of a particularly delightful book. They had said goodbye to Mrs MacFee the day before, but all the same, she was at her cottage door to wave to them as they went past early in the morning.

It was glorious weather. They lunched in Edinburgh and stopped briefly in York, then went on to Monk Fryston, a village to the south of the city where there was a hotel which had once been a twelfth-century manor house. It was set in idyllic surroundings, and was, Sarah considered, a most romantic place. Her bedroom was vast and luxurious, with a bathroom which could have done justice to one of the glossy magazines. Influenced by her surroundings, she changed for dinner, and put on a straight little dress in pale coffee silk, one of the village paragon's masterpieces. She added the earrings which Hugo had given her for good measure, and was rewarded for her pains when Hugo tapped on her door and then stopped short as he entered. He said at once:

'How pretty you look, Sarah—that dress is perfect

with your tan.' He raised quizzical eyebrows. 'And the earrings.'

She went a little pink under his admiring eye. 'Well, it's such a lovely place I felt I should try and do it justice.' She twiddled an earring absently. 'Hugo, do you always stay in this kind of luxury?' She stopped and frowned, then tried again. 'Is it because we're on holiday?' It still wasn't quite what she had meant to say; she had sounded rude. She peeped at him to see if he was offended. Apparently not. He leaned easily against the door, his hands in his pockets. He looked well turned out, idle and completely assured.

He said silkily, 'My dear good girl, I like comfort and the good things of life, and I shouldn't dream of offering you anything less than that—you are my wife.'

He was smiling, but he was also, she saw, annoyed. She took a step towards him and said contritely, 'There, I knew it sounded wrong when I said it—I didn't mean to criticise you, you know. I love having b-bathrooms all to myself and champagne at dinner, only what I meant was—I don't mind if I don't—I'm happy without them.' She added, still trying desperately to make herself clear, 'The cottage was perfect.'

She had a sudden vivid memory of standing at the stove in the early morning, frying bacon and eggs, watching Hugo through the open door, chopping wood in old corduroys and an open-necked shirt. She raised troubled eyes to his and said baldly, 'I didn't know you were so—so—rich—this sort of rich.' She waved an expressive arm around her. It was a relief to see that he was no longer annoyed. He left the door and came across the room to her and she felt the firm touch of his hands on her shoulders. He said gently as though he were talking to a child:

'My dear, you are surprisingly naïve, and it's

refreshing. My money isn't important. I have a good deal more than most people, perhaps, and I use it how and when I wish. . .'

She interrupted, 'Oh, Hugo, I do beg your pardon! I'm sure you use your money wisely and you're not in the least selfish—no one else would have bothered with Mrs Brown, and I expect there are quite a number of Mrs Browns you've helped, and Dick Coles told me that you're godfather to all his children and that you're always buying them presents. . .and Kate's Jimmy told her you gave Matron bottles and bottles of super sherry for the nurses' dance and didn't tell a soul. . .' She paused, a little incoherent and out of breath, to see laughter surging over him. She said crossly, 'What's so funny about that?' then smiled, albeit reluctantly because he was smiling at her—not laughing any more; staring at her in an odd speculative way. 'Am I a disappointment to you?' she asked slowly.

She felt his fingers bite into her flesh. 'On the contrary, my dear Sarah—you have been in many ways a delightful surprise.'

'Because I can cook?' she queried practically. 'People seem to think that if one is a nurse, one is incapable of doing anything else.'

He took his hands from her shoulders and said lightly, 'I believe you to be capable of anything, Sarah. And now shall we go down to dinner?'

They reached Richmond the following evening, and getting out of the car, Sarah thought what a lovely house Hugo's was. There were Bourbon roses out in the front garden, and the soft pink of a New Dawn climber mingled with the rich mauve of wisteria on the house walls. They went inside, to be welcomed by Alice's quiet warmth and to sit by candlelight in the dining room eating lobster Thermidor and the strawberries and cream she had served after it. Afterwards they sat in Hugo's study; he at his desk, reading a pile of correspondence, while she, having devoured the few letters which were hers, sat quietly doing nothing at all. There had been a letter from Kate, written in haste and excitement because Jimmy had got the Surgical Registrar's job—for Steven would be leaving when he married Anne Binns. The news was heavily underlined and surrounded with exclamation marks, then lost in a pageful of wedding plans. Sarah had put the letter aside, resolving to ask Kate over for the day. It would be nice to hear all the news, although hospital life had never seemed so remote. There were letters from her mother and father too, and her brother, who had flown over from his regiment in Germany for the wedding and to have a brief glimpse of the bride and groom. Apparently he thoroughly approved of Hugo and was looking forward to seeing them both again on his next leave.

Hugo's voice cut through her vague thoughts. 'Anything in your letters?' he enquired idly.

She told him about Kate, and about Steven too, and he said:

'Ah, yes. I'm glad Jim got the job—I had a word with Binns about him.'

She exclaimed warmly, 'How kind of you, Hugo—what a dear you are!'

She was sitting in a leather easy chair within the soft glow of a red-shaded lamp. She smiled at him, unaware of the beautiful picture she made. He glanced up briefly and then down again to his letters. When he spoke it was about quite another matter.

'We're bidden to a cocktail party to celebrate Anne Binns' engagement—er—Thursday week. Will you accept?'

She looked at him anxiously. 'If you were alone—I mean before we married, you'd have gone, wouldn't you? So we'll go—only don't leave me alone, Hugo.'

He put his letters down and sat back. 'No, I'll not

do that, Sarah——but it's a good idea to plunge in at the deep end, however cold the water.'

He got up and pulled up a chair to sit beside her. 'I've not opened these yet. They'll be invitations of one sort or another——shall we look at them together, and decide about them? There's a letter from my mother too, and my sisters,' he tossed them into her lap, 'and there's this.'

He handed her a card. It had a drawing of an unlikely-looking bride and groom standing under an archway of horseshoes, any available spaces being filled with cherubs and rosebuds.

'Mrs Brown,' said Sarah instantly. 'Bless her shaky old heart!'

The verse inside was as unlikely as the cover, and underneath it Mrs Brown had written in a careful, spidery hand:

'To dear Dr and Sister, knowing you'll be Happy.'

Sarah avoided her husband's eye. 'I suppose she doesn't think of us as Mr and Mrs.'

'Do you?' His question was unexpected.

She answered him, a little flustered, 'I don't know. . . I'd like to go and see her one day soon.'

'That's easily arranged. Come up to town with me in the morning. I'll drop you off somewhere and you can shop if you wish and we'll meet for lunch. While I'm at the clinic you can sit and drink tea with her. I want to have a look at her anyway.'

The morning sun was glorious. Sarah took advantage of it to wear one of her new dresses——a shirtwaister of silver grey lawn, cunningly pleated and tucked. She was aware how nice she looked as they strolled along Cholmondley Walk. There were few people about, the dogs had the place to themselves, and when Hugo whistled them to heel they obeyed him rather huffily, implying in a doggish manner that it was a day to spend out of doors.

Hugo dropped her outside Fortnum and Mason's.

She watched him drive away feeling a little lost, then turned to examine the tempting displays in the windows. He had bidden a cheerful goodbye and urged her to buy whatever she pleased and charge it to his account, and when she demurred on the grounds that no one in the shop would know her, informed her placidly that he had already taken care of that contingency. It was still barely half past nine. Sarah wandered round the food department, then found her way to the cosmetic counters where she spent a pleasant half hour choosing some new lip-sticks. They weren't a great deal of money and she had several pounds of her own in her handbag—she opened it and found a small roll of notes neatly ringed with a rubber band and bearing a message in Hugo's awful handwriting that it was an advance on her allowance.

She counted it stealthily while she had coffee—for an advance it seemed a lot of money, but presently she was rather glad, because she saw just the scarf her mother had been wanting for some time, and then exactly the gloves she had been searching for. She strolled up Regent Street and on an impulse pur-chased all that was necessary for the making of a *gros-point* chair cover, and was appalled at its cost, but it would take a long time to stitch and it would be pleasant to do when they were home in the evenings. All the same she was secretly a little appalled at her extravagance as she made her way to St George's Hotel where Hugo had said he would meet her at half past twelve. He was waiting for her, although she had taken care to be punctual, and took her up to the bar, where she admired the view while they drank their sherry and he talked of nothing in particular in his pleasant way. Sarah looked around while she sipped, and was glad she was wearing the shirtwaister and the white straw hat with its grey ribbon—it was a pert little hat and the ribbon matched her eyes as well as the dress.

She ate *sole el Mansour* because Hugo had suggested that she might like it. It was as delicious as he had said it would be; so were the raspberries and cream which followed it. They were drinking their coffee when he said reluctantly, 'We must go, Sarah, or my new OPD Sister is going to hate me for evermore.'

They both laughed because he had already told her that Sister Vines was exactly what he had wished for—middle-aged and married and pleasantly dowdy, poor fodder for the hospital grapevine.

He had left Sarah in Phipps Street, waiting patiently in the car until Mr Ives had opened the door and ushered her inside the dark little hall. She had turned to wave, and he had lifted a casual hand in farewell and driven away.

Mrs Brown was delighted to see her, but her delight didn't quite mask the fact that she wasn't well. Her elderly face was too pale and lined; her ankles, Sarah noted with a nurse's eye, were badly swollen. She had been twice to the hospital, she informed Sarah, driven there by someone whom she described as 'a kind old geezer in a bowler 'at', who Sarah guessed was a member of the hospital car service. . .and Dr Coles had seen her and suggested that she should go back into hospital, but she had refused. She ate a chocolate from the box Sarah had brought with her and enquired about the honeymoon. Over tea, Sarah told her about the cottage, and when Mrs Brown observed, rather wistfully, that it sounded rather like Hyde Park, she found herself fighting a ridiculous desire to cry. . .but Mrs Brown, for all the fact that she was making no progress at all, seemed happy. She welcomed Hugo when he arrived, submitted cheerfully to a lengthy examination and then sat, Timmy once more on her lap, answering a great many questions. When he had at length finished she said comfortably, 'I ain't so well, Doctor dear, and it's no use you telling me to go into 'orspital again, for it's of no use, and I'd rather be 'ere with Timmy.'

Hugo was sitting on the side of the bed, his stethoscope swinging from one hand. He said kindly, 'Then, you shall stay here, Mrs Brown. Your own doctor—Dr Bright, isn't it?—is back again. I'll ask him to visit you and our good friend Mrs Crews will perhaps pop in rather more frequently.'

He smiled and got to his feet, and Sarah, who had been quietly watching him, was aware that if ever she was ill she would want Hugo to look after her and no one else. His glance flickered over her and she got to her feet and said goodbye. Mrs Brown looked from one to other of them.

'It's nice ter see yer so 'appy,' she said. 'Come again, Sister dear, and you too, Doc.'

On the way home Sarah asked, 'Is Mrs Brown going to die soon?'

'Yes—within a few weeks. We could keep her alive a little longer in hospital, but she would hate every minute of it. I'll see that Mrs Crews understands the position.'

She said diffidently, 'I should like to go and see her—you don't mind?'

They had stopped at the traffic lights; he turned and looked at her coolly.

'My dear girl, why should I object? I'm your husband, not your keeper. Did you enjoy your shopping?'

She felt snubbed and she wasn't sure why; perhaps he didn't like her being inquisitive about Mrs Brown, but after all, she had known the old lady for a year or more when she had been in OPD. She replied in a subdued voice that yes, she had had a very pleasant morning, and remembered the money she had found in her handbag. It didn't seem quite the moment to mention it, but she said a little stiffly:

'Thank you for my allowance. It was thoughtful of you, Hugo.'

He didn't answer and after a pause she asked, 'Did you have a busy clinic?' With this remark she had better luck. He told her about it with no sign of ill-humour, so that she began to think that she had imagined it all. They stayed at home that evening, talking shop in a relaxed way for a good part of the time, and Sarah got out her *gros-point* and sat by the open window, and presently the talk turned to the garden and the house, and small everyday matters, so that she felt like a real wife.

The days passed quickly and smoothly. Sarah settled into a gentle routine which she found she enjoyed very much. She had thought that she would miss the busy life of hospital, but this was not so. Alice had proved herself to be a gem, handing over the reins of housekeeping without withholding her support, so that within a week Sarah was beginning to feel her feet. She took over the flowers for the house and a few odd dusting jobs and busied herself inspecting drawers and cupboards, and twice a week, when Alice was free, she cooked.

She took the Rover out several times and found that she wasn't as nervous as she had expected to be. Greatly daring, she drove to St Edwin's and brought Kate back to Richmond on her day off. Her friend had a great deal to say about everyone in the hospital, with the notable exception of Steven, so that when Sarah asked, with no sign of emotion, when he was leaving, Kate stared at her in surprise. 'Sarah,' she exclaimed, 'you aren't—you don't still. . .' She caught Sarah's eye. 'No, you couldn't possibly. Your Hugo's marvellous—you're the envy of every female at St Edwin's. Are you happy?' she demanded.

'Very,' said Sarah, very quickly and not giving herself time to think about it. 'I only asked because Hugo and I are going to Steven's and Anne's engagement party next week.'

Kate was all attention. 'What will you wear?' she wanted to know. It was an interesting topic of conversation and lasted them until it was time for her to go back to meet her Jimmy. Sarah drove her to the hospital very carefully, mindful of the rush hour, and on the return journey so busy with her thoughts that its terrors were quite dimmed. Hugo wouldn't be home for dinner, so there was no need for her to hurry. Alice was out too; she would have the house to herself for the whole evening. Hugo hadn't been home for dinner on Tuesday evening either; he had said he had work to do. She wondered what that work was, and thought wistfully that although they were such excellent friends, she didn't like to ask. She supposed that when one was married—really married, and loving one other—one didn't need to ask what the other one was doing, because life would be shared anyway. She sighed, deep in thought, and stalled the engine, and an irate taxi-driver leaned out of his cab to tell her what he thought of her, looked at her lovely, unhappy face and shouted instead:

'Hard luck, miss!' and waited patiently while she got noisily into gear.

The house was quiet when she got in. She went into the garden with the dogs, then went to the kitchen and made a sandwich because she couldn't be bothered to cook anything, and when she had tidied everything away, she roamed the house, looking at the portraits on the walls, and examining the china and silver, of which Hugo had a small but choice collection. In the end, she went to bed with a book, and read the same page over and over again before she shut it, turned out the light and lay awake listening for Hugo. When he came at last, she heard him pause at her door and call a soft good night, but she didn't answer.

CHAPTER FIVE

SHE overslept the next morning. It was Saturday and Hugo was free all day. Alice had called her, for her morning tea-tray was in its usual place beside the bed—she must have gone to sleep again. When she got downstairs Hugo was in the garden, reading his post. He looked up briefly and said pleasantly, 'Good morning, Sarah.' He smiled. 'Lazy-bones! It was barely eleven when I got in and you must have been asleep when I called goodnight.' His grey eyes were suddenly raised to hers. 'You weren't asleep, perhaps?'

She evaded a direct answer. 'I must have been tired—I expect it was the result of driving to St Edwin's twice in one day.'

'Did you? Good girl! Just for that I'll take you to the theatre and supper afterwards. . .the Mirabelle. I've got tickets for that show at the Comedy.' He tucked an arm into hers. 'Come and have breakfast—I'm famished.'

Sarah, dressing for her evening out, surveyed her person in the long mirror in her bedroom and decided that she didn't look bad at all. She had bought the dress in Salisbury with part of her father's cheque, and now she was glad that she had; it was sugar-pink organza with a scooped-out neck and long sleeves caught into a tight buttoned cuff—it looked faintly Regency, and she had dressed her hair to match it in a honey bun. The earrings looked fabulous with it too. She turned from admiring them as there was a tap on the door and Hugo came in. She caught up her purse and said, 'I'm ready—will I do?' in a happy, excited voice.

She revolved slowly, so that the dress blew out in soft folds around her, and stopped to face him. He was standing with his back to the door, with his hands behind him. He said gravely:

'You look like a fairy princess—I only hope you won't disappear during the evening.' He left the door and she saw the velvet case he was holding. 'You should have had this when we were married, but I had no opportunity to get it from the bank. It was my grandmother's—a gift from my grandfather when she was his bride, just as it is now a gift from me to my bride.'

There were pearls inside—a double string with a diamond clasp. She held them in her hands and said, breathless with delight, 'They're gorgeous—fabulous!' She gave him a long look, trying to read the expression on his face. But it wasn't for her to read; she gave up after a moment and said in a small voice, 'Thank you, Hugo—will you put them on for me, please?'

She felt his cool fingers on her neck, and then, hands resting lightly upon her shoulders, he turned her round to face him again. He put a finger under her chin and stood staring down at her, then released her and said lightly, 'Are you ready? Will you need a wrap?—it's a warm night.'

She answered him, not really aware of what she said; she had thought for one moment that he was going to kiss her, but he hadn't. And she was disappointed.

The evening was magic; the play was excellent and the Mirabelle a fitting background for the pearls. She hardly noticed what she ate, and they danced, not talking. They got back home at three o'clock and he kissed her lightly on her cheek and said, 'Up to bed with you.'

Sarah was suddenly petulant. She wasn't a little

girl, to be told when to go to bed! 'I'm not sleepy,' she said slowly.

He turned from locking the door behind them. 'Well, I am,' he said mildly, and she turned without a word and went upstairs to her room, only pausing at the door to say, 'Thank you for a lovely evening, Hugo. I enjoyed it.' She waited a moment hopefully, but all he said was, 'Good. Sleep well.'

She lay seething with a rage she didn't understand, and her last waking thought was that never—never would she wear the pink organza again. She was vague as to the reason for this momentous decision and she was suddenly too sleepy to bother, anyway.

It was on Tuesday again that Hugo called over his shoulder as he left the house that he wouldn't be back until after nine at the earliest, and would she mind being on her own. Before Sarah could utter the sharp observation which sprang to her lips, he had gone. She watched the car slide away with a smouldering eye, then tried to forget about it. But she thought about it a good deal during the day. Perhaps he went to his club, or visited an old friend—a cold reasoning voice at the back of her head asked what kind of friend, and she decided against pursuing this dangerous train of thought. One day, when the occasion was right, she would mention it. She had other things to occupy her mind, she told herself stoutly. There was the matter of a new dress for Mr Binns' party—she had several in the cupboard which would do very well, but there was no harm in looking around. She had a game with the dogs, talked house with Alice and then went to Harrods, where she found a very simple and consequently very expensive dress in honey-coloured silk jersey—it would be exactly right for the pearls. She bought it, and because the day stretched before her into a lonely evening, took a taxi to Phipps Street.

Mrs Brown was glad to see her—she was also very much worse, although she made no mention of this, merely asking Sarah in a small, breathless voice if she would make tea for them both. Sarah had brought her a bedjacket, a frivolous thing, pink and frilly. They admired it together and drank their tea, then Sarah, on the pretext of talking to Mr Ives, went in search of Mrs Crews and arranged for that good soul to let her know immediately if Mrs Brown should become worse. She went back to Mrs Brown and stayed another half hour or so before taking her leave. It was only four o'clock—she went home and took the dogs for a long walk, then went to bed early after a lengthy talk with her mother on the telephone, in which she gave a somewhat inaccurate account of life in Richmond in a voice which was a little too cheerful.

She was glad about the new dress when they arrived at Mr Binns' home, which was a splendid house in Hampstead, furnished to the last inch by a well-known decorator. It was like walking through the pages of *Ideal Home* but far less interesting, for nothing had been left to individual choice. Mrs Binns had obviously submitted to the dictates of the current fashion in furniture. Sarah, studying a peculiar chair as they crossed the imposing entrance hall, hoped that she was happy with it.

The rooms were full, but she knew a great many of the people there—Matron, the consultants, members of the Hospital Committee—she had an acquaintance with them all. There was a number of younger men and women too, friends of Anne Binns, she supposed. Sarah said the right things to Anne and thought she looked rather pretty in a mousy sort of way. Her dress was quite lovely, and a good thing too, thought Sarah waspishly; with a figure like that... Meeting Steven wasn't as bad as she had thought it would be; perhaps it was the new dress and the pearls, or the gentle pressure of Hugo's hand under her elbow, which made it possible for her to greet him so easily and congratulate him with every sign of sincerity. She had expected that the pain of meeting him again in such circumstances would be acute, but she felt nothing at all except a well-concealed embarrassment; perhaps that was what being numb with pain meant—probably she would feel dreadful later on. She went around the room greeting those she knew and receiving a great many good wishes in the process; it was probably coincidental that Steven joined the group she found herself with. She knew none of the people in it very well, some not at all. They went away one by one, leaving her with Steven.

He said rapidly, 'I want to talk to you, Sarah.'

She gave a polite smile. 'But I don't want to talk to you,' she said coldly. She glanced round the room as she spoke; Hugo wasn't to be seen, unless he was behind her, and she couldn't very well turn round and look.

'You're not in love with him,' Steven said roughly, 'you married him to spite me.' His eyes fell on the pearls, and he gave a sneering little laugh, so that Sarah felt rage bubble up into her throat. She went white, swallowed the rage and said softly, 'How dare you, and how insufferably conceited you are!'

This time she did turn round. Hugo was at the other end of the room, talking to Matron. With the most casual air in the world he strolled across the space between them, bringing Matron with him. He ignored Steven and said pleasantly, 'Darling, I've just been telling Miss Good what a phenomenal cook you are.' His manner was placid, but she caught the gleam in his eyes as he smiled down at her. She didn't stop to think what the gleam might be, but returned his smile with one of pure relief and said gaily, 'Oh, Hugo, have you been puffing me up?'

She transferred her smile to Matron, who said comfortably, 'And why not? And what is more, your husband has invited me to dinner on the strength of it.'

By some means, she wasn't sure how, Hugo had got between her and Steven. He stood close to her and had caught her hand in his and held it lightly while he asked Steven in a polite voice which wholly covered his dislike of him what his plans were for the future. Sarah felt they must present a picture of perfect wedded bliss, but the glow of satisfaction the thought had engendered faded into a peculiar hollow feeling that it was only a picture. She arranged a date with Matron, and when Mr Peppard joined them, answered his fatherly jokes with just the right amount of pertness, and presently, having bidden her hostess goodbye with the gentle good manners Hugo deserved of her, went home with him.

He hardly spoke on the short journey save for trivialities about the evening, but when they were home, sitting over a leisurely meal, he asked:

'What did Steven say to make you angry, Sarah?'

She hesitated, then, 'He was offensive.'

Hugo selected a peach from the dish before him and asked, 'Shall I peel it for you?' and proceeded to do so. After a moment he said gently, 'I am aware that he was offensive. I thought you would hit him.' He smiled briefly and his grey eyes, very compelling, met hers across the table. 'What did he say, Sarah?'

She said miserably, 'It doesn't matter, does it?'

'Not in the least. That's why I can see no reason why you shouldn't tell me.'

She looked at him with a smouldering eye, annoyed at his bland persistence, and said clearly, 'He said I wasn't in love with you and that I had married you to spite him.'

She hadn't known what he would say, she only knew that she was put out when he chuckled dryly.

'Conceited fool!' was all he said. He passed her a
plate with the peach on it, and took one for himself.
'By the way, I shan't be in tomorrow evening,
Sarah—perhaps you would like Kate or some other
friend to come to dinner and spend an hour or two.'

She put down her fruit knife with a hand which
shook ever so slightly.

She spoke with a certain amount of violence. 'No,
I would not! You. . .on Tuesdays and Fridays you
come home late!'

He glanced up with raised eyebrows, there was
the hint of a smile at the corners of his mouth. 'Yes,
I do, don't I?' he agreed imperturbably. Sarah waited
for him to say something—anything, but he didn't.
It was like having a door shut quietly in her face.
She put her napkin down on the table and got up
and ran from the room and upstairs, where, to her
own amazement, she burst into tears. She felt better
afterwards—probably it was the result of seeing
Steven again—she thought about him, and was surprised to find the process rather dull. She gave up
after a time and had a bath and went to bed. She
heard Hugo go out with the dogs and then lock up for
the night, but he didn't come upstairs. She guessed he
had gone to his study; it was past midnight when
she heard his quiet step pass her door and cross the
landing to his room.

She felt foolish and self-conscious when she woke
up the next morning, but when she went downstairs
at her usual time it was to find Hugo waiting as
though nothing unusual had occurred. It was a breathless day, the sun already brassy in a thunderous sky,
the river reflected the dull clouds, making it look
like sluggish oil. They strolled along by the water
and she talked a little wildly of anything that came
to mind, jumping from one subject to the next with
a fine disregard for context. When she at last paused

for breath, Hugo enquired, 'Are you going to visit Mrs Brown today?'

She hadn't thought to do so, but now that he had put the idea in her head she said yes, she rather thought she might.

'May I suggest that you don't take the car? I think we're in for a storm, and driving in blinding rain can be unpleasant. Take a taxi up after lunch.'

They turned for home and she answered meekly, 'Very well, Hugo,' secretly relieved because she hated thunderstorms anyway. She remembered then that Alice would be out that evening, and hoped it would have cleared away by the time she got home. She said so to him, then went scarlet, because it sounded as though she was getting at him because he wouldn't be home. He didn't answer, though, and after a minute she concluded that he hadn't been paying attention to what she had been saying.

It was raining by the time she reached Phipps Street. The taxi-driver looked at her curiously when she paid him outside the shabby little house, and when Mr Ives appeared in the doorway, scowling horribly, Sarah made haste to assure the man that there was no need for him to wait. She soothed Mr Ives, whose scowl was due to anxiety over Mrs Brown, and went upstairs to greet the invalid and arrange the flowers she had brought with her in a dreadful china vase with 'A present from Southend' written in gold across its front. It was one of Mrs Brown's treasures and the sight of it led the old lady to a series of reminiscences about day trips to that popular resort. It worried Sarah to see that she was in bed, sitting comfortably enough, it was true, with Timmy under the quilt, and her new bedjacket on. Doc, she assured Sarah, had told her it would be a good idea if she stayed in bed until her dinner, so after Mrs Crews had been to tidy her up, she popped back in. That it was now almost four o'clock in the afternoon seemed to have escaped her notice, and Sarah saw no point in telling her. They had tea, and she produced the chocolate cake Mrs Brown was partial to, then sat listening to the old lady's snatches of talk. Every now and then Mrs Brown dropped off into a light nap, and woke up apparently refreshed, to continue where she had left off.

Sarah hadn't meant to stay so long, but Mrs Crews would be coming at five, and it seemed a shame to leave Mrs Brown by herself. Thunder had been rumbling for the last hour or so; now there were fitful flashes of lightning; she wondered uneasily if she would be able to get a taxi. She was washing the tea things when Hugo walked in. He smiled and nodded at his patient and said to Sarah, 'I counted on you staying until Mrs Crews got here,' and proceeded to examine Mrs Brown in a casual fashion which didn't deceive Sarah at all. He hadn't quite finished when Mrs Crews arrived and without looking up he said quietly, 'Don't go, Sarah.'

So she stayed, standing with her back to the window so that she shouldn't see the lightning. He gave Mrs Crews some instructions and said goodbye, then waited while Sarah made her farewells and then followed her downstairs to where Mr Ives was waiting. She stood while the men talked, only half listening, but when they were at length on the pavement she stood stubbornly where she was.

'Jump in,' said Hugo cheerfully, but Sarah stayed where she was. 'I shall take a taxi, thank you,' she said with an hauteur which was spoiled by an ear-splitting crash of thunder. He looked up and down the empty street.

'Don't be mulish, Sarah. Taxis seldom come along here, you know.'

'If you think you have to come home with me,' she burst out, 'just because I said I didn't like thunderstorms—there's no need. I—I was joking.'

'You're a shocking liar, Sarah.' He laughed softly. 'I'm not taking you home, anyway. There's something I want you to see.'

She eyed him uncertainly. He looked quite serious. 'Get in, my girl. There's no time to explain now— I'm late already.'

She got in at that, and Hugo started the car at once without saying any more. The journey wasn't a long one; he picked his way through the maze of small streets between Bethnal Green and the Whitechapel Road and eventually turned into a drab street improbably called Rose Road, and stopped before a two-storied house, one of a row; and distinguished from its neighbours by the fact that its lower windows were painted white with the words *Surgery. Dr John Bright* written upon them in large black letters. Sarah let out a slow breath and turned to Hugo, but he said quickly:

'Not now, Sarah—come inside.'

She did as she was bid, following him meekly through the ramshackle door which led directly into a bare waiting room very full of people, all talking at the tops of their voices. They stopped as Hugo entered, however, and rather raggedly chorused a 'Good evening, Doctor' and stared at Sarah. Hugo paused on his way to one of the doors at the back of the room, drawing her to a standstill too. 'My wife,' he said to the room at large. 'She is a trained nurse and has come to help this evening.' There was a murmur of interest and Sarah smiled uncertainly, then coloured when a voice said, 'Cor, Doc, you got yerself the fairy orf the Christmas tree and no mistake!'

There was a little ripple of good-natured mirth in which Hugo joined before he took her by the arm again and ushered her into one of the rooms at the back. There was an elderly man there, going bald and stooping. He had rugged features and bright,

dark eyes; they searched Sarah's face as she went in
and he straightened up. Hugo said easily, 'Hullo,
John. I've brought my wife—Sarah, this is John
Bright who runs the practice. He's kind enough to
let me come along and help twice a week.'

The smile he gave her was wholly friendly, which
did nothing to lessen her feeling of guilt. She had
thought. . . Heaven knows what she had thought. . .
She raised troubled eyes to his, but Dr Bright was
speaking.

'I'm delighted to meet you, Mrs van Elven. Hugo
has told me so much about you; and don't believe a
word he says—he keeps this place going. I'd never
manage on my own, and well he knows it.' He
paused. 'There's a room next door where Sandra,
our clerk, sits. Would you like to sit with her?'

Sarah put her gloves and handbag down on the
hideous little mantelshelf. 'I'd like to help,' she said
simply. She looked at Hugo as she spoke. He was
smiling. 'Why not? Heaven knows we can do with
it, eh, John? Come and meet Sandra—I daresay she's
got some sort of white coat you can wear.'

Sandra was young and blonde and mini-skirted
and patently pleased to see a fresh face. She pinned
Sarah into a white overall, very starched and much
too large, and confided that the sight of blood fair
turned her up, and they'd get on a fair treat with
another pair of hands.

By the end of the evening Sarah wondered how
they had managed with only the three of them; she
undressed babies and struggled with small children
wearing clothes which were a little too small for
them and therefore not at all easy to peel off, let
alone put on again; she tested urine and took tempera-
tures and did a few simple dressings, and cleaned
the dirt from hands and faces and feet—good honest
dirt from good honest workers who told her sheep-

ishly that they hadn't had time to clean up before surgery hours.

The last patient went just after nine o'clock and Sandra, with a cheerful, 'So long', followed him. The doctors lighted their pipes and settled down to notes and forms. Sarah tidied up, turned off the gas from under the old-fashioned sterilizer and then sat down on the hard wooden chair in the tiny room used by Hugo. He looked up briefly, smiled and went on with his writing. She sat quietly, watching him, until Dr Bright put his head round the door and said, 'There you are, how about coffee in my flat?'

He looked a little wistful. She peeped at Hugo who wasn't looking at her and said at once, 'There's nothing I'd like better—I'm exhausted after all that hard work!'

She smiled at Dr Bright, looking, for an exhausted person, remarkably pretty and lively. Hugo hadn't looked up, but she sensed that he was pleased with her answer—perhaps they always had coffee after the surgery had closed.

Dr Bright lived alone on the second floor. He had a daily woman, he explained to her, who cooked and cleaned. He added stiffly that his wife had died several years ago and that he had a son, running a hospital in Mombasa. He led the way into a comfortable sitting room, very much cluttered up with books and papers and old copies of *The Lancet*; he swept a pile of them off a shabby but enormous armchair and invited her to sit down. Instead, she asked tentatively, 'Would you let me make coffee? I'm sure you and Hugo don't get much time for a good talk.'

She listened to the steady rumble of their voices as she boiled milk and found mugs, and then, inspired by a sudden idea, she put her head round the door.

'Are you hungry? How about some sandwiches, or have you had a meal?'

They hadn't, nor for that matter had she. The fridge

yielded a surprising hoard of comestibles. She took
in the coffee, and then, preceded by a delicious smell,
omelettes stuffed with bacon and tomatoes and mush-
rooms. When she returned with her own, they had
already demolished theirs.

'I told you she was a good cook,' Hugo commented as he got up to replenish their coffee mugs.
While he was in the kitchen, Sarah said quickly:

'Would I really be a help if I came every week?
Twice a week, isn't it?—with Hugo. I don't want to
be in the way. . .'

Dr Bright looked at her over the heavy rims of his
glasses.

'My dear Mrs van Elven, of course you will be of
help—we need someone desperately, but I can't
afford an assistant and I'll not let Hugo put his hand
deeper into his pocket than he has done already.' He
smiled. 'The omelette was delicious.'

She laughed. 'I'll make a cheese soufflé next
time—only it'll take a little longer.' She broke off
as Hugo came back. He said nothing, only smiled,
so presently Sarah cleared the dishes away and went
back into the kitchen, and when she had tidied up,
got ready to go home.

In the car, on the way to Richmond, she said half
defiantly:

'I told Dr Bright I'd come with you to help,' then
added hastily, because she had sounded overbearing,
'That is, if you don't mind. It would be nice to have
a little job. . .not that I'm bored or anything like that.
I can always find lots to do at home, and there's the
garden—and the dogs; but there's still time over. . .'

'You don't need to make excuses,' Hugo replied
shortly. 'We shall be glad of your help. It's a busy
practice,' and added as an afterthought, 'John and I
have known each other for years.' And that was all
he said. After a short silence, she began to talk, rather
aimlessly, about the weather, hardly noticing that he

did no more than make polite comments from time to time, because she was busy with her own thoughts.

Inside the house, in the dim-lit hall, he said almost curtly: 'I expect you're tired—I'll say goodnight. There's some reading I must do.' He took a handful of letters from the marble-topped side table and walked away from her to his study, went inside and shut the door with quiet emphasis. Sarah started up the stairs, getting slower and slower, until half way up she stopped, turned round, and ran down again and across the hall to the study door and went in before she could change her mind. Hugo was standing with his back to her, looking out of the open window, the dogs beside him, but he turned round as she went in and took a couple of steps towards her, saying, 'Sarah, is anything the matter?'

She stayed by the door. 'Yes, there is. I had no business to suggest to Dr Bright that I should work for you both—not without asking you first.' She sought for words. 'I thought you would be glad,' she said woodenly, 'but you're not. I—I pried into something private you didn't want me to know about. I'll write to Dr Bright and make some excuse...'

She turned to go, to be checked by his quiet, 'Just a minute, Sarah.' She turned to face him and he went on, 'If you choose to remember, it was I who—er—put the idea into your head to visit Mrs Brown.' She blinked and then nodded. 'I also suggested that you should not take the Rover.' She nodded again. 'And I counted on you—being you—staying with Mrs Brown until five o'clock when Mrs Crews arrived. I knew that if I left the last two or three cases to Coles I should find you still at Phipps Street.' He paused, staring at her. 'I could have brought you home even then, if I had wanted to.'

She gasped. 'You didn't mind me going to Rose Road.' Her voice rose a little. 'You wanted me to...' She frowned heavily and looked magnificent, but she gave no thought to that. 'Why couldn't you have just said so?' she demanded.

He said blandly, 'I should prefer you to—er—like me for myself, not for what I do.'

Sarah digested this in silence, understanding very well what he meant. It was romantic, even a little dramatic, that a successful Harley Street specialist, presenting an immaculate person to his own world, should choose to help out in a scruffy little surgery near the Whitechapel Road. It would impress any girl less level-headed than herself. She twiddled her wedding ring, admitting to herself that, level-headed or not, she was impressed too. She glanced up and found his grey eyes upon her.

'I see you understand me,' he remarked smoothly.

She said at once, 'Oh, yes. But you see, you need not have kept it a secret, because I like you already, and I can't imagine anything you might do making any difference to that. . .even though I don't know you very well.' She sounded forlorn, but only for a brief second, for she went on briskly: 'Why were you angry coming home just now?'

'Not angry,' he corrected her patiently. 'I was uncertain as to whether I had done the right thing after all. Rose Road is hard work, and dirty and smelly—far worse than OPD. I realised that perhaps I had let you in for a worse job than you had had before we married.'

Her ill-humour and unease quite evaporated. She smiled widely and asked, 'Was that all it was? But I shall like it very much, really I shall, and it's only twice a week.' She added with unconscious candour, 'I shall be with you too.'

There was no expression on his face, nor in his voice.

'Er—yes, so you will. I didn't realise you would wonder where I was.'

'Hugo, how ridiculous you are!' she remarked

roundly. 'Of course I wondered! I even thought that you—you wanted to get away from me or—or something. . .'

He said gravely, 'Never that, I promise you, Sarah.' His voice sounded strange, but she couldn't see his face clearly, because he had his back to the light. She said with relief, 'Oh, good! I'm glad we're friends again—I don't like it at all when we fall out; now I'm going to bed, for you must be wanting to be by yourself.' He didn't answer this, but gave a half-smile as she went to him and reached up and kissed his cheek. 'Goodnight.'

It was several days later that Mrs Crews telephoned. Sarah had just finished arranging a bowl of flowers on the dining table—it had taken her a long time to do, but was, she considered, well worth the trouble she had taken. The telephone cut across her gentle thoughts and she went into the sitting room to answer it. Ten minutes later she was in the car, thankful that the morning rush hour was over as she made her unhindered way to Phipps Street.

Mrs Brown was in bed, the awful pallor of her pinched little face in cruel contrast to the pink bed-jacket. She said in a thin, cheerful voice, ''Ullo, ducks. Funny, I was just thinking about you and the doc.'

Sarah smiled warmly at her. 'Now, isn't that funny,' she remarked cheerfully. 'Because I told the doctor that I was coming to see you today and he said he'd pop in later and take a look at you before we go home.'

Mrs Crews was at the sink, placidly preparing a dinner Mrs Brown wasn't going to eat. Sarah caught her eye.

'If you'd like to do your shopping, Mrs Crews, I shall be here for an hour or so.' They exchanged an understanding look. 'I'll come down to the car with you, there's something I have to bring up.' They went down together and at the door Sarah said, 'I've not had time to let my husband know. . . Did you get a message to Dr Bright?'

'Yes, 'fore I rang you, ma'am. He's out on a baby case—Sandra said twins.'

Sarah dug into her handbag, wrote a number on a leaf of her notebook, tore it out, and gave it to her companion. 'Dr van Elven will be at St Edwin's by now—it's getting on for two o'clock. Will you ring this number and give him a message from me? That Mrs Brown is very poorly and would he please come here when his clinic is finished.' She paused, frowning. 'There's nothing more to be done, you know. Mrs Brown doesn't want to go into hospital and there's nothing more to do for her. I'll be quite all right here, so don't rush too much.'

'You're alone in the 'ouse until four o'clock,' said Mrs Crews doubtfully. 'I'll pop in about three to see 'ow things are. It ain't right you should be on yer own.'

She trotted off, and Sarah went back upstairs, carefully carrying something she had taken from the car. She deposited it on the small table drawn up to Mrs Brown's bed and saw Mrs Brown's face light up. There had been no time to gather flowers from the garden—she had picked up her floral masterpiece from the table, and brought it with her, bowl and all. Mrs Brown gazed at it with pleasure. 'Cor!' she said in a whispering voice. 'All them lovely flowers— you shouldn't 'ave, Sister dear.' She stroked Timmy, lying under her hand. ''Ow about a cuppa?'

Sarah made tea and they drank it together, and Mrs Brown talked a great deal about everything under the sun in a voice which rapidly became more breathless, until she said, 'I think I'll 'ave a little nap.'

When she was asleep Sarah felt her pulse—it was almost imperceptible, as were the shallow breaths.

The old lady's face was very pinched and very tranquil. Sarah looked at her watch; it was a little after three—an afternoon had never seemed so long. She thought about Hugo, and longed for him to come.

Mrs Brown opened her eyes when Mrs Crews came softly in and they all had tea again, only this time Mrs Brown only took a sip or two, lifted carefully against her pillows by Sarah, who said comfortably:

'The doctor will be here presently.' There was no need for her to say more, because Mrs Brown had gone to sleep again, and Mrs Crews, after performing a soundless pantomime to show that she would be back again, crept away.

The old lady still slept when Hugo came quietly into the room. He stood in the doorway and gave Sarah a swift all-seeing glance before he turned his attention to his patient. He put his case down on the table in the middle of the cluttered little room and took his stethoscope from it and asked quietly, 'Where's John Bright?'

Sarah was still sitting by the bed, Mrs Brown's hand in hers. She looked at Hugo with eyes shining with relief. He seemed to fill the room; she was conscious of the confidence and calm and gentleness he had brought with him. Just for a moment her lip quivered, but her soft voice was steady.

'Mrs Crews tried to get him. He's out on a midder case—twins.'

He nodded and bent over the bed to put a large cool hand over Mrs Brown's and Sarah's as well. His touch was very reassuring but brief. He straightened up again and looked at her with the careful noncommittal mask of his profession upon his handsome face. She asked worriedly:

'Did I do right? Should I have got an ambulance?'

He shook his head. 'Perfectly right, my dear. No point.' His eyes left hers and studied Mrs Brown, who opened her eyes with the abruptness of a small child and said breathily, 'There you are.'

He lowered himself carefully on to the side of the bed.

'Hullo, Mrs Brown,' he said, and frowned with mock severity. 'What have you been doing the moment my back is turned?'

She managed a faint chuckle. 'Don't you be bamboozling me, Doctor dear.' She paused to get her breath. 'Because it ain't no use, for all you're a good kind man.' She closed her eyes and then opened them again. 'Thanks fer all yer've done—and ducks 'ere. Them flowers. . .'

Her glance invited Hugo to admire them, and he did so, concealing his astonishment at the sight of his highly valuable and prized Rockingham flower bowl gracing her bedside table, he murmured, 'Delightful,' and Mrs Brown said, 'Timmy—yer'll give 'im an 'ome?'

'Certainly—you can be sure that he will be happy and cared for.'

She sighed and slept again, to wake presently and fix Sarah with a tired eye. 'Me name's Rosemary— it's a nice name for a little girl.'

Sarah, knowing what she meant, said cheerfully, 'It's a lovely name. When—when we have a little daughter, she shall have your name.' She didn't look at Hugo as she spoke, but she didn't think he would mind her saying that, it was so obviously what the old lady wanted to hear. It was a harmless lie that would hurt no one—that wasn't true; she was conscious of her own deep hurt even as she smiled at Mrs Brown, who gave the ghost of a chuckle and closed her eyes and didn't open them again.

There were things to do, of course, and presently Mrs Crews came and Hugo said, 'Come along, Sarah,' and she found herself outside on the landing with him. It smelled of fish and chips and hot vinegar,

and the tap over the sink in the corner was dripping
steadily. She choked on a sob she was trying to
suppress and found herself in Hugo's arms, crying
into his waistcoat. She heard him say, 'My poor
darling, you have had a bad day,' and accepted the
handkerchief he offered, mopped her face and blew
her beautiful nose with resolution and said in a
watery voice:

'I feel better now, thank you. So silly of me!'

He still held her in a comfortable, impersonal grip.
'No,' he said in a kind voice. 'Not silly. I'm only
sorry I couldn't leave the clinic and come to you
at once.'

She looked at him in genuine astonishment. 'But
of course you couldn't—all those people waiting
for you.'

He looked as though he was going to say something at that, but instead he bent and kissed her
gently, then led her downstairs where Mr Ives was
waiting by the door. Hugo kept his arm about her
while he spoke briefly to him, and she stood quietly
within its comfort, not listening. When they reached
the pavement she said helplessly, 'Oh—two cars,'
and stood staring at the Iso in a helpless way until
Hugo took her handbag and got the keys before opening the Rover door and pushing her gently on to the
seat. He got in beside her, started up the engine and
said matter-of-factly:

'We'll leave the Rover at St Edwin's for the
night—perhaps you would come up tomorrow morning and drive it back. We'll pick up a taxi and come
back here and go home in the Iso.'

When they got back again to Phipps Street, he put
her firmly in the car and said firmly, 'Stay there,
Sarah, I shan't be long,' and went into the house.
Presently he came out again with the Rockingham
bowl under one arm and Timmy under the other. He
was followed by Mr Ives, who came across to peer

at her through the car window. He said hoarsely:

'I'll miss yer, Sister.' He put out a hand and shook hers solemnly. 'Be seeing yer,' he said.

They were halfway home when she roused herself to speak. She stared at Timmy, sitting on her lap, and asked, 'Who's going to see to. . .?'

'I've arranged things with Ives and Mrs Crews. Don't worry about it, Sarah.'

His voice was calm and very kind; she found that she wasn't worrying for the simple reason that he had told her not to.

Inside the house, she took Timmy to Alice and went back to the hall in time to meet Hugo coming in with the Rockingham bowl. She followed him into the dining room and watched him put it back on the table.

'I hope you didn't mind me taking it, Hugo; there wasn't time to pick anything—I was in a hurry, and I'd just arranged the flowers in it—it looked gorgeous.' She stopped, appalled to find her voice wobbling. 'I—I was going to wear my jersey dress when you came home because it matched so well. . .'

He was standing in the shadow, so she was unable to see his face very well. 'How delightful of you,' he said after a pause, 'although you look charming in that dress.'

She looked surprised. 'This one? Why, it's that old cotton thing I wore when I was at Mother's.'

'Yes, I remember.'

She found herself blushing and didn't know why. 'I'll run upstairs and change,' she said. 'I shan't be more than ten minutes.'

He talked about Mrs Brown during dinner, gently at first, then with a cheerful matter-of-factness, and presently led the conversation to other things. 'I think,' he said, as they drank their coffee, 'we might have a few people to dinner, don't you? We owe one or two already, don't we? Shall we have the Coles and Kate and Jim to start with, and then something more ambitious with the Binns and Peppards and Matron?'

'Black tie?' Sarah asked anxiously.

'Oh, yes, I think so, don't you? It will give you an opportunity of wearing one of your pretty dresses. . .the pink fairy-tale princess would be nice. There are plenty of roses in the garden to match it— you could do another centrepiece.'

She agreed, not sure if he was teasing and then sure he was when he asked:

'Not scared? You shouldn't be, you know. A colonel's daughter. . .'

She got up and said hotly, 'I'm not a colonel's daughter any more, but a doctor's wife—and proud of it!'

Her own words had surprised her; she had really no idea of saying them. To cover her confusion she went over to the piano and started to play. She played well, but with a regrettable lack of attention, for her thoughts were confused and needed sorting out. After a while she jumped up and said:

'I think I'll go to bed.' It was barely nine o'clock, but Hugo got out of his chair and went to the door with her without mentioning this fact. She stared up at him as they said goodnight, trying to read she knew not what into his placid, gently smiling face. She went upstairs, feeling confused.

CHAPTER SIX

DURING the next few weeks, Sarah found herself wondering about the state of her own feelings. For a few days Mrs Brown's death had occupied her thoughts to a certain extent. She had gone to the funeral with Hugo and Dr Bright and an astonishing number of people from Phipps Street. They had been bidden to the room on the top landing afterwards, where Mrs Ives dispensed strong tea, fish-paste sandwiches and slab cake stuffed with unlikely-looking cherries, and everybody had congratulated everybody else on the success of the whole undertaking. Dr Bright had seen her astonished look and explained, 'This is exactly what Mrs Brown would have wanted—I can think of no better memorial to her.'

She looked across the stuffy little room to where Hugo was talking to Mr Ives and the funny little man who lived on the landing below. He appeared completely at ease—she suddenly wanted to be beside him, sharing his feelings and thoughts. She turned back to Dr Bright, looking unhappy, but unaware of it, and he said briskly:

'You'll be along this evening, I hope, Sarah? It's such a luxury to have you to do the bandaging and cope with the babies—you're not sorry you started?'

She smiled. 'No—I like it very much, and I see more of Hugo.'

She enjoyed the sessions at Rose Road. She had bought herself some white overalls which fitted her, and called Hugo 'Doctor' in front of the patients, and if they exchanged half a dozen words of a personal nature during the evening, that was a rarity; yet they were together and she felt as though she was sharing at least part of his life, albeit a very small part. About his practice in Harley Street she knew very little indeed, and when, one day, she had made the suggestion that she should call upon him there, he had discouraged her, though in the kindest possible way. They walked the dogs each morning, it was true, but that was only half an hour at the most, and although he had never once given her the smallest hint that he preferred to be alone, she wished he would suggest that she sat with him in his study while he read his post, just as she had done that first evening. He was the pleasantest of companions, kind and considerate, and amusing too. . .she wondered if it was she who had changed, and had she really been content to see so little of him when they first married? And yet they enjoyed each other's company. They went out together frequently; she had everything she could wish for. He was generous to a fault. He had taken her down to spend a Sunday with her parents, and she hoped he would suggest a walk; but he didn't, preferring to discuss world politics with her father. And yet he had been quite delightful on their way home, although when she had thought about it afterwards, his conversation had been quite impersonal. The ugly little idea that he was beginning to regret their marriage crossed her mind and she suppressed it sternly as being unworthy of him; but it was there, all the same, to worry her in an unguarded moment. Sometimes, when she awoke in the night, she wondered if he still thought of Janet, and greatly daring, she essayed to bring her name into conversation, only to be quietly checked by Hugo, firmly introducing another topic.

It was during their first dinner party that she made an interesting discovery about herself. They had invited Matron and John Bright, as well as the Coles and Kate and Jimmy Dean. She sat opposite Hugo, well satisfied with the elegantly appointed table, with

its silver and crystal and the Worcester dinner service—she had conjured up a flower arrangement
almost exactly the same as the one she had taken to
Mrs Brown, and had put on the honey-coloured dress
and the earrings and pearls. Their glances met for a
moment and she felt a thrill of pleasure at the pride
and admiration in his eyes. She had spent a long time
in the kitchen with Alice, enjoying the planning of
the menu. They had come up with artichoke soup,
followed by roast beef with one of Alice's superb
Yorkshire puddings, the whole rounded off by *fraises
Empress* with a *sauce sabayon*. Now she watched
the results of their labours being eaten with every
sign of enjoyment by their guests. Hugo was a good
host; the wine was excellent; the company were
enjoying themselves. She was roused from her
pleasant domestic thoughts by Kate, who asked her
if she had heard the news that Steven was to marry
Anne Binns in October. Sarah stared at her, struck
dumb by the sudden awareness of a total lack of
interest in Steven. She hadn't thought about him for
days—weeks; she saw no reason ever to think of
him again. She went on looking rather vacantly at
Kate until Hugo's voice bridged the awkward little
pause. 'There you are, darling. A chance to buy a
magnificent hat!'

She turned her fine eyes upon him, still looking
astonished at her discovery, and said on a happy sigh,
'Yes, Hugo,' thinking how marvellous it was when
he called her darling, although it was only because
they had guests. She gave him a dazzling smile, and
mindful of her duties, pressed Matron to try a little
more of the *fraises Empress*.

When the last of their guests had gone, she wandered back to the drawing room and began to plump
up the cushions, while Hugo, who had lingered to
let the dogs into the garden, stood in the doorway

watching her. She peeped at him once and saw that he was smiling.

'Congratulations, Sarah. A most successful evening—it seems that I have a wife who is a first-rate hostess as well as a beautiful woman.'

She gave him a smile and began to rearrange the flowers in their vases. Surely he would mention Steven's marriage, then it would be easy to tell him. She started on the cushions once more, but when at last he said, half laughing, 'Did you want to tell me something, Sarah?' she said immediately and pettishly, 'No, I don't.'

She went up to bed soon after that, and cried herself to sleep without knowing why. She woke up during the night with the thought very clear in her mind that of course she couldn't tell Hugo that she no longer loved Steven—it would create an impossible situation: living with a man you loved and who loved another woman, even if that woman was a memory. Only if, by some miracle, he fell out of love with his Janet would she be able to tell him. She sat up in bed, made aware of what she had been thinking—it wasn't Steven she had loved at all, it was Hugo. It had always been Hugo, and like a stupid blind fool she hadn't known. And now that she knew, what was she to do about it? Impossible to tell him. She lay down again, telling herself to be thankful that at least he liked her enough to have made her his wife—perhaps in time he might love her. She went to sleep on the thought.

He was in the hall when she went downstairs in the morning. He had his back to her, bent over the morning papers. The sunlight shone on his grizzled head; he looked distinguished and elegant and very large. He turned his head and smiled at her and her heart thumped against her ribs in a way that it had never thumped before. She stopped on the stairs, quelling an urgent desire to fling herself into his arms and forcing himself to move across the hall towards him and wish him a good morning in her usual voice. She had the peculiar sensation that her feet weren't quite touching the ground, and when they left the house and he took her arm with his usual friendliness, she shook with excitement and happiness so that he asked her in some astonishment if she was cold. It was indeed a cool morning, but not sufficiently so to warrant a shiver.

She said lightly, 'It must be a goose on my grave,' which sounded so nonsensical that they both laughed, but she missed the penetrating look he gave her; only when she glanced up, she thought how happy he looked. They had crossed the river and were strolling along the Promenade, the dogs racing up and down, playing their own particular games.

'I think we might go to Holland in a week or so,' Hugo remarked. 'September's a good month for a holiday, don't you agree? I think I can manage the last ten days or so—if this weather holds, it will be delightful. We'll take the car—Holland's a small country, I can show you quite a lot of it in that time. We can visit my family too, but I think we will stay on our own, don't you? There's a good hotel at a small place called Vierhouten, not so very far from my parents, and within easy reach of Hasselt and Wassenaar where my sisters live. Gemma, my youngest sister, lives at Nîmes—we could drive down from Holland, and spend the night somewhere on the way, stay a couple of days at Avignon and visit her from there and return along the west coast to one of the Channel ports.'

Sarah agreed that it sounded delightful. He must have thought about it a good deal; no one could reel off a trip like that without having made a few plans first.

'What about your aunts in Alkmaar—the three old ladies?' she asked.

'Ah, yes. We must try and spend a few hours with them. . .it won't be too much of a rush for you?'

They were nearly home. She went through the gate ahead of him, her head full of the delightful prospect of having him all to herself for two weeks. 'I shall love it, Hugo. How marvellous to have two holidays in one year!'

He laughed, looking surprised. 'Well, I usually manage to get away several times. It's difficult to take more than two weeks at a time, otherwise it's merely a question of fitting appointments. . .have you enough money to buy any clothes you want?'

They were in the dining room, facing each other across the table. Sarah poured his coffee and as she passed it to him said in a wifely voice, 'You've only got ten minutes. I've still got some money left from my allowance.'

'Then you had better spend it, as your quarterly allowance was paid in at the beginning of the month; we've been married three months now, three months and ten days, to be exact.'

She went pink. 'Oh, do you remember it too?' The pink deepened, for she hadn't meant to tell him that she knew, almost to the hour, how long they had been married. He had gone over to the sideboard, and looked at her over his shoulder. 'I have a businesslike mind,' he observed. 'Would you like two eggs or one?'

She had no appetite. 'I'll just have toast,' she said, and saw his brows lift and heard the faint mockery in his voice.

'Slimming? I can assure you there is no need.' She shook her head as he came back to the table, to subject her to a bright searching look as he sat down. 'Feel all right?'

She said a little vaguely, 'Yes, thank you,' wishing with all her heart that she could tell him just how she felt. Instead she drank her coffee and broke her toast into small pieces, not eating any of it.

After he had gone, she wandered into the garden and then back into the house again, where she did a little desultory dusting and made out a list of groceries with Alice before getting her shopping basket. She enjoyed her visits to the grocer and the time spent choosing vegetables and fruit, and discussing cuts of meat with the butcher. She enjoyed, too, being addressed as Mrs van Elven. She mooned along the streets, savouring the delightful fact that she bore Hugo's name. It was strange that until that moment she hadn't thought very much about it, but now, because she loved him, everything was different.

It wasn't until after lunch, while she was pottering in the garden, that common sense once more took possession of her mind, reminding her that she had been living in a dream world all the morning, in which Hugo had most conveniently fallen in love with her. She had been aware of the foolishness of her thoughts and brushed the awareness aside because they had been so delightful, but now she sat down on the grass and began to tidy away the bits and pieces of her dreams—it wouldn't help at all to allow them full rein. She would have to be constantly on her guard with Hugo, so that he would never know. They had been happy so far; she had done her best to be the sort of wife he apparently wanted, she hoped with some success, although she was uneasily aware that she hadn't penetrated his deep reserve. Perhaps she never would. Janet would have been the only one to do that.

She got to her feet and started to garden with a furious energy which strove to overcome the sudden despair for the future. Her eyes blurred with stupid tears; it was only when she stopped to blow her pretty, reddened nose and wipe her eyes that she became aware that she had uprooted a flourishing

colony of carnation cuttings. She planted them carefully once more, sniffing prodigiously as she did so.

She went by bus to Harley Street, and found Hugo
waiting for her in the car. At the sight of him, misery
and love and delight at seeing him again caused her
to look so peculiar that he asked for a second time
that day if she was feeling all right. As she got into
the car he watched her with an expression she was
unable to read, but mindful of her good resolutions,
she said cheerfully that yes, she was feeling marvellous, and told him what she had done with her day
and then enquired with a somewhat overpowering
brightness if he had been busy. He gave her another
look before he replied, a thoughtful, frowning one,
and began to tell her, rather abruptly, about a chance
meeting with an old colleague.

Rose Road looked dingy and forlorn despite the
children playing on its pavements, and the dogs running to and fro between the idlers who had stopped
for a gossip and the hurrying figures intent on getting
home or round to the pub. The waiting room was
full too. Sarah said hullo to Dr Bright and went to
put on her overall in Sandra's slip of a room, and
then, armed with notebook and pencil, began to sort
out the patients. There were more than usual for
Hugo that evening, and several new ones as well as
the hard core of bronchitics and arthritics and
stomach ulcers. Sarah knew the regulars by name as
well as by sight now, and exchanged a word with
each of them as she made her way round the packed
room. They called her 'missus' or 'luv' and occasionally gave her a peppermint to suck or a banana. She,
in her turn, kept the vase on the centre table filled
with flowers from the Richmond garden. She was
gradually replenishing the vintage magazines too,
although no one read very much, preferring to talk.
The first once or twice she had been there, they had
gossiped unhappily in church voices, glancing at her

uneasily, but now she was accepted. She moved to and fro, making sure that they had their turns right, unruffled by the cheerful four-letter words which flew around her ears. A few of the words she had never heard before, and since that occasion when she had asked Hugo to explain one of them to her, and he had looked at her with outrage and told her that he would be damned if he would, she had thought it best not to bother about them.

The waiting room emptied slowly; there were still half a dozen people left in it when three youths came in and sat down together. They didn't speak at all but stared around them at the other patients, who glanced at them quickly and then looked the other way. Sarah, coming in from Dr Bright's surgery, sensed uneasiness in the air; she also smelled their cigarettes.

'No smoking here, please. If you want to finish your cigarettes, you can go outside. You won't be going in to doctor yet—I'll call you.' She smiled at them impartially. 'Names?'

The boy in the middle spoke. 'We don't want ter wait—we'll go in next.'

She looked at him coolly. 'People take turns here,' she said reasonably. 'And put out those cigarettes.'

They laughed and blew smoke in her face, and were disconcerted when she took no notice at all, merely asking, 'Which of you is the patient? And who is your doctor?'

They didn't answer. Sarah put her notebook back in her pocket and said, hiding a fast rising irritation, 'I suggest you go—you're wasting my time.' Before she could say anything else, the boy in the middle caught her by the wrist—not painfully, but she would have had to struggle to release herself. She stood still, annoyed but not particularly frightened. The boys were young and silly and inclined to bully. Out of the corner of her eye she saw the patient nearest

Hugo's surgery door get up and go through. He was elderly and slow, but the boys didn't notice. Seconds later, the same door was flung open, and Hugo, looking very large indeed in the bare room, had reached her in a couple of hurried strides.

He put an arm across her shoulders and the boy dropped her wrist, as though it had burned him. Hugo spoke without raising his voice, but it cracked around the boys' heads like a whip.

'You lay one finger on my wife and I'll thrash the three of you!' He inspected them deliberately down his patrician nose, while his fingers exerted a reassuring pressure upon her shoulder. The boys had drawn together. They threw their cigarettes on to the floor and ground them out hastily, while the youngest and cleanest made haste to say:

'Hey, doc, we didn't know she was yer wife— honest we didn't.' His companions joined in, all talking together. 'It was jist a joke—we 'adn't got nothing to do—we didn't do no 'arm.'

'Quite true,' agreed Sarah, still incensed, but fair by nature. 'They were only being annoying.' She took a quick look at Hugo. His face was stern and there was a gleam in his eyes which boded ill for the culprits. She added hastily, 'I'll accept their apologies if they'll offer them.'

She caught an unexpected sparkle of laughter in Hugo's look—but whatever he intended to say was drowned in a chorus of, 'Sorry, missus,' and, 'No 'ard feelings, lady.' The three of them began to edge towards the door, and almost reached it when Hugo said, 'Wait! Why did you come in here? And don't put me off with a lot of lies. . .there's nothing wrong with you except idleness. Bored stiff, I suppose?'

They shuffled their feet in deplorable shoes, shrugging their shoulders, and looking helplessly at him. Unwillingly they nodded and the boy who had held Sarah's wrist grinned sheepishly at her.

'You're none of you worth a brass button,' remarked Hugo almost lazily, 'and I don't suppose you know what work is. Come along next week. We could use some extra help—and don't expect to get paid for it!' They looked surprised, suspicious and eventually, pleased. When he said. 'Now—out!' in a manner conducive to obedience, they went.

When they had gone he looked down at Sarah, still held fast against him. 'I'm sorry, Sarah—did they scare you?' His tone was so light that she instantly took exception to it. She had secretly been just a little alarmed, but now nothing would induce her to say so. She said crossly, and decidedly loftily, 'Of course not. I'm not easily scared.'

He might at least have asked her if she felt faint or upset or something...instead, he said shortly, 'No, I imagine you aren't,' then took his arm away from her shoulders and went back to his surgery without another word, leaving her to smoulder.

Five minutes later she was required to bandage a septic finger he had just incised. She did it with an efficient calmness which covered the riotous tumult going on beneath the starch of her overall, and was on the point of slipping out after the patient when he leaned forward and caught her by the arm and said slowly, 'I should never have brought you here in the first place.'

The tumult exploded into a spreading wave of happiness. He hadn't been angry with her at all—only with himself. She gave him a glorious smile, and was shaken when he said silkily, 'You smile—perhaps you will tell me why?'

She gave him a puzzled look. 'Well, I thought just now that you were angry with me, and then I thought it was all right because you were angry with yourself—and now you're angry with me again.' She paused. 'And I'm not sure why,' she finished a little uncertainly.

They stared at each other for a long moment, then he let go of her arm and said in an exasperated voice, 'Oh, my dear girl. . .' and kissed her swiftly and brusquely on the mouth. He drew away from her almost at once. 'That mustn't happen again.' He spoke in his usual voice, calm, almost casual. She thought he was referring to the three boys, and tried not to think about the kiss, for she felt that it had been given by way of an apology.

Ten days later they gave their second dinner party. Sarah, who had enjoyed the first one enormously, wasn't quite so sure about this one; for one thing she didn't know the people who were coming very well, and they were all a good deal older than she was. But they were Hugo's colleagues, if not his chosen friends, and she quite saw that a certain amount of entertaining was obligatory. He had a great many friends, she was beginning to discover—young married couples, and some who had been married for some years and had children at school, and a handful of rather vague professors who, surprisingly, fitted in with everyone else.

She was beginning to realise too that he had been very considerate when they had first married, introducing her into his life gradually, so that she had never, at any one time, felt surprise at the number of people who made up his circle of friends. Now they were beginning to drop in informally from time to time for drinks in the evening, and occasionally an impromptu supper, and she and Hugo returned the visits. His friends had made her very welcome, and life was altogether enjoyable. That it could be a great deal more enjoyable was something which she steadfastly shut her eyes to, although she had the good sense to know that sooner or later she would give herself away, or worse, blurt everything out to Hugo.

She and Alice had spent a long time over the menu—they were to have *tournedos* with oysters, preceded by flamenco eggs and followed by grilled fresh peaches accompanied by whorls of Chantilly cream. She decorated the table with late pink roses and geraniums and verbena, and wore the pink dress, quite forgetful of her vow never to wear it again. Hugo was late home and she was already downstairs, putting the last-minute touches to the table, when he got in. She went to meet him as he opened the door and was halfway across the hall as he tossed his bag on to one of the wall tables and came to meet her. He stopped an arm's length away and studied her. 'I was beginning to think I should never see you in this dress again,' he said. 'I'm glad you're wearing it tonight—it's most becoming.'

She smiled with pleasure and thought how tired and strained he looked. They would be going on holiday the following week and he looked as though he needed it. She said now, 'Shall I get you a drink before you go up? I put everything ready—I thought it might save you a few minutes.'

He said briefly, 'Good girl. I'll change first and we'll have a drink together before they arrive.'

He went upstairs and Sarah went to the kitchen to make sure that Mrs Biggs had arrived to give Alice a hand, and found that she had. Alice as usual was in calm control of the culinary arrangements; there was nothing for Sarah to do but to stroll back into the dining room and then into the drawing room to switch on some of the lamps there. The room looked quite beautiful. She stood in its centre, loving it, and presently, because there was nothing further to do, sat down at the piano.

She was thundering through the noisier passages of a Beethoven sonata when Hugo joined her. She stopped as abruptly as she had begun and he fetched their drinks with the remark, 'You were playing as

though you were running away from something,
Sarah.' He gave her a piercing look. 'Are you nervous about this evening? You don't need to be, you
know—it's bound to be a success.' She didn't
answer, and he went on, 'I've got the tickets for next
week—the midday ferry from Dover. I think it will
be best if we spend a night in Amsterdam on the way
to Vierhouten. I telephoned for rooms this morning.'

She said, 'That sounds very nice, Hugo. I'm looking forward to it.' She smiled fleetingly and went
over to the window to let in Timmy and the dogs,
then stayed there, looking out into the garden. She
felt lonely, even though Hugo was standing, tall and
handsome and self-assured, on the other side of the
room. Only suddenly he wasn't on the other side of
the room at all, but beside her, and before she could
draw another breath he was holding her close, smiling down at her with a look which made her heart
stop and race on again wildly. He said quietly, 'Sarah,
there is something. . .' and was interrupted by the
clanging of the front door knocker. He released her
at once, said something forceful in his own language,
and then, mildly, 'Our guests, I imagine.'

It was the Sopers, a pleasant couple in their thirties,
who lived close by. John Soper was something in
the City and had known Hugo for years. Sarah liked
him; she liked Margery Soper too—a small, dark
woman, good-natured and lively and kind. The
Peppards followed hard on their heels, and lastly, the
Binns. Sarah greeted them all with a serenity which
successfully hid her annoyance. Hugo had been going
to say—what? She thought she would never know
now, for he hadn't meant to speak; the words had
been wrung from his lips—unpremeditated. She
thought that whatever he had been going to say would
never be said.

Then she dismissed the thought with an effort and
concentrated on her role of hostess with such success

that after dinner the ladies retired to the drawing room full of praise at her good management, leaving the men to talk around the dining table. 'And let's hope they won't be too long,' remarked Sarah, as she arranged her guests comfortably around the log fire. It hadn't been really necessary to light it, indeed all the windows were open to the quiet September evening, but the room looked so lovely with the firelight flickering and one or two lamps alight. Alice had brought in the coffee tray, and Sarah busied herself with the delicate little cups and saucers, to be surprised when the men joined them almost at once, and then covered in confusion when Mr Peppard said loudly:

'I saw no point in sitting around talking about politics and antibiotics and such dreary stuff when I could be here with you, Sarah, I shall sit beside you and you shall tell me what you thought of Scotland.' He drew up a chair and continued, 'There's an advantage in being elderly, my dear. One can do as one wishes and merely be labelled eccentric instead of ill-mannered.'

Sarah poured the coffee amid the ensuing laughter and then, obedient to Mr Peppard's whim, entertained him with her views on Scotland. But presently the conversation became general and she was free to look around her. Hugo was at the other end of the room, talking to Margery Soper, when Mrs Binns took advantage of a pause to enquire archly, 'I suppose this house contains some splendid nurseries—after all, it was built in a period when large families were the thing. I expect they're on the top floor.' She looked at Sarah. 'Will you use them?'

With admirable composure Sarah smiled at the wretched woman. She was aware that Hugo, as well as everyone else, was listening. She said evenly, 'As a matter of fact, there are some super nurseries on the first floor. They're separated from the front landing by a soundproofed door—such a sensible precaution, don't you think?'

Hugo's voice came pleasantly across the room. 'I've some happy memories of the nurseries in the house—it's virtually sound-proof, as Sarah has said. My sisters and I could quarrel to our heart's content while some poor housemaid acted as an uneasy referee. . .my grandmother was a little deaf, and my mother in a perpetual state of apprehension as to what we would do next.'

Margery Soper spoke quickly, as though she were picking up a cue.

'Do tell us—do you still quarrel with your sisters? I can't imagine you doing any such thing with anyone. I think you just go on getting your own way!'

Everyone laughed, although Mrs Binns' laugh was half-hearted—she wanted to know more about the nurseries. She knew, as everyone else present knew, that Sarah and Steven had been, at some time or another, in love with each other. It had been providential that Hugo had married her, leaving the way clear for dear Anne. . .and while she had no doubt that Sarah was happy, there was no avoiding the fact that she was a striking-looking girl and attractive to men. A baby—several babies—would keep her nicely occupied. She decided to pop in for tea one afternoon and ask a few tactful questions. . .

The last of the guests had gone by eleven o'clock. Sarah preceded Hugo into the hall from the front door. The evening had gone very well—at least, she thought so. Hugo said just behind her, 'Thank you, Sarah. Another feather in your cap. . .the evening was delightful.'

She stood still and he came and stood beside her in the dim-lit hall.

'I don't remember telling you about the nurseries when we went over the house.' His voice was bland,

and although it wasn't a question, she was aware that he expected an answer.

'No,' she answered, her voice very matter-of-fact, 'you didn't. Alice told me, because I asked her. You—you didn't want me to know, did you?' She turned round to face him. 'But I love this house—all of it. I wanted to see all of it, so I asked Alice. You don't mind?'

He said shortly, 'I should have preferred it if you had asked me.'

'Oh, I thought—as you hadn't mentioned it. . .'

His voice was all silk. 'I had forgotten your discretion, Sarah.'

She said nothing, for there was nothing to say—nothing, that was, that could penetrate the aloofness of his manner. She watched him walk past her into the drawing room and put the guard before the still smouldering fire. He said over one shoulder:

'Would you like to go to your parents on Sunday? It's rather short notice, but perhaps they would have us for luncheon.'

'I'd like that—and of course Mother won't mind short notice. Shall I telephone her tomorrow?'

He strolled back, hands in pockets. 'Yes, will you?' He smiled down at her charming and elegant and infuriatingly good-natured. Sarah's heart bounced against her ribs because he was near and at the same time she felt rage snatch at her good sense. She said with almost painful clarity, 'I wasn't being discreet, I was being kind—at least I thought I was. It must be—painful for you to talk about the nursery wing. It's empty; it could have had yours and Janet's children in it.'

She met his thunderous, astounded look briefly. 'Goodnight.'

She swept past him and started up the stairs. By the time she had reached her bedroom she had regretted every word.

She would have apologised the next morning, but he gave her no chance—there was nothing in his manner to indicate his true feelings. He discussed their forthcoming holiday and wanted to know if she could spare the time to go to Rose Road that evening, and presently left for his consulting rooms, leaving her to wonder if he had heard her at all.

Sarah arrived a little early at St Edwin's and went to sit in the car to wait for him. When he came through the gloomy archway which led from Out-patients, he had Dick Coles and Kate's Jimmy with him. They were deep in discussion, and once they all stopped and bent their heads over the papers he was holding. Watching him standing there, Sarah felt quite light-headed at the sight of him. But the face she lifted to his presently was calmly welcoming, and she greeted the three of them with a mild pleasure which gave no hint of the commotion going on inside her. It was quickly apparent that she was to be given no chance to apologise. Hugo, during the short drive to Rose Road, began a dissertation on a case of phaeochromocytoma which had been referred to him that afternoon. Sarah agreed politely with his deliber-ations over irregular cardiac rhythm, and marvelled silently that he found so much to say about it.

It was a relief to get to Rose Road and plunge into the cheerful hubbub of the waiting room. Sandra was on her summer holiday, but she had the somewhat erratic help of Shorty and Lefty and Tom, who, true to their promise, had indeed turned up to make them-selves useful at the surgery. She had despaired of them on their first evening, but now that they had been several times, they were beginning to be of help. Tonight she set them collecting names, so that she could get the cards from the filing cabinet. . .but there were several patients with dressings to be taken down and re-done, and any number of specimens to be tested. She began to wonder if half the residents in the area suffered from diabetes.

They were down to their last two patients when the door was flung open and a young woman carrying a bundle rushed in. She thrust it at Sarah, her face parchment white, struggling for words although she made no sound. But she had no need to speak, for the bundle was a very small baby. From the state of the charred tatters around it, it had been very severely burned. It was alive; Sarah thanked heaven for its faint wailing voice even as she winced for its pain. She went straight to Hugo's little surgery and put her bundle on the couch, indicated the mother and set about wringing out a sheet in saline solution. She had it ready as Hugo asked, 'Have you got. . .?' then stopped because she was already wrapping the mite very gently in it. He said then, 'Hospital—you take the baby, the mother can sit behind. I'll tell John.'

She sat beside him, her pathetic burden in her arms while he drove through the crowded streets. It was the only time she had seen him with his hand on the horn. . . Casualty were ready for them, because of course John Bright would have telephoned. She handed her tiny patient to a waiting nurse, then took the girl into one of the cubicles and gave her tea while she gently wormed from her all the information the hospital had to have. It seemed a long time that they sat there, though in reality it wasn't above an hour and at the end of that time Night Sister came to say that the baby had a fair chance and that the mother could stay the night in the hospital if she wished. The girl went with her, her face empty with shock. Sarah thought it probable that she didn't realise where she was. Dr Bright would have contacted her husband by now; perhaps when he came she would draw comfort from him.

There was no sign of Hugo. Sarah tidied the cubicle and took the tea cup to the sink and washed it, then started to clear the small cluttered treatment room. She was only half done when she heard a car stop outside and a moment later Dr Bright and a short, thick-set young man came in.

Dr Bright wasted no words. 'Where is she?'

'Children's—Special unit. I'll take Mr McClough up.' She started for the door, the pale-faced young man keeping pace with her. 'Will it be too late for us to come back to you?' she asked as she went.

John Bright was on his way out. 'Of course not— I'll be waiting.'

Children's was quiet, deceptively so, for there was subdued activity in the glass-walled cubicle at the end of the wide corridor. The cot was in the centre of the small room; she could see the plasma drip on its stand and Night Sister fiddling with it. . .and Hugo straightening his long back to speak to the Registrar. There was a nurse there too, and the baby's mother. She looked up and saw them coming and rushed out to meet them, not stopping to take off the white gown they had put her into. She hurtled through the door like a small whirlwind and hurled herself into her husband's arms. He held her close and despite his pallor said bracingly, 'Or'right, me darlin', 'ere I am, so yer don't need ter worry no more.'

He gave her a smacking kiss and Sarah half turned away, horrified at the envy she felt for the girl—to envy a woman so unhappy, because her husband loved her! She closed her eyes for a second and when she opened them Hugo had come out into the corridor too and was standing watching her. She turned and went back to Casualty then; there was nothing more to do but wait for him. He came presently, quite unhurried and said mildly:

'I'm sorry you had to wait, Sarah.'

They sat silent as they went back through the late evening. Lefty was hanging about outside the surgery. Sarah saw his quick glance before he looked away with studied indifference. She got out of the car and said, 'Hullo, Lefty, thanks for your help—we couldn't have managed without you.' Which wasn't quite true, although they were improving.

He grinned. 'Garn, missus! 'Ow's the baby?' His narrow chest swelled. 'I fetched 'er dad.'

Hugo joined them. 'I told you you'd be useful if you hung round here long enough. The baby will be all right—we hope.' He took something from his pocket. 'Split that with your pals.'

Lefty took a look at what he had been offered and gave a shrill whistle. 'Cor! Ta, Doc. You're OK.' He grinned. 'Missus 'ere, she's OK too.'

Inside, John Bright was waiting for them. He had made coffee and while they drank it Sarah made sandwiches, then took them into the sitting room, where Dr Bright said, 'What a woman you are, Sarah! I can think of quite a few women who would be sitting back complaining that they were tired or upset.'

She smiled gently at him. 'I hate to disillusion you; I'm both—but I'm hungry too.' She bit into a sandwich and said, 'I hope the baby does.'

'She's got a good chance, I hear. You looked very—lonely—when we got to Casualty this evening.' He looked at Hugo. 'You have a wonderful wife, Hugo.'

She tried not to look at Hugo, but it was impossible not to do so. He was staring at her very hard and half smiling. After a little pause he said, 'Yes, John, I have.'

She was disappointed. He could have thanked her on their way back from the hospital; he could have told her she was beautiful, and wonderful too, never mind if it were true or not. She remembered then how horrible she had been about Janet and the nurseries and conceded that it had been generous of him, in the circumstances, to agree with Dr Bright. She got up and collected the cups and plates and, refusing help, washed them up with a cheerful clatter.

They spoke very little on the way back to Richmond. Sarah could have told him how sorry she was a dozen times, but, sadly, she couldn't find the words.

It wasn't until Sunday after lunch with her parents, when she elected to take the dogs for a walk and Hugo unexpectedly joined her, that she plucked up her courage. They had reached the top of the hill and had paused to admire the sweep of country around them. She spoke quickly before she could change her mind.

'I'm sorry I was beastly the other evening, Hugo— it was a rotten thing to say. I beg your pardon, and if Janet were here, I'd beg hers too.'

He gave a rumble of laughter. 'If Janet were here your—er—regrettable words wouldn't have been uttered.'

She had been taken aback by his laughter until she realised that of course he was hiding his true feelings. She encountered the mockery of his smile as he observed, 'You know, Sarah, I can't remember feeling hurt. Should I have been?'

She went an indignant pink. 'Please don't joke, Hugo. You told me before we married how you felt about Janet. . .' She was very earnest.

He stopped smiling and stood staring at her with an expressionless face, his grey eyes a little bleak. He said at last, 'My dear, I'm sorry. I didn't realise that you had so much thought for my happiness. Shall we cry quits?'

He kissed her briefly and she managed a very credible smile, and presently began to talk about their holidays, resolutely ignoring her aching heart.

CHAPTER SEVEN

THEY arrived in Amsterdam in a wet dusk. The weather had been pleasant enough when they had landed at Zeebrugge—they had followed the coast road as far as Le Zoute and had tea there and then gone on to catch the ferry at Vlissingen. It was crowded with enormous lorries and long-distance transports, standing nose to tail, hedging them in on all sides. Hugo eased the car between them and they climbed the iron steps to the deck. Sarah had been momentarily taken aback to hear Hugo speaking Dutch to one of the drivers. When they were leaning on the rail watching the grey water of the Scheldt, she said:

'You know, I'd almost forgotten that you're Dutch. Your English is so perfect—well, nearly perfect.'

He smiled lazily. 'Dear me, do I drop my H's?'

'Don't be ridiculous! I didn't mean your grammar—it's just your accent; but only now and then.' She frowned. 'I wish I spoke Dutch—even a modicum. I suppose you couldn't teach me a few words?'

'Perhaps—a word here and there as you need it. My family speak English so you will have no difficulty there.'

She watched Vlissingen advancing towards them across the wide river's mouth; it looked grey and disappointing until she saw the row of houses along its sea boulevard. 'When we go home,' she said, 'perhaps I could find someone to teach me Dutch.'

Hugo laughed. 'Am I to take that as an invitation?'

She gave him a quick sidelong glance to see if he was serious. She was unable to tell. 'You would

141

never have time,' she said flatly, and then, in case she had sounded ungracious, 'Thank you just the same.'

They had said no more on the subject, as it was time to go ashore, and later, when they were crossing the flat countryside towards Bergen-op-Zoom, their talk was of the country around them. The road was good and fast, running through endless fields, showing a vista of villages and tall church spires under a wide sky, into whose empty blue bowl clouds were beginning to pour. They skirted Breda—a tantalising view of churches and steeples, gone in a flash, and then on to the Moordijk bridge crossing the Hollandsche Diep, worthy of a long explanation from Hugo.

Rotterdam was, to her, a jungle of flyovers and bridges and traffic coming at them from all sides. She hadn't quite got used to travelling on the other side of the road for a start, a fact which didn't seem to worry Hugo at all for he drove steadily through the confusion without hesitation, commenting upon the interesting aspects of the city as he did so. It was pleasant to leave the city behind at last, and the motorway with it. It was beginning to drizzle, but the country was pretty now, with small villages whose houses might have come from Brueghel's brush. As they slowed to go through Alpen-aan-der-Rijn, Hugo told her about the International Bird Park. 'If you like,' he said, 'we'll come over one evening for dinner. There's an excellent restaurant and the lighting is rather special, I think you might enjoy it.'

Sarah replied warmly, 'Oh, please, yes—I'd love it. How interesting it all is!' More than interesting— she was just beginning to realise that they would be together for two weeks or more. It hadn't seemed quite true; the idea was so delightful that her heart began to hurry. She was unaware that she was smiling until Hugo's hand came down on her own two hands clasped on her knee. 'Why do you smile like that?' he asked quietly. 'Are you happy?'

He had withdrawn his hand, but she still felt its warmth. He had never asked her if she was happy. She said now, 'Yes, I am—I haven't been so happy. . .' she paused, for she had been on the verge of saying since she discovered that she didn't love Steven; but of course she couldn't say that. 'For a long time,' she ended rather lamely, then added:

'That sounds as though I haven't been happy, but I have—I like being married.' It sounded naïve, but it was the truth anyway; as much as she would be able to tell him.

He said, his deep voice thoughtful, 'Thank you, Sarah. I believe that we—er—suit each other admirably.'

After that they drove in a companionable silence until he suggested that as they were nearing Amsterdam, she might like to study the map.

They were on the motorway again, passing Schiphol. She stared at it for as long as she was able, then applied herself to the map of Amsterdam.

'It looks like a spider's web,' she said, to be told that she was a clever girl because that was exactly what Amsterdam was. He sent the car racing past an articulated lorry to join the steady fast-moving stream of traffic making for the city's heart. 'Our hotel is in the heart of Amsterdam,' he explained. 'A pity we aren't staying longer, but next time we'll spend a week here—or we can fly over for a weekend.'

They were in the city now. Sarah peered out at the tall thin, quaint houses and the multitude of shops and the ever-recurring canals, and thought privately how nice it was to be able to take casual weekends whenever one felt like it. Her own family weren't poor, but more than one holiday a year would strain the finances. It seemed that Hugo hadn't exaggerated when he had told her not to worry about money. It was a pleasing thought.

Hugo had slowed down. The street they were in was lined with shops and she craned her neck to look at them until Hugo said cheerfully:

'I can see we shall have to have a quick look round before we leave tomorrow—as a matter of fact, we don't need to get to Vierhouten until the evening, that will give us the whole day here.'

She said hastily, 'Oh, I don't mind—really. Only it's all strange and foreign and I'm as curious as a cat.'

He laughed. 'Well, we're almost there. Here's the *Munttoren*; the hotel's across the bridge.'

The hotel was delightfully situated close to a canal and inside it proved to be quietly and comfortably luxurious. Moreover, Hugo had been there before and was remembered. Sarah, standing beside him while he signed the register, wished that she understood even a little of what was being said, and even as she thought this, he remarked in English, 'Forgive me speaking Dutch, Sarah. You'll find the staff speak English—they'll get you anything you want.'

Her room was pretty and very comfortable and had a view of the canal. She stared out of the wide window for a few minutes, then wandered through the intervening bathroom to Hugo's room. He looked up as she went in through its open door.

'Will dinner in half an hour suit you? You can have the bathroom first.'

She nodded. She wanted very much to unpack for him and talk, but there was an air of aloofness about him which prevented her from suggesting it. She went back to her own room and presently, dressed in a silk jersey dress printed in a glorious mixture of pink and cream, accompanied him down to dinner. That her appearance drew a number of admiring glances mattered not at all to her. What did matter was Hugo's pleasant, 'How charming you look, Sarah!'

She ate her dinner with an excellent appetite and in a warm glow of content, and when they had finished their meal, accompanied him on a stroll through the nearby streets. The Rokin housed some mouth-watering antique shops, and although she wasn't very knowledgeable about such things, she knew enough to appreciate the treasures he pointed out to her. There was some particularly fine Friesian silverware, and a variety of golden trinkets which, he explained carefully, probably constituted part of the dowry of some wealthy farmer's daughter two hundred or more years ago.

They parted in the hotel presently, he to read the papers, she to go to her bed, armed with a guide to Amsterdam and the latest Paris edition of *Vogue* which he had conjured from thin air for her delectation. Leafing through it, she decided that one of the many reasons why she loved Hugo was because he was untiringly considerate of her without once drawing attention to that fact.

She was busy with her hair when he knocked on the door in the morning, and although she called a muffled 'Come in' through a mouthful of pins, he merely opened the door a couple of inches and after enquiring if she had slept well, asked her if she would make her own way down to breakfast when she was ready and he would meet her at table. It was another ten minutes before she was ready. She was wearing a new suit for the first time—a toffee and white tweed with a silk blouse beneath its jacket. It had swinging pleats and rather nice buttons. Sarah had been horrified when she had asked its price, but it had suited her when she tried it on, and now, taking a long careful look at herself, she had to admit that she had done well to buy it.

Hugo was waiting for her, leaning against the

table, reading *De Telegraaf*. He looked up as she approached and said to please her mightily, 'That's new—I like it.'

She sat down, a little pink with pleasure, and at once perceived the small package by her plate. She looked at it and then at Hugo, who said, 'Go on, open it—it's for you, Sarah.'

It was an old Friesian watch chain which she had admired the previous evening, remarking that it would make a gorgeous bracelet. She took it from its box exclaiming, 'Oh, Hugo, it's lovely! How kind of you, and thank you!' She studied his face across the table; perhaps she would see something more than his habitual calm expression. She didn't.

'A trifle to remind you of Amsterdam,' he observed, and took the chain from her and wound it round her wrist. 'I'm glad you like it.' He smiled then—the kind of smile, she told herself hopelessly, that her brother might have given her; mildly affectionate and good-natured.

They had almost finished their breakfast when Hugo was hailed by a man who had just entered. He made his way rapidly towards their table and Sarah had time to observe that he was as tall as Hugo, although of a heavier build and about his age. Hugo held out a welcoming hand.

'Jan, how delightful! What are you doing here? You must meet my wife.' He looked at Sarah. 'Sara, I must introduce you to one of my oldest friends in Holland—we went to school together. Jan Denekamp.'

She shook hands and smiled delightedly when the big man said:

'I've been wanting to meet you, Sarah—I may call you Sarah? We have all heard such tales of Hugo's bride—all of which are understatements.' He laughed, a deep, jovial rumble, and Hugo said, 'We've almost finished, but do have breakfast.'

His friend sat down at once, but declined his offer. 'I breakfasted hours ago—saw you as I passed. I'm on my way to meet Jacoba and the children.' He turned to Sarah. 'You must meet my wife, and if you can bear the idea, my six children.' He gave her no chance to do more than nod, but rattled on, 'What do you think of Amsterdam? Do you stay long? You will visit Hugo's family, I suppose.'

Sarah said quickly before he could start again, 'We arrived yesterday evening. . .'

'And leave today,' interposed Hugo. 'I want to show Sarah something of Holland, and we plan to visit Gemma.'

Jan raised his thick brow. 'Quite a trip! I take it you've got the Iso Grigo with you. Do you like fast driving, Sarah?'

'With Hugo, yes, I do,' she answered promptly, and was rewarded by the look on Hugo's face. Jan Denekamp rumbled pleasantly, 'There speaks a good wife! But there, you have a good husband, unless he's changed in the last year.'

In another five minutes he took his leave, repeating his invitation to visit his home when they had the opportunity. 'Next time you come, eh?' he queried genially. 'Now it would not be kind to ask you, for you are not long married and you wish to be together.'

During the morning she asked Hugo if Jan was a doctor too—a question which made him laugh very much. 'Heaven forbid!' he replied. 'He's in shipping. Do you like him?'

'Yes, very much. Does he ever come to England? I should like to meet his wife.'

'They usually come over for a few days or so before Christmas. We could have them to stay—you'll like Jacoba.'

'And the six children?'

'You'll like them too. I daresay we can find room

for them all, could we not?' He added, 'Jan and Jacoba are devoted to each other.'

She said slowly, 'Yes, I thought perhaps they were. I mean, you can tell. . .the way he said her name.' She paused. 'Anyway, you can tell,' she reiterated defiantly, just as though he had contradicted her, which he had made no attempt to do, saying merely, 'Yes, I daresay you are right.'

She had the absurd suspicion that he was secretly amused, but when she stole a look at him, he was contemplating a somewhat way-out trouser suit in the boutique window she had stopped to study; his eyes were half shut and there was no expression upon his face.

They lunched at *De Borderij*—they had chicken on the spit and an excellent burgundy which she found a trifle heady, and then, because it looked so delicious, she ate trifle piled with whipped cream, remarking happily as she did so that it was fortunate that such things made no difference to her weight. Hugo, who had chosen cheese, agreed with her, pointing out with a twinkle that, under such a happy circumstance, she would be able to eat all the whipped cream she wished to—she had merely to ask.

After lunch, he took her along the *Nieuwe Spiegel-straat*, which, Sarah was quick to point out, was not in the least new, its houses having been built a good two hundred years previously although they were now, almost all of them, antique shops. They strolled along its length and Hugo obligingly purchased her a carved *koekeplank* because she thought it might look rather sweet in the kitchen at Richmond. From there, the shops in the Singel were but a step, and in one of them, Sarah having been much taken with some old Dutch prints in its window, Hugo waited patiently while she chose a selection of them. While they were being wrapped and paid for, she prowled

off on her own and when he joined her she was
standing before a small bowl—a creamy porcelain,
painted exquisitely with puce and pink flowers,
touched with green and blue and yellow. When he
enquired whether she liked it she said guardedly that
yes, it was charming. She loved it, in fact, but if she
said so, Hugo would buy it. 'Where does it come
from?' she wanted to know. 'I've not seen anything
quite like it.'

'Weesp,' said Hugo knowledgeably. 'Some time
in the eighteenth century. It's charming.'

She forgot to be guarded. 'It's absolutely
gorgeous!' She moved away. 'Hugo, I should like to
give you a present too. Is there something you like,
something you could use or—or look at every day?'

He said immediately, 'Yes, there is. A pewter inkstand in the window, for my desk.' He smiled at her
charmingly. 'Shall I leave you to buy it?'

'Well—yes. Shall I be able to speak English?'

'Certainly—and I'm here to help.'

The inkstand was nice. Sarah bought it and opened
her purse to pay, then asked, 'Hugo, can I pay with
English money?'

'Of course. Presumably you have a good reason,
for I seem to remember that you had a considerable
amount of Dutch money with you.'

She counted out her English pounds and while the
dealer dealt with change she said, 'Oh, yes, I have.
It's a silly reason. I want to pay for your present
with my own money—money I earned. I had some
left. You don't mind?'

'It makes it twice as acceptable, Sarah. Thank
you.' He strolled away to talk to the shop owner and
presently she saw him handing over some money—
probably, she surmised, paying for the prints.

They left the hotel after tea. Vierhouten was some
sixty miles away, but the late afternoon was pleasant
and there was no hurry. Hugo forsook the motorway

as soon as they had left Amsterdam behind them and took the road through Hilversum and Weesp, then turned into the small byroads which he seemed to know so well. The country was well wooded and the small towns looked prosperous, with villas set in neat gardens and here and there a solid, square house standing well back from the road, half screened by trees. At Soestdijk, Hugo drew up obligingly so that Sarah could take her fill of the royal palace, at the same time furnishing her with a concise history of the House of Orange, then circled away again, back to the country roads through the Veluwe, until they reached the hotel. It sat delightfully in a pocket of woodland—not large as hotels went, perhaps, but comfortable to the point of luxury. Sarah, changing her dress, looked round her room and reflected that Hugo was a man who expected, and obtained, the best things of life.

Later, as they sat over dinner, he asked, 'You like this place, I hope, Sarah? I have always found it pleasant. It has only been reopened for a couple of years, but it's comfortable and the food is good.'

She was eating smoked eel by way of a starter.

'It's delightful. Tell me, Hugo, do you know all the best hotels in Europe?'

'Oh, my dear girl, you credit me with too much,' he answered carelessly. 'And to be honest, I have never found anything better than my—our home.'

'The cottage?' she asked, and saw his eyes smile.

'Ah, the cottage—my bolthole, shall we say? Or rather, our bolthole now, isn't it? Each time I go there, I have the feeling that something wonderful will happen.'

'Perhaps it will,' said Sarah, forgetting to be non-chalant. Her grey eyes stared into his, momentarily lost in a dream world which held her and Hugo and the cottage.

'Don't you feel like it anywhere else?' Her voice

was eager, and he gave her a brief, bright glance before replying. 'Now you mention it,' he answered blandly, 'I have recently experienced the feeling on several occasions—and what is more, I have—er—no doubt that sooner or later that same feeling will become substance.'

Sarah fell silent. Surely he wasn't expecting to meet Janet again, not after all those years? She opened her mouth, intent on asking him, when he said quickly, 'You were asking me about the Veluwe—let me explain. . .'

The explanation lasted for the rest of the meal, and continued throughout the stroll they took afterwards. Presently Sarah went to bed, stuffed with useful information, and quite out of humour.

They spent the following day doing nothing because Hugo had said that she needed a quiet day before embarking on a round of visits. They walked in the countryside in the morning, and in the afternoon played tennis. Sarah, who was rather proud of her game, was soundly beaten, but consoled herself with the knowledge that Hugo had paid her the compliment of playing his usual game. She was consoled still further in the evening by being taken to dine at *De Ouwe Stee*—a restaurant housed in an eighteenth-century farm. Its interior was exactly what Sarah had been led to expect from her perusal of Old Dutch interiors, and she quite forgot her dinner while she stared around her, asking a great many questions which Hugo answered with competent brevity. Finally he said on a laugh, 'Look, my girl, if I promise to bring you here again, may we dine now?'

She smiled enchantingly, showing a dimple in one cheek which he hadn't previously noticed, and answered him saucily, filled with a reckless desire to egg him on. She knew that she looked nice—she was wearing the pink patterned jersey again, and the soft lighting was most helpful. She allowed her long curly lashes to sweep her cheeks, and allowed the dimple to appear once more. She asked demurely:

'Have you been here before?'

'Oh, yes, several times. With Jan.'

'Just the two of you?' she wanted to know.

He began to smile. 'Naturally Jacoba was with Jan; did I not tell you that they were a devoted couple?'

Sarah studied the fine diamond of her engagement ring as though she had only just recognised its magnificence. 'Oh? Three's such an awkward number.'

'I must agree with you,' he answered in a hatefully bland voice. 'But of course we were a foursome.'

She poked at the *poulet Grand'mère* on her plate with a pettish fork wishing with all her heart that she had never begun the silly conversation. As though she minded with whom he had been! And if he was going to be secretive about it, she couldn't care less. . .

Hugo chuckled. 'Do ask,' he invited.

She gave him a fleeting, fuming glance. 'Ask what?' she demanded.

'Don't you want to know about the girls I brought here?'

She raised her eyebrows in what she hoped was a dignified surprise, and then, because she couldn't help it, met his amused look.

'I don't care,' she said crossly, and was dumbfounded when he said instantly and with an air of patience:

'Why, Sarah, of course and quite rightly, you don't care. That's why our marriage is so—er—rational. We are, after all, two level-headed and mature people, not young things whose good sense is blinded by our emotions.' He smiled blandly at her and she wished rebelliously that she was a young thing, and not a mature woman whose emotions didn't seem to take age into account. She heard him say:

'I can recommend the ice pudding—would you care for some?'

She said 'No, thank you—just coffee' in a politely wooden voice which barely concealed curiosity and rage and frustration, but he didn't appear to notice but beckoned the waiter and gave the order, and went on talking as though she had never interrupted him.

'The first time I came here I brought a—let me see—yes, she was blonde, tall and handsome.' He frowned in thought. 'And for the life of me I cannot recall her name. No matter. She ate a great deal—no, don't look like that, Sarah—you appreciate your food as you appreciate everything else in life. She had no interest in anything else.' He sighed. 'She was a dead loss.'

Sarah stifled a giggle and then looked severe, but he went on, undeterred, 'We came again a year or so ago. I brought Elsa—a charming redhead, very small and dainty; she had a dainty appetite too because she was dieting—she ate almost nothing and we, perforce, with her. I remember when I had taken her home, I returned for Jan and Jacoba and we went to a village café and ate *Kaas Broodjes* and *Patat Frit* and washed them down with Pils. Jacoba was charming about it, but she is a charming woman.'

Sarah stirred her coffee and observed with a faint choke in her voice:

'How unfortunate you were in the choice of companions.'

He nodded cheerfully. 'Yes, wasn't I? But third time lucky, as they say. Perfection, my dear Sarah—the right size, the right shape, beautiful, intelligent—a charming voice, a healthy appetite. . .'

'How nice for you!' Sarah spoke with asperity, giving him a smouldering look. He was lounging back in his chair, his gaze intent, his eyes puckered in a smile which brought the colour to her face. She said rather feebly, 'Oh!' and then, because she wasn't much good at dissembling, 'You mean me?'

He said gently, 'I mean you, Sarah. I suppose you cannot object to a husband, however rational, paying his wife a compliment?'

Her heart was in her throat, she swallowed it back to its rightful place before replying. 'Of course not. Thank you—I don't deserve it after being so inquisitive.'

Her heart was still being troublesome. It would perhaps be a good idea to change the conversation. She asked presently, 'What time do we leave in the morning? Are we expected for lunch?'

She didn't know whether to be pleased or sorry that he seemed quite willing to follow her lead.

Before she went to sleep that night, Sarah had promised herself that she would never again give way to the childish impulse to know more about Hugo's life before they met, for even when her curiosity was satisfied, her peace of mind suffered.

Hugo's home proved to be a fair-sized square house, with a pointed scalloped roof, cut square on top, standing in its own grounds well back from the quiet country road. The village was only a mile or so away—nearer, perhaps, but the thickly wooded country around it made it appear more isolated than it was. It had an iron railing fencing it in, a low stone balustrade enclosing a formal garden in the front of the house, and a pair of formidable gates which stood invitingly open.

Hugo said nothing as they mounted the short double step to the front door, and Sarah was glad because she was a little disappointed with the house. From its exterior, she fancied it would be filled with late Victorian furniture of a particularly repulsive sort, and a good deal of red plush. They were admitted by an elderly maid, who exclaimed at some length over Hugo and would doubtless have done the same over Sarah if they could have understood each other. As it was, she uttered a terrifyingly long word in her own language and clasped Sarah's hand. Hugo said gently, 'Mien is congratulating us upon our marriage,' then looked pleased at Sarah's careful, *'Dank je.'*

Mien looked pleased too as she threw the inner door of the entrance lobby with something of a flourish, so that they might enter. Sarah, completely taken by surprise, stopped short, and said, 'Oh!' She had been utterly mistaken. It wasn't Victorian at all, but pure Old Dutch—there were the black and white tiles, the carved staircase, the white plaster walls above shoulder-high panelling, the great Delft plates separating groups of dim family portraits. There was a scattering of tables along the walls and one or two outsize William-and-Mary chairs and an enormous stone chimneypiece.

'Rather unexpected?' asked Hugo from behind her. 'The ancestor who built this house owned a fleet of East Indiamen and made a fortune. He collected his furniture over the years, but refused to part with the furniture he had inherited, so the place is a kind of museum—a very comfortable one, mind you, and if one is born here, as I was, one loves it. I hope you will come to love it too.'

They had crossed the hall as he was speaking and Mien opened the door into what Sarah rightly supposed was the drawing room. She had time to see that it was large and lofty, that its windows were vast and draped with floor-length curtains, and that the walls were white-painted wood picked out with gold leaf; then Hugo's hand under her elbow urged her gently towards the marble fireplace, flanked by two enormous chesterfields and several comfortable easy-chairs, from two of which Mijnheer and Mevrouw van Elven rose to greet them with a warmth which put Sarah entirely at her ease within a couple of minutes.

They lunched in comfortable state in a dining room which she judged to be furnished in the French Empire style; the chairs were heavy and leather-covered, the side table ornately elegant—she wasn't sure if she liked it, but perhaps it would grow on her; in any case, she wasn't going to let it spoil her appetite. She had been a little nervous of visiting Hugo's family, but now she found that she was enjoying herself. It was strange and a little disturbing to see this new aspect of Hugo. In hospital he had seemed remote, all-sufficient—or so she had thought during the years she had worked for him. She had obeyed his requests there without question, and seldom thought of him as a person. . .and now, because she loved him, she could never learn enough about him.

After lunch, Hugo and his father retired to the latter's study to discuss what his mother called family matters, but which she informed Sarah as they started on a tour of the house, would be disposed of in so many minutes, so that they could enjoy a comfortable dissertation on their shared love of medicine. As they climbed the staircase together, her mother-in-law said kindly:

'We are so glad to welcome you into the family, Sarah. You are so right for Hugo; you understand his work and will be such a help to him. He told us how you go with him to Rose Road. How pleased he must be about that, and how you must enjoy working together—such a worthwhile job, my dear. Of course, when the children come, it won't be easy for you.'

Sarah, behind her hostess, and thankful for it, murmured suitably, fiercely dispelling a pleasant vision of a bunch of children, all bearing a marked resemblance to Hugo, trooping upstairs in the wake of a loving Dutch Oma. It didn't bear thinking about. She concentrated upon the portraits lining the walls of the corridor they were traversing and presently recovered her spirits sufficiently to take a real interest in the various rooms they inspected, wandering in and out in a leisurely way while Mevrouw van Elven kept up a gentle flow of small talk.

'Next time you come, my dear,' she said, 'you must stay here with us. We quite understood when Hugo told us that he intended to show you something of Holland in the week or so that you are here, and it is easier for you to stay in hotels instead of coming back here each evening. But he usually comes over several times in the year even if it is only for a couple of days, so we hope to see you very soon.'

Presently they went back to the drawing room and in a little while tea was brought in, followed by the men. They had finished tea and were preparing to go when Hugo's father got up from his chair and came over to sit by Sarah. He gave her a half smiling look which made him look very like his son, and said:

'Sarah, there is something we wish to give you— we were unable to bring it with us to your wedding, and you must forgive us for that, but now you shall have it, as Hugo can arrange things with the Customs.' He put a small velvet box into her hand. 'It is old, you understand, two hundred years old, and now that you are one of the family we wish you to have it. When Hugo inherits'—he waved an arm— 'you will of course have what jewels there are, for then they will be yours by right. This little trifle is their forerunner.'

Sarah opened the box. The 'little trifle' was a diamond crescent brooch of a splendour which would bear comparison with her ring and earrings.

'It's beautiful! Thank you both, and thank you for wanting to give it to me. I'll treasure it, but I'll wear it too, because it's too lovely to keep hidden away.'

She bent forward and kissed him on one cheek, then kissed her mother-in-law as well, feeling a little overcome. She was grateful to Hugo when he caught her hand and drew her to stand beside him. 'We'll go somewhere special so that you can wear it,' he promised lightly. 'And now fetch your things, my dear girl—I'll take you out to dinner. . .'

They were to go again within the week, and still again for the family dinner party Hugo's mother had arranged. In the car she said:

'How lucky I am! Your mother and father might have disliked me.'

Hugo was driving slowly, sitting relaxed behind the wheel. 'Not very likely, I fancy. You're my wife, Sarah, and as a family we share the same tastes and views about the more important things in life.'

Her heartbeats deafened her. 'Am I important?' she asked. He glanced at her, his eyes sharp. 'Of course; I'm old enough to regard a wife as a vital as well as a permanent part of a man's life.'

She swallowed; perhaps this would be the right moment to try and tell him. She drew a steadying breath, but before she could speak, he remarked, 'It was a good day, don't you think? You like my home?'

She swallowed disappointment with resignation. 'Very much, only I didn't know it was going to be quite so—so grand.'

He looked incredulous. 'It doesn't seem grand to any of us, and it won't to you when you know it better. We shall come over quite often, you know. When my father dies, and I hope that won't be for many years yet, and I inherit the house—could you consider living there?'

Sarah didn't need to think. She said at once, 'Oh yes, of course! I should like it very much. Did you think I shouldn't?'

'No. I think I know your likes and dislikes, Sarah,

but if you had set your face against it, then we would have dropped the whole idea.'

She digested this in silence. 'You consider me too much, Hugo. I don't expect you to alter your whole life to please me.'

She heard the laugh in his voice as he answered. 'My dear Sarah, let me be the judge of that.'

They did a great deal during the next week. They explored the Veluwe thoroughly; they dined, as Hugo had promised, at the Avifauna's attractive restaurant; they visited Arnhem, where Sarah spent a couple of enthralled hours in the open-air museum and shopped for presents to take home; they went back to Amsterdam so that she might enjoy a trip along its canals, and a brief glimpse of its museums. He took her to lunch at the Hotel de Nederland near Hilversum, and to Alkmaar to see his aunts, three dear old ladies who lived in a house which must have rivalled any museum she had yet seen. They adored Hugo and were prepared to adore her too and made her promise, with a gentle persistence there was no gainsaying, to return soon and spend a few days. She heard Hugo agree to visit them again in the early spring, and bring her with him.

They went to Hasselt too, to spend the day with his sister, Joanna. The September sun shone on the small, partly medieval town, lying, peaceful and old-fashioned, so unexpectedly near the main road. Joanna lived on the very edge of the town, with her husband—the local doctor—and her four children. The children fell upon their uncle once they had offered a polite hand to Sarah, and he had at once disappeared with them to examine a boat they had just acquired. Their father came in from his rounds presently—a rather silent man who obviously adored his wife. The three of them sat over coffee, and Sarah decided very quickly that she liked them both immensely. By the time Hugo had returned with the children, she was firm friends with Joanna, and from the shrewd look he gave them both as he entered the room, Sarah deduced that he had made himself scarce deliberately.

He did the same thing at Wassenaar, romping with lazy good nature with his two small nephews while his sister Catherina and Sarah got to know each other. Catherina was younger than Joanna and pretty, with Hugo's grey eyes and quiet manner. She took Sarah over the house—a large thatched cottage in one of the leafy lanes of Wassenaar. It was delightfully furnished; it must have taken time and thought and money too; but Hugo had said that her husband was a highly successful solicitor. Sarah met him at lunch, and was surprised to find him a quiet, unassuming man with the kind of face she could easily forget. She tried to get Hugo to talk about the children on their way back to the hotel, he was so obviously devoted to them, but he rebuffed her gently, and she went to her room thinking with something like panic that life was by no means the simple clear-cut affair she had imagined when they had married. But then she hadn't been in love with him.

They spent a day in the Noordoost Polder, because Hugo said it was a miracle of reclamation. Sarah found it flat and bleak, even though she could appreciate the magnitude of the task the Dutch had performed. She listened with interest while he explained what had been done.

'We spend our lives keeping our country from slipping back into the sea,' he remarked finally.

Sarah stared at him. She said after a pause, 'It's strange, in England I never thought of you as anything but English— Oh, I know from time to time your accent betrays you, but here you're all Dutch, even while you speak English to me.'

He began to laugh. 'You know, Sarah, I begin to

wonder if you gave enough serious thought to marrying me.' He was still laughing, but his eyes studied hers intently so that she flushed and said hastily:

'Oh, but I did—at least I wasn't quite sure at first. It was. . .that is. . .' she faltered a little before his bright stare, and he caught her by the arm and said, with a return of his usual placid manner:

'Poor Sarah! I'm only teasing. Let's go to Kampen and have lunch and then go and see Mother.'

The rest of the day was perfect. Hugo's parents made much of her over a lively tea and the talk was of the Richmond house, and Scotland, and the possibility of a visit to London later on. 'Come for Christmas,' invited Hugo, 'and perhaps we can persuade Sarah's mother and father to come up at the same time. Would you like that, Sarah?' He turned to smile at her, looking handsomer than ever, so that just looking at him sent her off into a daydream in which he suddenly and overwhelmingly fell in love with her. When he said 'Darling?' in a gentle questioning voice, it seemed, for one blissful moment, part of the dream which had somehow come true.

She caught her mother-in-law's smiling eye and went scarlet, saying hastily, 'That would be marvellous, Hugo,' and was relieved to feel the blush subsiding even though her heart was bouncing against her ribs. She would have to learn not to blush—it was too ridiculous. Apparently Mevrouw van Elven didn't share her view; for she nodded approvingly and said, to no one in particular:

'A lot of girls would give their eye teeth to colour up so prettily.'

Sarah said miserably, 'Would they? But I'm not a girl—I'm twenty-eight.'

She heard her father-in-law chuckle from the depths of his chair.

'I should have said that you are very much a girl,

my dear. And if you're still uncertain, why, you can
ask Hugo when there's no one else about.'

This remark almost had the same effect of making
Sarah blush all over again. She was saved by Hugo,
making some trivial remark which turned the attention on to himself. She gave him a grateful look
which he acknowledged with a faint smile and a
twinkle which had a bad effect on her pulse again.
She turned from him with resolution and applied
herself to taking her mother-in-law's advice about
Dutch cooking.

Two days later, they were back again—this time
for the dinner party. Sarah dressed with care in the
honey crêpe, because the diamonds needed something simple. She was standing with the pearls in her
hands when Hugo came in. 'Will I look gaudy?' she
asked anxiously. 'I did want to wear everything.'

He studied her carefully and at leisure. 'That dress
is very plain and a lovely colour; you won't look in
the least gaudy.'

He took the necklace from her and fastened it,
then turned her around to face him. 'You look very
beautiful, Sarah,' he said. She thought he was going
to kiss her, but he took his hands from her shoulders
and said lightly, 'Shall we go? We don't want to be
too late leaving Mother's. If we get away by nine
tomorrow we should make Nevers in time for
dinner.'

They were the last to arrive, although not late,
and were immediately engulfed by the family. Sarah
found herself talking to Catherina's husband, Franz,
and discovered that his nondescript face covered a
quick wit and a sense of humour she hadn't expected.
She sat next to Huib, Joanna's husband, at dinner,
and he was nice too, although neither of them could
hold a candle to Hugo. He was at the other end of
the table on the opposite side, and although he gave
her an occasional smile they had no chance to speak,

and when they all went into the drawing room he went and sat with his mother, apparently content to see Sarah talking to Joanna. She felt resentful and neglected, and although she knew she was being silly, she contrived to turn her back. Which was a pity, because he stared at her most of the evening.

She had recovered her temper by the time they were ready to drive back to the hotel. They chatted about the evening and his family until she asked, 'Hugo, I thought your sister was called Joanna, but Huib called her something quite different. It sounded like Shot.'

She felt him laugh in the dimness beside her. 'I think you mean *Schat*. It's a term of endearment—er—treasure. It's used a good deal between mothers and children and husbands and wives.'

'Is that the only word—what do they say for darling?'

'We don't use darling as the English do—everyone is darling, are they not? Go to any party in London, and the air rings with the word. We say *lieveling*, but not very often in public—and *liefje*—little love. Perhaps we don't use endearments as much—I don't know. What I do know is that when we say them we mean them.'

They had arrived back at the hotel, which Sarah found annoying, for the conversation was promising. She waited while he put the car away, hoping that he would continue. Evidently he considered there was no more to be said on the interesting subject. He reminded her kindly that she would have to be up early in the morning, and wished her a good night.

They left on time. Sarah, who had spent some time looking at a map before breakfast, was secretly appalled at the distance Hugo intended to cover. The car was a fast one and supremely comfortable, but by her reckoning it was a distance of almost five hundred miles. Over their coffee she mentioned this fact to Hugo. He passed his cup to be filled again and enquired in an irritatingly bland voice:

'Nervous, Sarah?'

'No,' said Sarah snappishly, 'I'm not. Won't you get tired?'

He raised a derisive eyebrow. 'No, I seldom get tired driving. I know the road; the car can more than hold her own. Besides, there are long stretches of motorway where there is no speed limit.' He took some toast and buttered it lavishly. 'Still,' he continued, 'we can easily take another day over the trip and spend another night on the way.' His tone was gentle and mocking. Sarah choked on her coffee.

'Look,' she said, being sweetly reasonable with an effort, 'I told your friend Jan that I liked driving fast with you. Not driving fast, full stop. With Father or—or anyone else I can think of, I might be scared, but not with you. And I really was worried about you getting tired.' She added with a little burst of temper, 'Did you think I was pretending when I told Jan I liked travelling fast with you?' She frowned severely at him across the table. She looked delightful.

Hugo stared at her for a long moment and said suddenly, 'Dishy—that's the word I want.'

She stared at him open-mouthed. 'What do you mean?' she demanded, 'and have you heard a word I've been saying?'

'You're dishy,' he said deliberately, 'decidedly dishy, despite the fact that you're as cross as two sticks...and I heard every word you said.'

Sarah put down her cup and strove for dignity. 'I'll get my coat,' she began, and spoilt it by giggling. 'This is the silliest conversation!' she remarked, suddenly good-tempered again, then caught her breath as he stretched an arm across the table and caught her hand.

'May I not call my wife dishy if I wish?' he asked.

There was something in his voice which made her
look at him. He was smiling, but there was no mockery this time, and his eyes were bright. For a brief
moment she thought she saw something in his face
which she had never hoped to see, and then it was
gone. Probably wishful thinking, she thought,
allowing common sense to take over. All the same,
when she went upstairs to collect her things, her heart
sang. . .

They lunched, rather late, in Arras, then sped south
for Paris. At Bapaume they joined the motorway,
and then after half an hour Sarah remarked, 'I used
to wonder why you drove an Iso Grigo; now I know.'

He kept his eyes on the road ahead. 'Did you
wonder about me, Sarah? I always had the impression
that although we were good friends you barely knew
what I looked like.'

She gave a little gurgle of laughter. 'Don't be
absurd, Hugo! And anyway, you must know that
you're one of the most discussed consultants at St
Edwin's.'

'Not any more. You forget, I'm now a married
man. Which reminds me, I must send a picture card
to OPD. We'll stop for a cup of tea in Fontainebleau
and buy one.'

They had tea as he had promised, and, also as he
had promised, they drew up before their hotel in
Nevers as the September dusk was falling, apparently
as fresh as when they had set out that morning. They
set out again the following morning after a breakfast
of coffee and croissants. It was a mere two hundred
and twenty miles to go, as Hugo said, and Sarah,
hypnotised by yesterday's speed, found herself
agreeing cheerfully that they would be in Avignon
for tea. They were to stay there, so that she might
see something of the old town and go over to Nîmes
to visit Gemma. Hugo turned off the N7 at Lyon, on
to a quieter road running more or less parallel with

it, then beyond Valence turned off again to eat lunch
at a restaurant in Privas. He had been there before,
he explained, and the food was good. Sarah, eating
what was set before her with a healthy appetite,
thought how nice it was that Hugo always seemed
to know where to go and how to get there, and did
so without the least fuss. She supposed that if he
were to find himself in Siberia or Brazil or some
other far-flung spot, he would still contrive to get
the best of what was to be had in that particular
region.

The walled city of Avignon charmed her. Over tea
in their hotel, she asked, rather doubtfully, if there
would be time to see the Papal Palace.

'Of course there will,' Hugo replied promptly.
'We'll go and dance on the Pont d'Avignon, too.'
He smiled nicely at her. 'Tomorrow morning—
before we go over to Gemma's. She won't expect
us before noon. Now let's take a look round the
town, shall we?'

She was almost happy. They walked arm-in-arm,
looking in shop windows, and after a while sat at a
table outside one of the cafés in a square, and drank
Pernod. 'The first drink we had together,' Hugo
remarked as he gave the order. On the way back to
the hotel he asked for the second time in a few weeks,
'Are you happy, Sarah?'

She stopped in the narrow street and looked up at
him. 'Yes, Hugo. Happy and spoiled too—I haven't
lifted a finger since we started out, and we've been
to the loveliest places and you bought me that bracelet and the prints and. . .'

He stopped her laughingly. 'You're not in the least
spoiled, and I'm enjoying myself just as much as
you are.'

'I'm glad; and it's fun, being together.' When she
had said it she went pink because she hadn't meant
to sound so enthusiastic, but he didn't seem to

notice—so she went on quickly to cover her slight confusion, 'I am a fool—you know, I can't remember the name of our hotel.' She started to walk on. 'I must be in a dream.'

He gave her a keen look. 'Yes, I think perhaps you are. It's the Europe—easy enough to remember if you should get lost. But there's not the remotest chance of that, because I shan't let you out of my sight.'

They dined gaily and grandly from the *menu gastronomique*—scrambled eggs with truffles, fillet steak *aux moelles* with baby courgettes and *pommes mousselines* and to follow this richness, Carlsbad plums with thick cream, the whole washed down with Chambéry. It seemed wise, for the sake of their digestions, to go for another stroll in the still, warm darkness, talking, as they always did when they were together, about everything under the sun.

It was overcast the next morning, but still bright enough for Sarah to look across the Rhone to the distant Alpilles. She danced a few steps on the old bridge, as unselfconscious as a child, influenced by her surroundings and the memory of the old French song. She had put on yet another new dress—a Givenchy model in white Crimplene with short sleeves and a little collar. It was tied with inspired simplicity by a chocolate brown leather belt, exactly matching her buckled shoes. It was just right for the weather, which was warmer than it had been in Holland. They walked back to the hotel, turning their backs on the four remaining arches of the bridge, followed the path outside the walls of the little city, and presently entered it again by the massive gate, and so to the Papal Palace, which she found awe-inspiring, towering out of the rock, shading the town beneath it. She found it gloomy too, and was glad that they didn't stay very long.

Hugo's sister lived in one of the old houses lining

the road which led through Nîmes to its famous gardens and the Tour Magne. They were admitted into a narrow hall and then into a small salon, overlooking the canal running down the centre of the road, but the view from the windows was restricted by reason of their narrowness. The room was very French, its treasures screened from the passerby by heavy brocade curtains. Not that Sarah fancied any of the furniture with which it was adorned; indeed, she doubted if any of the fragile-looking chairs would bear Hugo's weight. She was unable to test this interesting theory, however, because the door was flung open and Gemma burst in, to fling herself at Hugo and hug him violently, and then to embrace Sarah with an equally sincere warmth. She was small and pretty, and younger than Sarah, and it was obvious that Hugo loved her very much. She spoke a jumble of English and Dutch and French, and said at once, 'Come away from this awful little room—we never use it—only to receive visitors we do not like.' She twinkled at Sarah with Hugo's eyes, and slipped an arm through hers.

'I've been longing to meet you, Sarah. Hugo told me that you were beautiful, but of course you are so much more pretty than he described. I am so glad to have you in the family.'

As she spoke, she led them upstairs to a large comfortable room at the back of the house, with wide windows overlooking a small garden. There was a baby lying on its stomach in a playpen in the centre of the carpet, and a very small boy rolling on the floor with a spaniel.

Gemma waved at them airily. 'Hugo, here is your new niece, Simone. Pierre, come and say hullo to your Uncle Hugo.'

They sat talking, the baby sitting plump and round-eyed on Sarah's lap, while Pierre climbed on to Hugo's knee to examine his watch and cuff links and waistcoat buttons while his uncle imperturbably drank sherry. When Gemma's husband joined them, tall and slim and dark, and speaking excellent English, Sarah felt no surprise to hear that he, too, was a doctor.

The children were whisked away, and they lunched in an increasingly friendly atmosphere, afterwards going into the garden, leaving the men to talk over their coffee. Sarah sat beside her hostess, and talked about clothes and children and housekeeping, and presently Gemma said:

'Hugo is a good husband.'

Sarah smiled at her widely. 'Marvellous. There isn't anyone like him.'

Gemma nodded in agreement. 'He's a dear. You know about Janet, of course. He would never have married you without telling.'

Sarah replied composedly, 'Yes, I know about Janet,' and Gemma went on, 'Then we do not need to talk about the tiresome woman, eh? I was a little girl, you know, and then I was not able to understand how he felt, and of course he told me nothing. . . Come, we will go for a little walk in the gardens while the children sleep and the men talk.' She got up. 'Doctors!' she uttered in disgust. 'When two of them get together!' She threw up her hands in mock horror. 'They have no need of us.'

They looked at the Tour Magne and the Temple of Diana, then went into the town to inspect the Amphitheatre and the Maison Carrée and a few of the shops, and in one of them Sarah bought a leather pocket book for Hugo—he had one already, but she was filled with an urge to give him something.

They left after tea, with the promise that Gemma and Pierre would dine with them the following evening at their hotel in Avignon. Sarah spent the first ten minutes of the journey in silence, deciding what to wear. Gemma had been beautifully dressed; she would doubtless be rather eyecatching.

'A penny for them,' said Hugo idly.

'Not worth it,' she replied. 'Just wondering what I shall wear. . .'

'That's easy. We'll go out tomorrow and buy something.'

She shot him a horrified look. 'But, Hugo, I've several dresses.'

He shook his head. 'Nothing pink. I like you in pink—there are some good shops in Avignon.'

They found the pink dress—a finely pleated silk in pale rose. Its astronomical price had no visible effect upon Hugo, although Sarah was shattered by it. As they left the shop he looked at her face and said briskly, 'My dear girl, if you disapprove so much, I shall give it to Gemma.'

She whirled round on him so suddenly that she almost overbalanced.

'You wouldn't! My lovely dress! I—I don't disapprove.'

He took her arm in a firm grip and steered her to one of the little tables outside one of the cafés in the square they were crossing. When he had ordered their drinks, he leaned back dangerously in the flimsy chair and said mildly, 'Well, my dear?'

She had recovered herself very nicely by then. 'Hugo, please understand. You give me such lovely things—not just now and then, but all the time. . .'

'And shall continue to do so,' he interrupted her. 'I should warn you Sarah, that I am a man who likes his own way.'

He smiled at her, and her heart jumped because she saw that same look on his face again—at least, she couldn't be quite sure, for it had gone again. She said breathlessly, 'I did warn you that I might say some silly things. . .'

His hand reached for hers; his eyes puckered in a smile.

'Sarah, did I not once say "never silly"? I'll say it again—and remember this; you are being all, and more, than I asked of you.' He crossed his long legs and the chair creaked under him. 'And now, what shall we drink? A long one, I think, don't you? Will a Dubonnet suit you?'

She nodded and smiled a little uncertainly, and said almost in a whisper, 'It's a gorgeous dress, Hugo. I didn't mean to be ungrateful. Thank you very much—I'm looking forward to this evening.'

'Good. I'm told that there will be dancing at the hotel. Do you want to do anything special today?' And when she shook her head, 'Shall I take you to the Pont du Gard? It's not far, and the scenery is well worth the trip—we can have a meal at the hotel there.'

They went back to their own hotel and she hung up the new dress with care and then went down to join Hugo in the car, and after a pleasant drive was suitably awed by the magnificence of the Roman aqueduct.

They waited for Gemma and Pierre in the hotel bar, and when they arrived Sarah was instantly glad that she had on the pink dress, because it competed so successfully with Gemma's pale green gown. They complimented each other happily upon their appearances, and well satisfied, enjoyed their drinks, conscious that they were attracting admiring glances from most of the men present. Gemma, settling down beside Sarah, blew her brother a kiss and said pertly, 'Do we not look nice together? It is to be hoped that our husbands realise how very pretty we are. I shall enjoy myself.'

They all enjoyed themselves. The evening, after a leisurely dinner, passed all too quickly. They danced, and presently Pierre asked:

'Dance with me, Sarah? I am but a poor substitute for Hugo, I know. . .'

Sarah disclaimed this remark charmingly, while secretly agreeing with him. Hugo was dancing with Gemma—she watched them across the dance floor; Gemma seemed to have a great deal to say, and Hugo was listening very intently. Pierre saw her look.

'I think that my dear little Gemma is telling Hugo what a wonderful wife he has found for himself. I imagine he knows that already!'

They had a last drink together and after Gemma and Pierre had gone, Hugo suggested, 'One more dance, shall we?' and whirled Sarah away for a blissful five minutes, during which there was no past and no future—only a delightful present.

They left early next morning, going via Le Puy and stopping to lunch at a village inn a few miles short of Clermont-Ferrand. The inn was small, but the cooking was superb. They ate breast of chicken with a mushroom sauce, which Sarah followed by a chocolate soufflé, thoughtfully ordered for her by Hugo, before they had their coffee and Courvoisier. There was still more than two hundred miles to go, for he intended to spend the night at Tours; but she found it no distance at all. There was so much to talk about, that she found herself wishing that it had been twice that distance, and that Hugo would drive more slowly. . .

She wanted the day to go on for ever. All too soon they were in Tours; tomorrow they would be back in England, and back, too, to the brief glimpses of Hugo before he left for his consulting rooms or the hospital. There was still Rose Road, of course, and she thanked heaven for that—and the weekends although she suspected that with the oncoming winter they would entertain and be entertained more frequently, which would mean less time together and a consequent withdrawal of the intimacy they had discovered while they had been on holiday. Perhaps if she could be patient until they went to the cottage in the spring. . .she went to sleep on that resolve.

England welcomed them with a soft grey October sky and a fine rain as Hugo took the road out of Southampton, but the weather had no effect upon their good spirits. The journey from Tours had been, from necessity, fast, but the crossing had been smooth and they had walked the deck, talking endlessly. True, upon reflection Sarah realised that she had done most of the talking, with Hugo contributing a quiet word from time to time; but he appeared to have enjoyed her company as much as she had enjoyed his.

The house at Richmond looked very pleasant as they stopped before its door. Alice was waiting for them, with Edward and Albert and Timmy. There were flowers in the hall, and soft lamplight. Sarah stood in the doorway, glad to be home. She said so to Hugo as they went inside. He was bending over the dogs, making much of them, and didn't look up when she spoke.

He said quietly, 'I'm glad of that, Sarah.'

When she came downstairs again from taking off her things, he was still in the hall, and on one of the wall tables stood the porcelain bowl she had so much admired in Amsterdam.

CHAPTER EIGHT

IT was a few days after their return, while they were sitting at breakfast, that Hugo asked:

'Will you meet me in town this morning, Sarah? I'm free after eleven-thirty until the clinic...we might lunch together.'

Sarah looked up from the letter she was reading, to find him watching her intently. She put the letter down and said at once and happily:

'Oh, yes, lovely! Shall I come to your rooms?' But to her disappointment he said, as he always said, 'Well, no, I think not. Let me see—could you manage New Bond Street—er—somewhere we can't miss each other? How about Asprey's? Take a taxi— I daresay you can fill in the afternoon, can't you? If you don't feel like coming to St Edwin's, I'll pick you up.'

'Gracious, there's not the least need of that.' She looked quite shocked. 'I'll be there as usual and wait in the car. Dr Bright said on the phone that he expected a crowd this evening, and you won't want to be held up.' She poured more coffee for them both, and greatly daring, tried again. 'You're sure you don't want me to come to Harley Street? I'll have loads of time.'

It was no good; he countered her request with a smiling blandness which was nevertheless as definite as if he had said a bald 'no', and presently he got up to go, leaving her sitting at the table, a prey to a number of unhappy thoughts, not the least of which was the possibility that his receptionist was some lovely curvaceous blonde. She pondered about this for quite a few minutes, then, having made up her mind, went to find Alice, before she could change it again.

She got to Harley Street just about eleven. She had dressed carefully in the new suit, and had complemented it with her Jourdan shoes and a matching calf handbag and gloves, and had crowned her lovely head with a wide-brimmed hat which gave her a decidedly dashing air.

Hugo's rooms were on the first floor, according to the neat, impeccably shining plate upon the discreet front door. The door stood open; Sarah went inside and up the stairs and walked in through another door which invited her to enter. The room was discreetly comfortable and very restful, and save for the woman sitting behind a large desk in one corner, was empty. She was a round, cosy person with a sweet face, and, Sarah noted with soaring spirits, unmistakably middle-aged. She went across the room to her, her smile dazzling in its relief.

'Forgive me for just walking in. I'm Mrs van Elven—you must be my husband's receptionist. I'm so glad to meet you.' She held out a hand. 'Miss Trevor—have I got it right?'

Miss Trevor got up, beaming with pleasure. 'Well,' she said, 'I am glad to meet you, Mrs van Elven—I'll tell the doctor you're here.' She glanced at the clock. 'He's got one more patient to see—she telephoned to say that she would be a little late. . .' She looked at Sarah enquiringly.

'Don't tell the doctor I'm here—I'll surprise him.' Sarah smiled again and put her hand on the door handle, which rattled slightly because her hand was shaking.

Hugo was at his desk, writing. It was a large desk, and for a doctor, very tidy. He got to his feet when he saw her and said with his usual air of calm, 'Sarah, this is a surprise.' He didn't look in the least surprised, however, but then he was adept at concealing

his feelings. It was impossible, looking at him, to
have the least idea as to his reaction to her sudden
appearance; probably he was annoyed.

She advanced a few steps into the room. 'I was
early,' she explained. 'You don't mind if I wait for
you here? Miss Trevor says you have one more
patient—I could sit in the waiting room, if you
don't mind?'

He was lounging against the desk, his hands in his
pockets, staring at her. 'No, I don't mind. That's a
fetching hat.'

She went a little pink and a dimple appeared for
a devastating moment.

'Oh—well, yes.' She sounded guilty and he said
gravely, his eyes dancing, 'I wonder what you have
done to make you look so apprehensive. Spent all
my money?'

She gave him a swift look and smiled. 'No—I've
not had time to. . .' she stopped and felt her cheeks
getting red. She had been on the point of telling him
that there had been no time to even look at shops,
otherwise she would never have got to Harley Street
in time. She peeped at him between her lashes. He
was looking down at his desk and she couldn't see
his face; perhaps he hadn't noticed. She said chattily:

'What a nice room this is—so restful.'

'Naturally,' he agreed amicably, 'I endeavour to
exercise a calming influence.'

He was still standing by the desk, screening something she had seen as soon as she entered the room.
Her eyes, unbidden, lighted upon it once more,
although there was only very little of it to be seen.
A photo frame—a rather old-fashioned one, she
thought, probably silver. It was a pity she couldn't
see it—perhaps Hugo didn't want her to. Her heart
plummeted into her fashionable shoes. Perhaps this
was why he had never encouraged her to come; perhaps Janet's photo was on his desk—after all, he

couldn't very well have it at home. Impelled by some strong feeling she didn't stop to analyse, she whisked past him to have a look. She had been right about the frame, it was silver shell-back, a riot of cherubs' heads and true lovers' knots and roses; it housed two photos, and she had been wrong about those—they were of herself. One, a coloured snapshot her brother had taken the previous summer—she was standing in the garden with her hair hanging round her shoulders, laughing; the other was a portrait she had had taken to please her mother, very serious in her sister's uniform. She stared at them foolishly and then said in a small voice:

'Oh, it's me!'

Hugo was no longer lounging by the desk. He asked, at his most urbane:

'Why are you surprised? Whom did you expect to see, Sarah?'

She was for once, speechless, and even if she could have thought of something to say, she couldn't have said it, by reason of a lack of breath. Hugo laughed and took a purposeful step towards her, and then stopped as the buzzer on his desk broke the silence. He stopped short and said softly, 'Damn—my patient!' and Sarah, who wasn't at all sure what he had been going to do, added an unspoken swearword of her own and said out loud, 'Yes, of course, I'll go,' and slipped through the door he had gone to open for her. A bony old lady was talking to Miss Trevor. She gave Sarah an appraising stare as she swept past to where Hugo was waiting and broke into immediate speech, cut short, to Sarah's regret, by the gentle shutting of the door. She would have liked a little time to think, but Miss Trevor evidently thought that it was her duty to engage her employer's wife in small talk, and Sarah was too kind-hearted to do anything else but carry on her side of the conversation, trivial though it was.

The old lady reappeared after ten minutes or so to be ushered firmly to the door by Hugo, when he said, 'Five minutes, Sarah,' and disappeared into his consulting room again, but it was less than that and she had had no time to sort out her thoughts, and because he seemed disposed to be silent, she felt it incumbent upon her to talk, although she had very little idea of what she was saying. They took a taxi, and because she thought that she had been curious enough for one morning, she forbore from asking where they were bound for. When they alighted half-way down Bond Street and were on the point of entering a famous furriers, she stopped in its entrance. 'Why are we here?' she wanted to know.

Hugo was opening the door, a firm hand urging her gently forward.

'A winter coat. . .' was all he said, and then when she stopped again, 'Don't worry, Sarah, I know your views about wild animals being slaughtered for furs. You'll be shown only ranch mink.'

She tried on several, uncertain which to choose, because Hugo hadn't mentioned price, and nor, for that matter, had the saleslady. She decided at length looking a little anxiously at Hugo, who smiled blandly back at her. When the saleslady took it from her, remarking, 'A lovely coat, madam, and an investment, if I might say so—real value for nine hundred guineas.'

She sailed away and Sarah made a terrible face at Hugo and said in a small voice, 'Hugo, it's nine hundred guineas,' to be stopped by his calm, 'And very good value for the money, I imagine. I'll tell them to send it, shall I?'

She tried to thank him as they walked to Claridges for lunch, but it was difficult in the street, so she made another attempt when they were seated in the Buttery, only to be firmly but kindly discouraged.

'My dear Sarah,' said Hugo, 'must I remind you

that you are my wife and as such can expect to be the recipient of an occasional gift from me?' Sarah, spearing hors d'oeuvres, lifted her awed gaze to his as he continued. 'And if that high-flown speech had no effect upon you, I assure you that I can think up half a dozen more as good or even better.'

He smiled, his eyes twinkling and she gave a gurgle of laughter.

'Hugo, you sounded like a Church elder—a very nice one, of course! I could wear it to—to Anne's wedding, couldn't I? and Kate's. I shall need a new hat.' She contemplated an olive, lost in thought, and was taken aback when Hugo laughed.

'Now what have I said?' she asked. 'And that reminds me—shall I get Kate's present today? I could bring it with me and give it to her before I meet you at St Edwin's.'

'An admirable idea,' agreed Hugo, 'provided it's of a carryable nature. What had you in mind?'

'Well, they won't have an awful lot of money—I thought table linen or a great many towels.'

'An excellent choice,' he agreed, 'though I doubt if young Dean will be very enthusiastic. I think I'll send him half a dozen bottles of claret...just for himself, you know.'

'Well, how horrid!' protested Sarah. 'He's going to share the towels and things with Kate, so he'll have to share the claret with her too.' She caught his eye across the table; he was laughing at her silently. She said hastily, 'I shall go to the White House this afternoon.'

She waited until the waiter had substituted *poulet demi-deuil* for the remains of the hors d'oeuvres and said with commendable tenacity:

'I don't know how to thank you properly for my lovely coat.'

Hugo put down his knife and fork. He said gently, 'What a persistent woman you are, Sarah! I thought

I had made myself clear.' He gave her a mocking smile; his voice had an edge to it. 'My dear girl, you don't imagine that I'm trying to bribe you?'

'B-bribe me?' she uttered. Her saucer eyes, despite the smart hat, made her look like a surprised child, an effect considerably heightened by the bright colour which flooded her cheeks. She opened her mouth several times, only to close it again—speech, while her thoughts were so incoherent, would be useless. They clarified all at once into the tiresome fact that now it would be extremely difficult to show her true feelings—for if she did, he might construe them as the acceptance of the bribe he had so hatefully suggested she had suspected. He would never believe her. She choked upon a delicious morsel of truffle and swallowed it with as much pleasure as she would have downed a pill, then said finally, 'No, Hugo, I don't imagine any such thing—I tried to express my gratitude. You see, it's a marvellous present, even the most level-headed woman would be thrilled to have it.' She paused and went on briskly, 'Will you be busy in OP this afternoon?'

Hugo's mouth twitched a little at its corners, but he said in a perfectly ordinary voice, 'I expect so—there's a backlog of patients, naturally, but I'll do my best to get finished. By the way, I'm told the burns baby is doing well.'

They were on safe ground again; they talked amicably until he looked at his watch and said, 'I simply must go.'

They were on their way back from Rose Road after a busy evening, when Hugo told her that he was going to America. They were going over Putney Bridge and Sarah stared at the lights reflecting in the water below, as though she had never seen them before. She said at last, inanely:

'How nice. North or South?'

'North,' he answered casually—'Philadelphia, Boston, Baltimore, Washington—not in that order of course, and a number of smaller places.'

For all the world, she thought, as though he were just going into the next street. 'Will you be away long?' she asked. Her voice, she was pleased to hear, sounded politely interested, no more.

When he said laconically, 'Three weeks, give or take a day,' she felt her heart jerk and then resume its beating with a deplorable lack of rhythm. 'Isn't it all rather sudden?' she wanted to know.

He drew up in front of the house and turned to look at her in the dimness of the car. 'No,' he answered coolly, 'I've known about it for some months.' She waited for him to say something else; apparently he found that that was sufficient. She went ahead of him into the house, and wandered aimlessly in and out of the rooms, fiddling with the flowers until he came in from putting the car away.

'Why didn't you tell me?' she asked at once. She didn't look up from the chaos she was making of a vase of chrysanthemums.

'My dear girl, I saw no need; it isn't as though you are coming with me.'

She tried again. 'Why not?'

'What would be the point?' His voice was silky. 'We have just been on holiday, have we not? I shall be lecturing, shall I not?'

'You don't want me. . .?'

'Shall we not rather say that there would be no purpose in your coming?' The silky voice had a bitter thread in it.

She surveyed her wrecked vase. 'Oh! Is that why you bought me the coat?'

He bolted the front door with deliberate quiet and said over his shoulder, 'I shan't even bother to answer that, Sarah.'

She drew a breath. 'When do you go?'

'Tomorrow evening.' He had crossed the hall and had a hand on the study door. 'I have to telephone St Edwin's—shall we say goodnight?'

He smiled at her quite kindly and in such a manner that Sarah felt she had somehow been at fault.

In her room, she sat down to think. Something had gone wrong somewhere. This morning at his rooms she had thought for a moment that he was going to tell her something—she wasn't sure what. Perhaps that he was a little in love with her—and she could have told him, and they could have started afresh. It was as though he wanted to get away from her, but if so, why did he bother to have her photograph on his desk, where he would have to look at it all day— and why did he buy her a valuable fur coat when her allowance was sufficient for her to purchase something quite nice for herself?

Perhaps it was some sort of fashion which dictated that doctors should have their wives' photographs on their desks. . .and as for the mink, could it be that Mrs van Elven, the wife of a highly successful consultant physician, was expected to wear nothing less? The thought was unworthy of Hugo, but she chose to ignore that. She sat on, stony-faced, while the same few ideas whirled through her aching head. At length, because she had grown cold, she went to bed, where she lay shivering with mingled chill and misery and hopeless rage.

Hugo greeted her the next morning with his usual placid manner. That he gave her a swift penetrating stare while her head was bowed over the coffee cups, she was unaware. She had taken great pains with her pale face, and was under the impression that she looked much as usual. She was surprised when he told her that he intended to go to Harley Street as usual. Somehow, because North America seemed so far away, she had imagined that the preparations would be lengthy, but Hugo was travelling light with one suitcase, which, he blandly informed her, was already packed.

She asked politely, 'Would you like us to have dinner early?'

'No, thank you, Sarah. I leave about seven—I'll take the car and leave it at the airport. I'll be home just after three, though—we could have tea together.'

He got up to go soon after, enjoining her to have a pleasant day, and she answered woodenly, 'Oh, yes. I'll take the dogs,' and then remembered to ask, 'You don't mind if I go to Rose Road while you're away?'

He paused in the door. 'Why ever not? You've got the Rover. I'm not your master, Sarah—you're free to do as you choose.'

The day seemed never-ending. At three o'clock she went to the kitchen and fetched the tea-tray, because Alice had the afternoon off. She had made a fruit cake, the kind Hugo liked, and Alice had made some muffins. Sarah arranged these delicacies upon a small table before the sitting room fire, with the muffins ready to toast. It was almost four when she heard his key in the door. She flew to the kitchen, and was putting the kettle on to boil when he strolled in. He said:

'Hullo, Sarah,' then asked casually, 'What shall you do with yourself while I'm away?'

She was prepared, for she had thought that he might ask it. She answered lightly, 'Tea won't be a minute. I shall go and see Mother and Father and perhaps stay for a day or two, and Kate wants me to go shopping—a real spree lasting two or three days—and the Coles asked me to go over weeks ago. Mary wanted me to spend a day with them. She's not very well, but of course you know that, and I want to shop for myself. . .'

He said, half laughing, 'Stop! My dear girl, I'd

better extend my tour, so that you'll have enough time to do all you want.'

He took the tea-tray from her, and she went ahead of him into the sitting room, delighted that her exaggerated half-truths had sounded so plausible. She knelt in front of the fire, toasting the muffins, while he sat in his great armchair, glancing through his post with the relaxed air of one who has nothing better to do for the rest of the day. It was hard to imagine that in a couple of hours or so he would be starting on a three-thousand-mile journey. . . She became momentarily lost in a reverie in which she, with the ease of all dream happenings, accompanied him at the last minute, to be jerked back to reality by his voice enquiring if she liked her muffins burned to cinders.

She took the charred ruin off the end of the fork and started again, this time with more success, and presently they had tea. They had almost finished when Hugo said, 'I've arranged for the bank to cash any reasonable amount for you, Sarah—and Simms has everything in hand.'

She drank the last of her tea. 'Oh? What does he have to have in hand?'

'My affairs.' He spoke rather impatiently. 'This is an excellent cake—Alice has done us proud.'

Sarah said, her mind on what he had just said. 'I made it. . . Will you fly everywhere in America— could you not go by train?'

'Certainly not—I should be there for months if I did. The arrangement with Simms is merely routine. You can contact him if you need to—er—know anything. What did you put in this cake?'

She told him, her manner abstracted, while her imagination painted vivid little pictures of air disasters with Hugo injured, or worse still, dead— thousands of miles away. She looked unseeingly at him when he said, 'Don't Sarah. I've always considered you a woman of great good sense.'

His light derisive tone, more than his words, had the desired effect. She was making a fool of herself. She pulled herself together with an effort, uttering some not very intelligent remark about travel in America, then continued talking rather feverishly and with great brightness upon a variety of paltry subjects until Hugo got to his feet with the laconic remark that he had better change his clothes.

He came down again presently, just as the bracket clock on the mantelpiece reminded them in its silvery voice that it was seven o'clock, and went straight out to the car with his case. Sarah had gone out into the hall, but he had ignored her. It seemed that he neither wanted nor expected anything more than the most casual of farewells. He came back into the hall and shrugged himself into his car coat, looking huge and prodigiously handsome, and she wondered with a sudden spurt of jealousy how many women would meet him and think the same as she did. She went a little nearer, a smile pinned firmly to her pretty mouth, feeling cold and sick inside. He put a hand lightly, briefly on her shoulder and said, 'Well, *Tot ziens*, Sarah. I'll let you know how I'm getting on.'

He kissed her with an almost businesslike brevity, straightened up, and kissed her again, hard and fierce on her mouth, then went through the door before she could so much as say goodbye.

She was sitting over her solitary breakfast when the telephone rang. She had been up for some time, and had taken the dogs for a walk because she hadn't slept too well, thinking about his kiss. She got up now and walked across the hall, calling to Alice not to bother to answer it, as she went. It was probably Kate.

She lifted the receiver and Hugo's voice, very close to her ear, said, 'Hullo, Sarah.' She was silent for so long that he said again, 'Sarah?' This time she managed to say 'Hullo, Hugo. I'm a—a bit surprised. I didn't expect you—did you have a good trip?'

'Yes—dull, though. I slept most of the time. What are you doing?'

'Having breakfast—I took the dogs out.' She stopped because her voice was wobbling so stupidly and he asked, 'Why are you crying, Sarah?'

She sniffed, and said at once like an unhappy child: 'Oh, Hugo, I do miss you, and you're so far away!'

Even as she said it, the sensible part of her brain told her that she was going to regret those words... but she was beyond caring. She heard him sigh—was it with relief or triumph? She didn't know until he said, 'I hoped you might. Do you know why I came, Sarah? Why I left you behind? Well, you will when I come home.'

Her heart beat faster. 'Can't you tell me now, Hugo?'

'No—I want to see your face. I have to go now, dear girl. 'Bye.'

He telephoned her every day, and the fourth or fifth time she ventured to say, 'Look, Hugo, if you're busy... I'm all right now. It's lovely to talk to you each day, but it's costing you a fearful lot of money.' The words weren't very satisfactory, but apparently he understood, for he said mildly, 'I'm lonely too, Sarah, and I can think of no better way of spending my money,' and then more briskly, 'How is Rose Road?'

After that, she got into the habit of saving up all the scraps of news to tell him each day—Alice's awful cold, the Christmas puddings they had made, the beautiful boots she had bought herself, and the utterly ravishing housecoat she intended to buy Miss Trevor for Christmas... It seemed he didn't want to talk about himself, although sometimes he made some small reference to his tour, and once he told her that he was a little tired and she had said quickly, 'Hugo, do take care!' and he had replied on a laugh, 'What of, Sarah? Too many parties or demos or beautiful girls?'

'All of them,' she said promptly, and then 'Are there a lot of beautiful girls?'

'I daresay—I haven't noticed. Did you think I would?'

She said carefully, 'Well, if I were you, I suppose I would because you're the sort of man women look at. . .'

'Dear Sarah, your delightful mind is as muddled as your grammar!'

His phone call became the high point of each day. She rushed back from her parents, terrified that she would be too late, although mostly he telephoned fairly early each morning, and it was on one such morning when he said, 'I'll be home tomorrow, Sarah. About eight in the evening.'

A day had never been so short, nor had there ever been so much to crowd into it. Sarah was happily busy—there was extra shopping to do, naturally, and a visit to the hairdresser and flowers to arrange, and of course, the careful planning of a meal which wouldn't spoil if Hugo arrived later than he had said. She went to bed that night tired and very happy.

She changed her mind at least three times during the following day as to what she should wear for his return. She wanted to look beautiful for Hugo—all the doubts and fears which she had experienced before he went away seemed to have disappeared; she felt almost sure that he was beginning to love her. Janet had become a wraith in a slowly forgotten past. She finally decided on a red wool crêpe dress, the colour of claret, with a whirly skirt of unpressed pleats and a soft scarf collar. It went very well with the red and bronze chrysanthemums she had massed in the downstairs rooms, and its colour gave a flattering warmth to the pallor of her excitement.

She was dressed far too soon. She toured the house once more to make sure that everything was perfect and then went into the drawing room, where the animals were drawn up in a tidy row before the fire. She sat down beside them and opened a novel— there was at least an hour to kill—and read the same page steadily for five minutes before throwing the book down and picking up her knitting, but after two rows of this, hopelessly botched, it went the way of the book...and barely fifteen minutes had passed. Her restless eye lighted upon the piano, and presently the room echoed to a hotch-potch of music, played rather inaccurately and far too loud.

When the animals rose suddenly from their sleep and looked towards the door, she stopped playing and told them to settle down again, because there was at least half an hour to wait. But they took no notice of her, but raced to the door, jostling each other to get there first. She got to her feet, her heart pounding, to stop and pound again even harder as the door opened and Hugo stood there. He caressed the animals with a kindly hand, and said quietly, 'Hullo, Sarah.'

Sarah started across the room, her face alight with happiness and not caring in the least that it might show. She had taken perhaps three steps when he spoke again. 'I've brought someone with me—you'll never guess who.'

She halted, suddenly and miserably certain that she was perfectly able to guess who her guest was. The happiness on her face was replaced by a look of polite welcome as he stood aside to allow a tall, dark woman to enter the room.

Sarah said in her charming voice, which, she proudly noted, held not one single tremor, 'But I think I do know. You're Janet, are you not?'

She looked at Hugo then, smiling a little, her brows raised in a faint enquiry. She derived some sort of satisfaction from his disconcerted look as he answered her, 'Yes, this is Janet—how did you know, Sarah?'

She gave a gay little laugh; listening to it, she wondered fleetingly why she had never taken up a stage career—obviously she was a born actress. Before he could say any more, she gave her hand to Janet and said smilingly, 'How very nice to meet you, Janet—you're exactly as I had pictured you, you know. I'm so glad Hugo brought you back with him.'

Janet smiled—a nice smile in a nice face—not pretty, but arresting and lively. Her eyes were brown and smiled too. Sarah was confused to find that she rather liked her.

'I didn't want to come like this, but Hugo persuaded me.' She looked at Hugo who was staring at Sarah. 'I met Janet on the plane,' he explained, 'and insisted on her coming back for a drink.'

Sarah said instantly, 'Of course—and dinner too. Alice and I have concocted a rather special meal, and you simply must stay.' She led the way to the fire and sat down beside Janet on the great chesterfield before it. 'You must see Alice, because she told me that she knew you when you were last in England. Have you returned to live here?'

She accepted sherry from Hugo with a smile that was quite empty, and held it in both hands, because they were shaking.

'I've a job here,' said Janet. 'Medical Registrar at St Kit's—it's a six-month appointment—that'll give me time to settle my future.'

Sarah took a long drink of sherry. Probably whisky or brandy would have done her more good, but the sherry would have to do. She was very cold inside; it prevented her from thinking, which was perhaps a good thing. Was her own future to be settled along with Janet's?

She put her glass down carefully and looked at Hugo, leaning against the side of the fireplace. 'And was the trip successful, and did you enjoy it, Hugo?' She tried to put some warmth into her voice, without much success—he hadn't even pretended to greet her or to ask how she was. He said now coolly, 'I hope it was successful. I can't say I enjoyed it. You've been all right, I hope?'

Sarah answered that yes, she had been fine, and would they excuse her while she just told Alice. She hurried to the kitchen, fighting a strong urge to go back to the drawing room and see what they were doing.

It was almost eleven o'clock when Janet got reluctantly to her feet saying that she really would have to go. Sarah, egged on by some perverse desire to hurt herself even more than she was already, begged her to stay the night, but it seemed she had already booked a room at a hotel and left her luggage there. Hugo had got to his feet too. 'I'll run you back,' he offered pleasantly, and when Janet demurred, said, 'Nonsense, it will take no time at all, there's not much traffic about—besides, if it hadn't been for my insistence, you might have been tucked up in bed by now. . .'

Sarah accompanied them to the front door and wished a friendly goodnight to Janet, murmured meaninglessly to Hugo, and went back to the drawing room to wait for his return. She waited an hour, then went upstairs to bed, to lie awake until at last she heard his quiet footfall on the stairs. When he had shut his bedroom door, she turned on the bedside lamp and looked at the time. It was well past three o'clock.

She heard him go downstairs early, before seven o'clock, and go out with the dogs. Probably he intended to go through his post before breakfast. When she went down he was just coming from his study, a handful of letters in his hand. They exchanged civil good mornings, and talked during breakfast like polite strangers who find themselves at the same table. They had almost finished when Sarah mentioned Anne Binns' wedding in a week's time, followed the following week by Kate's. Anne's was to be rather a grand affair at a Knightsbridge church, and Hugo, frowning, said. 'Oh, lord, I'd forgotten. Top hats, I suppose. What did we send them?'

'Fish knives and forks in a magnificent case,' Sarah replied, and when he laughed briefly and asked why, she went on, 'Well, I should have loathed them myself.'

He looked at her in surprise tinged with amusement. 'My dear girl, you sound quite malicious! I have always thought of you as being the epitome of kindness.'

She shook her head. 'Then you will have to change your opinion of me. I can be as mean and nasty as they come.' She stared at him, and he stared back, his eyes searching and hard. He said suddenly:

'There was absolutely no need to have asked Janet for dinner last night, you know.' His voice was mild, at variance with his eyes.

She gave him an innocent look. 'But, Hugo, Janet's an old friend—more than a friend. To have sent her away after a drink would have been unthinkable. Besides, you enjoyed talking to her. You've a—a lot of time to catch up on. I thought we could have her to dinner again—or a weekend perhaps. . .'

He was angry, a quick peep sufficed to tell her that, but nothing of it showed when he spoke. 'You don't mind her coming here?'

She allowed a look of bewildered amazement to take possession of her face. 'You yourself,' she said gently, 'said we were level-headed and mature.' She took a slice of toast and crumbled it absently into fragments on her plate. 'It's marvellous that you should have met again, isn't it? Fate is remarkable!'

He said savagely as he got up, 'I'm glad you feel like that about it; I don't need to feel guilty when I see her,' and went out of the room without bothering to say goodbye, leaving her sitting there with a white face.

He didn't refer to their conversation when he returned home that evening, and there was nothing in his manner to indicate that it had ever taken place. On the surface they seemed to be back on their old footing, and during the next day or so this appeared to be the case. Janet was never mentioned, but neither were their daily telephone calls. Sarah found herself wondering if Janet had been with Hugo when he made them, although she was aware, deep in her mind, that he would never do such a thing. It would be easier to bear if only she could think of him as a deep-dyed villain!

They went to Rose Road together, as they always had done. It had been far too busy for them to talk, and afterwards, in Dr Bright's flat, she had made a pretence of being busy in the kitchen, so that she had no need to join in the conversation. Only when they were on the point of leaving, John Bright gave her a penetrating stare and said:

'You're not your usual self, Sarah—does this work make you tired?' and she had said hastily, 'Goodness, no! I feel fine—perhaps I'm cooking up a cold.' She had smiled at him. 'And I hope I'm not, because you know how I like coming here.'

It was the Binns wedding the following day; it gave them something to talk about in the car on the way back to Richmond, but she couldn't help but know that Hugo's thoughts were far away.

The wedding was something of an ordeal, despite the pleasure of wearing the mink coat and a simply gorgeous hat, and being accompanied by Hugo. The bride looked almost pretty in her white satin and lace, and the bridegroom. . . Sarah studied him as he led his bride down the aisle. He was smiling, but the smile covered indifference and there were lines of ill-temper marring his good looks. She looked away from him and instinctively up to Hugo, to find his grey eyes fixed on her so searchingly that she coloured and looked away.

They were quickly separated at the reception. Sarah could see him towering above his companions, immersed in talk, and looking as though he was enjoying himself. She wandered from group to group, and when she could escape retired to a corner with Kate, who was quite obviously longing to talk. They settled themselves comfortably, sipping Mr Binns' excellent champagne, and Sarah said, 'You're bursting to tell me something, Kate, and do be quick, my dear, because we'll never be left to ourselves for more than a few minutes.'

Her friend eyed her doubtfully. 'I don't know whether to tell you or not, but I think I'd better, though I can't see that it matters now you're married to your nice Hugo. His old girl-friend—Janet, I think her name is—is back in London.'

Sarah said calmly, 'Yes, I know. She's been to dinner—and she's a perfect poppet. Not pretty, but attractive. She wears the most lovely clothes.'

Kate was not one to be put off by even so interesting a red herring as clothes. 'He's been seen several times at St Kit's, talking to her. She's Medical Registrar there.'

Sarah said airily, 'Oh, the grapevine!' and came to a stop as Kate went on, 'Sarah dear, this wasn't the grapevine—it was Jimmy. Sarah. . .oh, hell, why did the woman have to come back?'

'I've been wondering that myself,' commented Sarah, in such a forlorn voice that Kate said, 'You mind dreadfully, don't you? Can I help? Surely she can't make all that difference now you're married to Hugo. Perhaps it's just a flash in the pan.'

'After fifteen years?' Sarah asked bitterly.

Kate gave her a look in which doubt, suspicion and pity were almost equally blended. 'Sarah,' she began, when Hugo said from behind her, 'You two look as though you're conspiring to kill someone.'

Kate stood up. 'I don't know about Sarah,' she said sweetly, 'but that was exactly what I had in mind,' and went away without another word.

Hugo took her seat, removed the glass from Sarah's hand and remarked mildly, 'A charming girl, but I fancy she rushes her fences sometimes. Do you suppose we've done all that's necessary here? The—er—happy pair are about to leave. I thought that we might slip away as soon as they've gone.'

It was still only a little after half past three; the November dusk was just beginning to cloud the river as they reached home. Indoors, Sarah said, 'Alice is out until six or thereabouts. I'll get some tea.'

Hugo looked at his watch. 'Don't bother for me, Sarah—I'll change at once. I've an appointment for five-thirty and I'll only just make it.' He started up the stairs, and she asked from the hall, looking up at his broad back, 'At Harley Street?' knowing what the answer would be before he answered shortly, 'No...if I'm not back by seven-thirty, don't wait dinner for me,' and disappeared into his room.

Sarah shrugged off the mink as though it were her old gardening coat, tossed her hat after it, and went into the kitchen. She hadn't eaten much at the reception; in fact, thinking about it, she couldn't remember eating anything except a morsel of wedding cake. She wasn't hungry anyway. She put on the kettle to boil, and walked up and down the kitchen with the teapot in her hand. A woman of courage and self-respect would doubtless go upstairs and ask a few straightforward questions, but even if she did, would she get straightforward answers?

The kettle boiled and she ignored it while she went to the back door to let Timmy in. He glared at her because she hadn't been quick enough and she picked him up, still in the open doorway, and asked, 'Timmy, what shall I do?'

'Do what?' Hugo had come into the kitchen. He turned off the steaming kettle without comment and crossed the room and took the teapot from her and made the tea, then said, 'Well?' He shot her a keen glance, and went on casually, 'If you stay there, you'll catch your death of cold, as they say.'

She came inside then and shut the door. 'I was only asking Timmy if he wanted his tea now or later,' she said. She didn't look at him because she wasn't a very good liar and she wasn't sure how long he had been in the kitchen. She put Timmy down, and he stalked off to join the dogs in front of the sitting room fire. She picked up the tea-tray and followed him; it held only one cup and saucer, for she wasn't going to ask Hugo a second time. He followed her into the room, and asked, looking at the tray, 'Aren't you going to eat anything?' He was putting on his coat as he spoke.

'After all that lovely food at the Binns'?' she answered brightly.

'All you ate was a miserable slice of cake.' It seemed he had the eyes of a hawk behind those lazy lids. She said woodenly, 'I wasn't hungry.' Which remark he must have found unworthy of an answer, for he made none but walked to the door and when he got to it said:

'I think perhaps I had better say I won't be in for dinner, Sarah. I'll see you later.'

He lifted his hand in a vague goodbye, leaving her to pour her solitary cup of tea and vow that on no account would he see her later. So she went to bed early after telling Alice that the doctor had an important engagement and she herself couldn't face another morsel after the wedding reception. Alice listened and nodded, and presently when Sarah was in bed, she appeared with a nice hot drink. Sarah drank her Horlicks under her motherly eye, aware that nothing short of a blow on the head with some heavy instrument would ensure sound sleep for her that night, but she yawned to give Alice the satisfaction of seeing that her remedy was taking effect, and asked her to put out the light as she went away.

It was barely half past eight—the night was going to be long. She heard Hugo come in about ten, and closed her mind firmly to the vivid picture of him and Janet dining together somewhere quiet, where they weren't likely to be seen. She sat up in bed, hugging her knees, trying to decide what to do for the best. Should she go to him and say 'Look, Hugo, do you want a divorce?' She frowned, trying to remember if there wasn't a law about getting divorced before a certain length of time; but what length of time? She didn't know. Perhaps that was why Hugo had said nothing; perhaps he was waiting for her to say something. She remembered how he had kissed her when he had gone on his lecture tour, and how he had telephoned her; but that of course was before he had met Janet again.

It was very quiet in the house. Hugo was still downstairs, for she had heard the front door open and shut and the dogs scuffling in the hall, and a little later, she heard Timmy's low cacophonous grumble at her door. He usually slept with Alice, but it would be nice to have company. She let him in and got back into bed, holding his elderly furry body close. He fidgeted around for a bit and finally went to sleep, and later, much later, Sarah went to sleep too.

She overslept the next morning; by the time she got downstairs, Hugo had been out with the dogs

and was already at breakfast. He wished her a
pleasant good morning and she was shocked at the
white weariness of his face. She said 'Hugo' before
she could prevent herself, then stopped, because his
expression would not allow her to ask him anything
at all. There was no need, anyway, she knew how
he must feel. To meet again the woman he had loved
for so many years and not be free to marry·her. . .it
must be awful for Janet too. She drank some coffee
and he said, 'You're not eating anything, Sarah. Alice
tells me that you had no dinner. Do you feel
all right?'

She said sharply, 'Yes, of course. I've a headache,
that's all. A walk with the dogs will cure that.'

After he had gone, she went and sat at the little
desk under the window and made out her shopping
list. She would shop first, then come back for the
dogs—it would fill an empty day. She put on her
outdoor things and collected a dress for the cleaners
and was reminded that there was a suit of Hugo's to
take as well. She went to his room and found it, laid it
upon the bed and began to go through the pockets—
though she didn't expect to find anything; he wasn't
given to hoarding bus tickets or bills. She
remembered the inside breast pocket just as she was
folding the jacket and swept a rather careless finger
within it. There was a small box there—a red velvet
jeweller's box. She looked at it for a long moment,
then opened it. There was a ring inside; a gold ring
set with precious stones—seven of them. Sarah
frowned, for there seemed no pattern in their arrangement at all. She took it out and held it in her hand,
looking at them. A diamond, an emerald, an amethyst
and then a ruby, another emerald, a sapphire, and
lastly, a topaz; a peculiar colour combination which
struck a chord in her memory. She was putting the
ring carefully back when she remembered. Such rings
had been popular in bygone days—a man would give

such a ring to the girl he loved; the gems spelled 'Dearest'.

There was a folded paper which had fallen out of the pocket at the same time as she had found the ring. She picked it up, and stood looking at it, and then very slowly opened it. It was a letter written in Hugo's handwriting—there was no address and no date. She folded it up again and then just as quickly, opened it again and began to read.

'My dearest darling,

It seems strange to write to you, for it is a long time since I have done so—and I shall be seeing you again very soon now, but in the meantime perhaps this ring will tell you a little of how I feel. . .'

Sarah read no further, but folded the letter and put it carefully back in the pocket, and the little box with it. She put back the odds and ends she had turned out of the other pockets too, and hung the suit back in the closet. She did it all mechanically, reflecting that she had got her just deserts for a mean and despicable action. When she had tidied everything away she went down to the kitchen where Alice was standing at the table, making a cake. She stopped her whisking when she saw Sarah and asked anxiously:

'Madam, are you all right? You're as white as a ghost.'

'It's only a headache, Alice—a brisk walk will cure it. I was going to take some things to the cleaners. I've put a dress out, but I haven't gone through the doctor's suit—the grey one. Would you do it for me and take them down to the cleaners? I meant to do some shopping, but I won't bother now. I'll take the dogs and have lunch out somewhere. Have the afternoon off, Alice—I'll get myself some tea when I come in.'

Sarah walked until she was exhausted and even the dogs began to flag. But she felt better for the exercise, and when she got home she was glad to see that she had some colour in her face again. Alice was still out; Sarah had tea and went upstairs to change her dress. She was downstairs again, in the kitchen with Alice, when Hugo returned. She had got into the habit of going into the hall to meet him, but now she stayed where she was, the kitchen slate held before her rather in the manner of a shield, but when he came into the kitchen, he said merely:

'Hullo. Something smells good,' and accepted the slice of cake which she cut for him, and went to sit on the kitchen table to eat it. He had eaten most of it when he asked, 'Has my grey suit gone to the cleaners?' giving her at the same time such a piercing look that she very nearly told him about the ring and the letter, but she could see his worried frown and the strained look around his mouth. She returned his stare with an innocent look of enquiry. She said, 'Yes—today.'

He still stared. 'Was there anything in it?'

She was saved from perjury by Alice, who answered for her.

'Yes, there was, Doctor. It's in the top drawer of your bureau—a little. . .'

'Yes, thank you, Alice,' he interrupted her swiftly, got off the table, went to the door and held it open. 'Come and have a drink,' he invited, his eyes still upon Sarah. She went, perforce, with him, and went and sat by the fire while he fetched their drinks before coming to sit down beside her. She was more or less prepared when he asked, 'I thought you usually went through my clothes before you sent them to the cleaners, Sarah.'

She said with a sangfroid which secretly pleased her, 'Yes, I do. But just this morning, I decided I'd go out with the dogs—my headache, you know'— she reminded him, 'and I asked Alice to do it for me. Do you mind? Was there something important?'

He said coolly, 'Yes. . .but only to me. I don't

object to Alice doing such things; why should I? She always did, you know, before we married. Did you have a good day?'

She was at some pains to tell him just how good the day had been. When she had finished he made no comment but said:

'We haven't been out for quite some time, have we? Supposing we take Janet down to Rose Road one evening, and the four of us go out to supper afterwards?'

She agreed at once, for what else could she do? 'Shall it be tomorrow?' she wanted to know. 'Because it's Kate's wedding the day after that... and we're going to the Coles next week...or will Janet need more time?'

'I think not,' he answered carelessly. 'I mentioned it to her the other day and she thought it was a good idea.' He was staring at her again, waiting for her to make some comment. She said brightly:

'Well, that's settled, isn't it? Is Janet happy at St Kit's? I hope she's made some friends. Why don't we have her to dinner one evening? Saturday perhaps—if she's free?'

'By all means,' Hugo said smoothly, 'if you would like that.'

'Will you ask her when you see her?'

'Yes, of course. What makes you think I shall be seeing her?'

She flushed and avoided his eye; they were getting on dangerous ground again. 'Well, you know. The grapevine—and people...'

'Ah, yes, that grapevine,' he said evenly. 'And people—do you believe all you hear, Sarah?'

She shook her head. 'No,' and was taken by surprise when he asked then, 'Do you still love Steven, Sarah?'

She got up, making rather a business about putting her glass down on the little work-table beside her.

She didn't know what to say—there were pitfalls whichever way she answered. She had better not say anything. 'I'll see if dinner's ready,' she said breathlessly, and sped from the room.

The following evening she met Hugo as she usually did, only this time they went to St Kit's to pick up Janet. Sarah, sitting in the back of the car, couldn't fail to see how Hugo and Janet suited each other, for Janet was big too—they looked wonderful together. She talked to Sarah over one shoulder on their way to Rose Road, but she talked a great deal to Hugo too with the ease of an old friend, and he answered her in like vein. Sarah was glad when they reached Dr Bright's and she could go to Sandra's little room, put on her overall and plunge into her work. She supposed Janet would stay with Hugo, and told herself that she didn't care in the least. But Janet spent the evening with John Bright, and chose to sit in the back of the car with him on the way to supper afterwards.

They went to a restaurant close to St Paul's and ate delicious steak and kidney pudding which Sarah was quite unable to appreciate. Hugo had brought up an interesting case of septicaemia he had been dealing with that evening, and though she was included in the conversation, they occasionally forgot that she was there and that she was completely out of her depth. The look of interest on her face became a little fixed after a time, and when Dr Bright turned to her and said, 'Sarah, how quiet you are,' it was quite an effort to smile. She said, so softly, that only he heard her, 'Am I? It's all a bit above my head.'

He gave her a sharp look and to her consternation said loudly:

'Well, I don't know about anyone else, but I must get home.'

His words had the effect of breaking up the party, and although he didn't speak to her again on their way back, she was surprised and touched when he bent and kissed her when he got out of the car. His simple action made her feel sorry for herself, which was perhaps why, when they reached St Kit's, she was so gaily persuasive with Janet.

'You simply must come,' she urged. 'Hugo will fetch you.' She glanced at him and encountered a cold stare which she ignored. 'We never do anything on Saturdays.' And that was a lie—when they had first married, they had gone out to dine or to a theatre. 'Come to tea and stay for dinner.'

She talked with almost feverish gaiety all the way back to Richmond, pretending not to notice that Hugo's responses were both curt and abrupt.

It was Kate's wedding the next day, a small affair compared with Anne Binns' grand occasion, and yet a great deal more fun, for there were only family or close friends and everybody knew everyone else. Kate looked so beautiful that Sarah felt her own heart would break; she didn't dare to look at Hugo beside her for fear her own feelings would show. Luckily there were so many people to talk to at the reception that she had no time to think. The wedding had been at two o'clock, but it was well after five before they left the pleasant house in Finchley where Kate's parents lived. When they reached the Marylebone Road, Hugo turned left, and after she had waited a few moments for him to say why, she asked, 'The hospital?'

'No—I want to call at my rooms. I shan't be more than a minute or two.'

He went inside, leaving her in the car. She watched him cross the pavement and disappear inside, tall and elegant and distinguished and more of a stranger than he had ever been. She had Janet's reappearance into his life to thank for that.

He was back again within five minutes and as he

slid into the seat beside her, she said waspishly, 'I suppose you telephoned Janet.'

She was horrified at herself the moment she had spoken, but he said mildly, 'Yes—I forgot to give her your message.'

She seethed silently. Presently, when she had her rage and her breath under control, she asked sweetly, 'Was she able to change her free time after all?'

He gave her a brief, unsmiling glance. 'Yes.'

Sarah took great pains with the dinner. Hugo had fetched Janet, apparently delighted to do so, and they had tea round the fire and Janet had been sweet— in any other circumstance, Sarah would have liked her very much. Now she went to the kitchen to make sure that everything was just so. They were to have *oeufs Maritchu* and *Poularde Niçoise* and an apple flan with clotted cream for afters. She went back to the sitting room, satisfied that the food, at least, would be a success, and found Janet and Hugo in earnest conversation which ceased abruptly as she entered.

Dinner was the success she had anticipated, so, for that matter, was the rest of the evening. Perhaps it was the excellent Pouilly-Fuissé which Hugo had opened, to mark, in his own words, a delightful occasion; or the fact that he laid himself out to be charming and amusing and it was impossible not to respond. At ten o'clock Janet had made as if to go, but Hugo had said at once:

'Not yet, Janet. There's an article in last week's *Lancet* I want you to see. There's something in it I can't agree with.'

He got up and she with him, and Sarah watched them go, side by side, across the hall to his study. He had turned at the drawing room door and said quite charmingly, 'You don't mind, Sarah? We shan't be long—it's hardly a drawing room topic.'

She nodded smilingly, longing to tell him that

during the course of her nursing career she had listened to a great many topics that were decidedly not fit for drawing rooms, and had learned not to be squeamish about them either. She remembered quite vividly several particularly repellent subjects which he himself had discussed with her not so many months ago.

It seemed like a hundred years of time before they returned, though it was barely ten minutes, and she said at once, 'I'll get some more coffee,' so that it was another half hour before Janet finally said good-bye, and then only after Sarah had begged her to stay the night. She stood on the step, shivering in the night air, waving in answer to Janet's cheerful goodnight. Hugo had called goodnight too. Presumably he would be back very late, or, she thought with a faintly hysterical giggle, very early.

The weather had worsened in the morning and on Hugo's suggestion she didn't join him in their usual walk, although she had never allowed the weather to keep her indoors before. They were dining with friends that evening, which left the afternoon to spend in each other's company. They spent it in the sitting room, reading the Sunday papers by the fire and discussing the news with a friendliness which wasn't quite effortless. Sarah welcomed it, and responded eagerly, with the dim idea that perhaps, if they could get back on to their old footing, it would be easier for her to talk to him about Janet. She longed to ask him what he had meant when he had telephoned her from America—he had said that he would tell her why he went. Had it been to meet Janet? She couldn't believe that somehow—meeting her had been one of those accidents Fate arranges from time to time. Rather desperately, she made one or two tentative overtures, to be checked by a bland-ness as effective as a high stone wall.

It was much colder the next day; Sarah hadn't

intended to go out, but the day, viewed from the hour of half past nine, stretched endlessly, and Hugo had said he might be late home. She put on the mink coat and a little velvet hat; she would go shopping for Christmas presents. She was actually in no mood for such a pleasant occupation, but it would fill the day until teatime. She was in Fortnum and Mason's, having coffee, when Janet and Hugo came in. They didn't see her, for she was at a small table set against a wall, almost out of sight, and in any case, they were far too deeply engrossed in talk, and went to a table on the far side, at an angle to her. She sat watching them, unable to take her eyes away. Hugo was talking earnestly; his whole attitude expressed concern, and when he stretched out a hand and took Janet's, Sarah closed her eyes for a moment, knowing that she couldn't go on any longer.

She had already paid her bill, so she got up quietly, thankful that her table was so near the door. She went through it blindly and started down the stairs, to be almost swept off her feet by a man coming up at a great speed. He stopped his headlong rush long enough to set her upright, apologise with a strong American accent, raise his hat and smile rather charmingly before tearing on again, leaving behind him an impression of scarcely controlled excitement. She forgot him at once as she hurried down the stairs and outside, where she hailed a taxi. All the way to Richmond she sat in a corner of it, a look of deep concentration on her face. Presently she nodded to herself, by the time she alighted before her front door, she knew exactly what she was going to do.

Once inside, she went first to the kitchen, to tell Alice that she would be out until the early evening, and there was no need to worry if she was a little late home, and then to her room, refusing Alice's offer of a little something on a tray as she went. If she ate, she would choke; besides, she had a lot to do. She hung the mink carefully away and changed into a thick tweed skirt and a sweater, then packed a case with a modicum of clothes—more sweaters, slacks, a warm dressing gown and undies—before putting on the duffle coat she wore when she took the dogs out. This done, she went to the small locked drawer in her dressing table and took from it the diamond brooch and earrings in their boxes, added the pearls and then, after a moment's hesitation, her engagement ring, before taking them across to Hugo's room and locking them, with scarcely a second glance, in the top drawer of the tallboy there. Finally she sat down and counted her money. She had been to the bank that very morning and she still had a few pounds of her allowance, more than enough for her needs.

There only remained the letter she must write. She would have liked to have walked out of the house—and out of Hugo's life—without a word, but that would be hardly fair. It took her a little while, and a great many sheets of paper, before she was satisfied with her efforts. She wrote at last:

Dear Hugo,

I'm going away so that you can get a divorce and marry Janet. I tried to talk to you about it, but you wouldn't let me, and when I saw you both in Fortnum's today I knew we couldn't go on any longer. Make any arrangements you want; I'll agree to anything so long as you can be happy again. I'm taking the car—I hope you don't mind, but I've left the jewellery you gave me in the tallboy drawer in your room. I've plenty of money and I shall be quite all right because I can get a job very easily. I'll let Mr Simms know where I am, later.

She signed it 'Sarah' and read it through. It was a bit businesslike and bald, but that was a good thing, although the whole of her cried out to let him know how much she loved him. And a lot of good that would do, she told herself fiercely.

She could hear Alice in the kitchen; she picked up her case and went quietly downstairs, propped the letter on Hugo's desk in the study, and let herself out of the house, taking care not to look back.

There was plenty of petrol in the tank. Sarah flung her case on to the back seat and drove the Rover carefully out of the garage at the end of the private road. The AA map was open on the seat beside her; she had studied it with a hasty intelligent eye in her bedroom. Once she got to Smethwick she would be all right, because there she would join the road they had travelled on to Scotland. Once on it, she would remember it well enough. She reckoned she would have to spend two nights on the way, perhaps three. At any other time she would have been terrified at the idea of the motorways, but now she didn't care. She turned the car towards Watford, where she would join the M1. It was barely two o'clock; she should be able to reach Manchester in the early evening and find somewhere to sleep in a nearby village. Not that the details of the journey bothered her; her one longing was to reach the cottage in Wester Ross and hide herself until the sharp edge of her grief had blunted itself a little.

Hugo, home later than he had intended, was met in the hall by an anxious Alice, who said without preamble:

'I'm worried about Mrs van Elven, Doctor. She came home about half past twelve, looking quite ill. She told me she would be going out and I wasn't to worry if she wasn't in to tea, but it's eight o'clock, sir, and no sign of her, and it's not like her not to ring up—she's always so considerate.'

Hugo had gone a little white, though he spoke

calmly enough. 'Don't worry, Alice, I expect she's been held up. Did she take the car?'

'I don't know—she didn't say she was going to.'

'What was she wearing?'

'Her mink coat and that pretty little blue velvet hat.'

'Then she must be visiting. I'll telephone round and see if I can locate her—the car may have broken down, if she took it.'

He flung his coat on to a chair and went into his study and immediately saw the envelope on the desk. He stood looking at it for a long moment, his face expressionless, then opened it slowly and read Sarah's letter just as slowly and read it again before folding it neatly and putting it into a pocket, before going upstairs, two at a time, to her room. He saw the mink coat at once. He looked at it with a kind of quiet despair and went to search the closet—but Sarah had a great many clothes; it was difficult to see what she had taken with her, but he was reasonably sure that most of her things were still hanging there. Which meant that she had taken only sufficient for a few days. She was quite possibly at her home.

On his way downstairs again, he was already making a mental list of people she might be with. He telephoned them all in turn and was still at his desk when Alice came in to enquire for news. 'And your dinner's ready, Doctor,' she ended. But Hugo took no notice of this remark. He looked at his watch, and said, 'I'll try the hospitals. . .'

She came back presently with a tray. 'You can eat while you telephone, I'll take the dogs out, then you'll be here when Mrs van Elven comes.'

But Mrs van Elven didn't come.

CHAPTER NINE

THE first snowflakes were falling as Sarah took the unwieldy key from its hiding place and fitted it into the lock of the cottage's stout front door. It was very cold inside, but not in the least damp. She lighted a lamp and put a match to the Aga which the worthy Mrs MacFee had faithfully left ready, then wearily fetched her case from the car before putting it away in the garage. When she at length got indoors, she was shaking with cold and tiredness and the aftermath of driving hundreds of miles, spurred on only by the knowledge that Hugo would never love her now that Janet had come back into his life.

The journey had been a nightmare experience of icy roads, fog, wrong turnings and the dreadful monotony of the motorway, coupled with the dread of losing her nerve as the fast traffic tore past her for mile after mile. She had spent the night at Kendal and started off again in the dark, grey morning, which never really became any lighter. She had stopped for coffee and sandwiches, although she couldn't remember where or when; she only knew that she wasn't hungry. She made tea and unpacked, and presently went to bed without bothering about supper.

She slept the deep sleep of exhaustion and wakened in the late morning to find that it was still snowing. The countryside was blanketed, blotting out roads and hedges and walls. She dressed quickly in slacks and thick sweater, and went, rather anxiously, to inspect the store cupboard. But here again Mrs MacFee had kept her word. Sarah sighed with relief at the plenitude of its contents. She stoked up the Aga, made breakfast, and then, in gumboots and an old anorak, went to clear the short, steep run-in from the lane to the garage.

It took her longer than she had expected, and there was still the path to the top of the back garden where there was the potato clamp. She shovelled doggedly, uncaring of the snow falling steadily to obliterate her hard work—that didn't matter, she told herself with false cheerfulness, she could do it all again the following day, and the day after if necessary; it would give her something to do. When she finally finished, the early dusk was already darkening an already dark sky and it was almost three o'clock. She dug some potatoes, not very easily, from the clamp, put away her spade and went indoors. The little sitting room, once she had got the fire going and the lamps lighted, was warm and cheerful. She had a bath and changed into the warm dressing gown, to sit cosily by the fire, eating a meal, half lunch, half tea, and listening to the wind's whispered howling outside. It looked as though the weather was worsening. . .a surmise confirmed by the weather forecast which predicted heavy snow, gale force winds, and drifts to be avoided.

Sarah switched the radio off because she wasn't sure if there were any spare batteries, then presently, in search of something to do, she searched through the cupboards and found some *gros-point* she had started when they had been there in the spring. She sat with it in her lap, remembering how happy they had been. She picked it up and began to stitch carefully, but in a little while put it down again, unable to see what she was doing for the tears which filled her eyes.

The snow continued. Each day she cleared the paths, glad of the work, then went back indoors to the warmth to cook a simple meal and work or read by the light of the one lamp she allowed herself. There was plenty of oil and coal, but it was imposs-

ible to get down to the village, and there was no way
of knowing how long the bad weather would last.
Sarah had attempted to make her way down the hill
one morning and had plunged into a drift which it
had taken her so long to get out of, she hadn't dared
to try again. The telephone line was down, had been
since the day after her arrival, and she didn't think
that anyone knew that she was in the cottage. Not
that it mattered; she had enough of everything for a
long time yet and she was comfortable, and the longer
she could keep away, the more quickly Hugo would
realise that she had meant what she had written in
her letter.

She had been there more than a week now, and
the snow, which had stopped for several hours, had
started again. She had seen the snow-plough on the
road running beside Loch Duich; it had looked very
small in the surrounding whiteness of the empty
countryside, with the Kintails looming in the icy
distance. It had cleared the road and disappeared
again, but before any traffic which might have followed it could do so, the wind became a howling
gale and obliterated its painstaking work. That same
wind drove her indoors too, for it whipped up the
snow into a blizzard which had made her painstaking
shovelling a mockery.

She had her lunch early and spent the short afternoon turning out cupboards which were already as
neat as Mrs MacFee's hands could make them, but
it was something to do. She had thought that once
she was alone in the peace and quiet of the cottage,
she would be able to think calmly about the future;
but that led to thoughts of Hugo, and she couldn't
bear to think sensibly of him—not yet.

The wind died down towards morning and because
she hadn't slept overmuch she got up early, before
it was light, and had breakfast in the snug kitchen
and did the chores, and because she didn't hurry over

them it was after ten before she got outside. The snow had stopped, leaving great drifts against the garage door and blotting out the garden. She tackled the run-in first—not that she could have moved the car in or out, but at least she could get to it. The garden path was a more difficult job; she worked steadily at it until she reached the hedge which bounded its end and then stopped, leaning on her shovel, staring down the hill towards the hamlet below.

She didn't know what made her turn round, some slight sound perhaps. When she did, Hugo was standing quite close. He put up a slow hand and took off the dark glasses he wore when he drove long distances, and she could see how tired he was—there were lines she had never noticed before, etched deep between nose and mouth. She let out a sighing breath, unconscious that she had been holding it, put her spade down carefully, and went down the path towards him. She was bewildered and surprised and at a loss for words, and so, it seemed, was he. She said the first thing she thought of.

'How lucky I cleared the snow from the front of the garage. However did you get the car up here?'

His tired mouth cracked in a grin. 'I didn't. I left it at Glenmoriston and got a lift on a snow-plough as far as Shiel Bridge.'

She said in amazement, 'You walked? It must be six miles at least. . .the drifts are shockingly deep too. How long did it take you?'

He glanced at his watch. 'Four hours. The snow's pretty firm, you know, and there are plenty of landmarks.'

They stood and stared at each other until she said, 'You must be tired,' and went past him, down the path to the cottage. 'I'll get you a meal and then you can have a bath and sleep.'

She knew she sounded like a bossy schoolmarm,

but at least it was better than just standing there. . . and it would be something for her to keep her mind on until she could collect her wits. She kicked off her boots at the back door and went to poke up the Aga while he pulled off his own gumboots and shrugged out of his sheepskin jacket. There was a covered milk can on the table. He saw her glance at it and said:

'I thought you might be getting a bit low with the tinned stuff.'

She was busy with the frying pan and the coffee pot and didn't look up. 'That was thoughtful of you—it must have been a nuisance to carry.'

He said politely, 'Not at all. I've some spare batteries for the radio too.' He had come to sit in the Windsor chair pulled up to the table. Sarah broke two eggs into the pan and then a third—he was a large man and would be hungry. She said at last, her thoughts once more under control:

'Why did you come, Hugo? I know there are papers to sign and—and things, but you could have gone ahead with whatever you needed to do. I told you I would agree. You didn't have to come all this way.' She drew a quick breath. 'How did you know I was here?' It was funny that she had only just thought of that. He didn't answer her question.

'I had to see you, Sarah.'

She dished up the bacon and eggs and put the plate down before him, and spoke her thoughts out loud without knowing it. 'No one knew I was coming here.' She picked up the coffee pot. 'It's something legal, I suppose,' she went on in a determinedly cheerful voice, 'and you're hung up until I sign something.'

'There's something I have to say to you, Sarah.'

She poured his coffee, studying his face. He was asleep on his feet.

'Yes, I know, Hugo.' She spoke soothingly and

with authority, just as she would have spoken to a patient panicking in OPD. 'But you're going to eat now and then have a nap, and you can tell me after that and not before.' She cast around in her mind for a suitable topic. 'The telephone's out of order, I'm afraid—all this snow,' and before she could help herself, 'Did Janet know you were coming?' she interrupted herself and answered her own question, embarked on a spate of talk she couldn't stop.

'I hope you managed to telephone her from Inverness—at least she'll know you got there safely. If the snow stops they'll send out the plough and you'll be able to get a lift back to the car. I expect you can't wait to get back.' She stopped because of the look on his face; if he hadn't been so desperately tired she could have sworn that he was laughing silently. 'Was the journey very bad coming up?' she enquired. 'Where did you spend the night?'

'I came straight through.' his voice sounded harsh, perhaps because he was so exhausted.

'Straight through?' she echoed, her voice a horrified squeak. 'In this awful weather—it's hundreds of miles!' She turned away and poured herself some coffee, swallowing back a great surge of tears. He must have thought it worth while. She took a scalding gulp and said with all the politeness of a good hostess, 'Do try some of this bread—I made it. I've got quite good at baking.'

Hugo took no notice of this remark. He said again, very quietly: 'I have to talk to you, Sarah.'

She put her cup down so sharply that some of the coffee spilt, but her voice was gentle. 'Yes, I know. But not now.' How could she explain to him that she was holding out for a few more hours before she had to listen to him telling her? 'You're too tired now and I must make up your bed. The water's hot— you'll find all you need in the bathroom.'

She was already halfway up the little staircase as

she spoke, holding her thoughts fiercely in check. She had almost finished making his bed when he came upstairs, and without speaking to her went into the bathroom and turned on the taps.

Downstairs, she cleared the table and washed up, then went to the cupboard to collect the makings of a stew—Hugo would want a meal when he woke; it would have to be something that wouldn't spoil however long he slept. She made some dumplings, then got out her boots and anorak again and made her way to the shed halfway up the garden where the apples were stored. Baked apples would go very well after the stew and they could go on top of the Aga.

She managed to keep herself occupied with these homely tasks for quite some time, and then, forgetful of lunch, went into the sitting room and got out her *gros-point*. It was calming work, and she would need to be calm when he came downstairs. She stitched steadily, waiting for her mind to clear itself, so that she could plan what to say. . .but it did no such thing; indeed, her thoughts piled one upon another, each one more incoherent than the last. The only one that made sense and remained permanently clear was that she loved Hugo. The one fact, she told herself with hopeless, wry good sense, which was of no use to her.

The day wore on; when daylight began to fail she stopped her sewing and lighted a lamp, then went to look at her stew and then to find her handbag and make up her face with meticulous care and do her hair. She peered into the little mirror on the kitchen wall and decided that she didn't look too bad. She had got a bit thin and her face had little colour, but provided she remembered to smile. . . She tried out one or two smiles and was heartened to see how normal she looked. Hugo's pity was the last thing she wanted.

It was quite dark by now, and still no sound from

upstairs. Sarah made tea and set a tray with a plate of scones and some jam Mrs MacFee had made and left in the cupboard, carried it into the sitting room and set it upon the little round table by her chair. She sat down then, to pour herself a cup of tea, only to leave it to get cold while she thought about Janet. It was absurd how much she liked her; she supposed she should really hate her for returning to England and ruining her life.

Which train of thought led, inevitably, to the future. She would have to decide what to do now. She would find a job, here in Scotland, and start again. She contemplated a bleak vista of years with something like loathing, and became so deeply immersed in her broodings that she failed to hear Hugo until he was at the foot of the staircase. He had put on the Aran sweater she had knitted rather laboriously while he fished, and some old corduroys, and he had found the red leather slippers they had bought together in Inverness. Her throat ached suddenly at the sight of them, but all the same, she remembered to smile.

'I've just made the tea,' she remarked simply. 'I hope you slept.' He looked as though he had—the lines had almost gone; he had shaved and he bore the well-scrubbed alert look of a well-rested man ready for anything. Well, so was she, she told herself.

He sat down opposite her and she poured his tea and handed it to him, and he in turn put the cup and saucer down again, staring at her in a silence so profound that she felt sure that he could hear her heart pounding. To forestall this possibility she made haste to ask him if he had slept well, quite forgetting that she had already done that, and when he replied that yes, he had, she added the interesting information that the beds in the cottage were very comfortable. This remark called forth no response, so Sarah took a sip of her cold tea, and picked up her embroidery frame and began unhurriedly to stitch, willing her hands to be steady, her lovely face bent to the glow of the little lamp; waiting patiently for him to tell her whatever it was that had necessitated his travelling almost six hundred miles in mid-winter. That he would tell her as kindly as possible she had no doubt. They had been—and still were—good friends. She thanked heaven silently that she had never allowed him to see that she loved him. All the same, when he spoke, she pricked her finger.

'It took me a week to find you, Sarah,' he said at last. 'You see, this was the last place I thought of. You said—do you remember?—that only the direst circumstance would force you to drive up here alone. I didn't remember that at once. I wasted precious days looking for you at your mother's and the hospital and Rose Road. I even went to see Mr Ives. . .and a dozen other people. You have so many friends. I tried Kate and Dick Coles and the bank, even old Simms. . .'

Sarah sucked her pricked finger. She said quietly, 'I'm sorry, you see, I didn't tell anyone because I didn't think you'd want to know.'

He said on a sigh, 'Sarah, my dearest Sarah! I've been half out of my mind.' He stopped. 'I love you,' he said suddenly and fiercely. 'I fell in love with you years ago. . .you were staffing on Men's Medical. It wasn't too difficult persuading Matron that you were just the type I wanted in OPD.'

She dropped her embroidery at that, and stared at him, open-mouthed.

'Oh, yes,' he went on, still fiercely. 'Only to discover that you and young Steven. . . I waited three years. And then I married you, knowing that I would still have to wait while you recovered from Steven; knowing that you weren't ready for my love. That's why I allowed you to go on believing in that hoary legend about Janet and me.'

Womanlike, she fastened on that. 'But you loved her!'

He smiled at her, with such tenderness and understanding that she caught her breath. He said quietly, 'Perhaps, for a year—two years.' And she nodded, remembering how she had felt about Steven. Her heart was thudding violently now; she picked up her embroidery again and began stitching as though her very life depended upon it, pushing the needle in and out of all the wrong holes with a complete disregard for the design. Hugo got up and took the maltreated canvas from her shaking hand, plucked her out of her chair and pulled her close so that her voice was muffled against his shoulder.

'Hugo!' she wailed. 'I've loved you for—months and months—long before I knew about it!'

Apparently this muddled remark made sense to Hugo, for he put a finger under her chin and stared down at her and kissed with slow gentleness and then, while she was catching her breath, kissed her again, not gently at all. When at length he loosed her a little she put her hands against his chest so that she could look up into his face.

'Janet—' she uttered. 'Why did you bring her home after you had been so—so nice when you telephoned? And why did you go away and leave me?'

'I thought that if I went away you might miss me—and you did, my darling, did you not? And as for Janet—my sweet Sarah, you gave me no chance to explain.'

'You didn't come back until after three o'clock,' she interposed pettishly.

He kissed her again before he answered. 'I parked the car and sat wondering how I could make you love me. You see, I had come home thinking...and you were quite waspish with me, dear love, and I began to think that you would never care for me.'

Sarah said in a rush of words that ended in a sob,

'Kate said you went to St Kit's to see Janet and you telephoned her, and you were in Fortnum's. . .' She was kissed into silence.

'Dear Sarah,' said Hugo. 'Listen. If you had shown me just once that I was more than just a good friend, I would have told you everything, but all you did was to fling Janet at my head. I would have told you that she's married and unhappy and had left her husband. That's why we were at Fortnum's—I persuaded her to meet him.'

'The man on the stairs who knocked me over,' observed Sarah, well pleased that the jigsaw of their conversation was making sense at last. Hugo lifted an enquiring eyebrow but forbore from questioning her; instead he said firmly, 'And now you will talk no more nonsense, dear heart, nor will you leave me again.'

He drew her close, but just for a minute she held back.

'Hugo, dear Hugo, there's something I must tell you.' She lifted a woebegone face. 'I—I found a ring in your pocket and I lied to you about it and I never will again; and there was a letter and I—' She gulped. 'I read it—not all of it, just the first line or two, and I thought it was for Janet.'

She sniffed to hold back the tears, because if she cried it would look as though she was trying to get his sympathy.

Hugo crushed her so tightly to him that her ribs ached. 'You addlepated woman! Why didn't you read the whole letter while you were about it, then you would have known that it was for you. I wrote it in America and then decided that I would give you the ring myself. Of course, I didn't know that Janet was going to be there, or that you would ask her to stay to dinner.'

Sarah wriggled in his embrace. 'I told you I should be silly,' she murmured, and reached up and kissed him, to be kissed, most satisfactorily, breathless.

Outside the cottage the snow fell, unhurried and unheeded, and in the little kitchen, the stew, forgotten, bubbled fragrantly on.

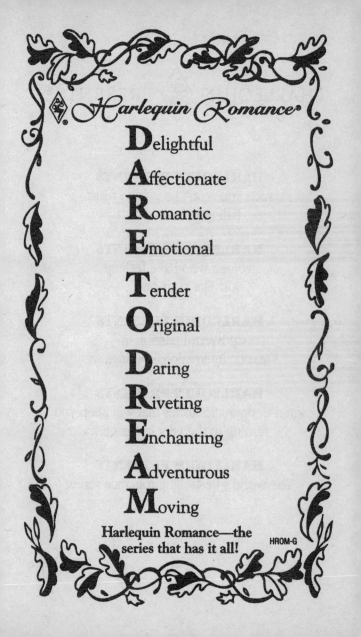

Harlequin Romance®

Delightful

Affectionate

Romantic

Emotional

Tender

Original

Daring

Riveting

Enchanting

Adventurous

Moving

Harlequin Romance—the series that has it all!

HROM-G

HARLEQUIN ◆ PRESENTS®

HARLEQUIN PRESENTS
men you won't be able to resist
falling in love with...

HARLEQUIN PRESENTS
women who have feelings
just like your own...

HARLEQUIN PRESENTS
powerful passion in
exotic international settings...

HARLEQUIN PRESENTS
intense, dramatic stories that will keep you
turning to the very last page...

HARLEQUIN PRESENTS
The world's bestselling romance series!

PRES-G

Harlequin® Historical

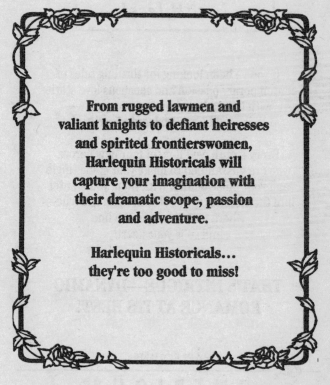

From rugged lawmen and
valiant knights to defiant heiresses
and spirited frontierswomen,
Harlequin Historicals will
capture your imagination with
their dramatic scope, passion
and adventure.

Harlequin Historicals...
they're too good to miss!

HHGENR

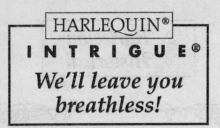

HARLEQUIN®

I N T R I G U E®

We'll leave you breathless!

If you've been looking for thrilling tales of
contemporary passion and sensuous love stories
with taut, edge-of-the-seat suspense—
then you'll *love* **Harlequin Intrigue!**

Every month, you'll meet four new heroes
who are guaranteed to make your spine tingle
and your pulse pound. With them you'll enter
into the exciting world of Harlequin Intrigue—
where your life is on the line
and so is your heart!

THAT'S INTRIGUE—DYNAMIC
ROMANCE AT ITS BEST!

HARLEQUIN®

I N T R I G U E®

INT-GENR